A TERRIFYING CLIMB!

He moved slowly, testing each hold and
stance before he used it and
scraping the snow away carefully with
his hands and feet. His body felt drained and
strengthless, and his arms and legs
were like bars of lead. He stumbled, slipped,
caught himself, moved on—and slipped again.

He had stopped. He kicked his numb feet
against a rock. He held his hands under
the red shirt until again he felt the stirring of
blood. He looked up into the mist
—and beyond it, at last, the sky was brightening.

No! He would not fall. He would not fall.

As he moved again his lips were
tight and grim. He was Rudi Matt, the son
of Josef Matt. And he would make it.

He would make it. . . .

BANNER IN THE SKY

JAMES RAMSEY ULLMAN

AN ARCHWAY PAPERBACK
POCKET BOOKS • NEW YORK

**POCKET BOOKS, a Simon & Schuster division of
GULF & WESTERN CORPORATION
1230 Avenue of the Americas, New York, N.Y. 10020**

Copyright 1954 by James Ramsey Ullman

Published by arrangement with J. B. Lippincott Company

ISBN: 0-671-56081-6

First Pocket Books printing September, 1967

20   19   18   17

AN ARCHWAY PAPERBACK and ARCH are trademarks
of Simon & Schuster.

Printed in the U.S.A.

For
JIM—BILL—DAVID
and also
(why not?)
SUSAN

Author's Note

THERE are many ways in which this story resembles the true story of the first climbing of the Matterhorn. The date—1865—is the same. The imagined town of Kurtal is much like the actual town of Zermatt. The name of Rudi Matt has been derived from that of the great mountain, and Captain John Winter, both in name and role, is more than distantly related to its real-life conqueror, Edward Whymper. Throughout, I have drawn on fact for the making of fiction.

But this book *is* fiction. Its people, places and happenings are imaginary. Most particularly, both Rudi and the Citadel are imaginary. Beginning with various circumstances of the true Matterhorn adventure, the story branches out on its own trail, to its own mountaintop.

I hope it makes for good climbing.

J. R. U.

The Chapters

CHAPTER 1

A Boy and a Mountain

In the heart of the Swiss Alps, on the high frontier between earth and sky, stands one of the great mountains of the world. To men generally it is known as the Citadel, but the people of the valley beneath it seldom call it by that name. They call it the Rudisberg— Rudi's Mountain. And that is because, in the long-gone year of 1865, there lived in that valley a boy called Rudi Matt. . . .

MOST of the boys of the village were tall, broad and strongly built. Rudi was small and slim. But to make up for it, he was quick. In all his sixteen years he had probably never been quicker than on a certain summer morning when he slipped out the kitchen door of the Beau Site Hotel and into the alley beyond. When Teo Zurbriggen, the cook, turned from his stove to get a jar from the spice shelf, Rudi had been at his usual place, washing the breakfast dishes. But when, five seconds later, Old Teo turned back, his young helper was gone.

The cook muttered under his breath. But, almost at the same time, he smiled. He smiled because he knew what the boy was up to, and in his old heart he was glad.

1

Outside, Rudi did not follow the alley to the main street. He went in the other direction, came to a second alley, and ran quickly through the back part of the town. He made a wide detour around his mother's house; another around the house of his uncle, Franz Lerner. Fortunately he met no one who knew him—or at least who knew he was supposed to be working in the kitchen of the Beau Site.

Soon he came to the edge of the town and a roaring brook. Across the brook lay a footbridge; but, instead of using it, he worked his way upstream around a bend and then crossed over, leaping agilely from boulder to boulder. From the far side he looked back. Apparently no one had seen him. Scrambling up the bank, he plunged through a clump of bushes, skirted a barnyard and picked up a path through the meadows. Here, for the first time, he stopped running. There was no living thing to be seen except a herd of grazing cows. The only sound was the tinkling of their bells.

The meadows rolled gently, tilting upward, and their green slope was sprayed with wildflowers. The path crossed a fence, over a rickety stile, then bent and rejoined the brook; and now the cowbells faded and there was again the sound of rushing water. Rudi walked on. Three or four times he passed people going in the opposite direction, but they were only *Ausländer* —tourists—and nothing to worry about. Whatever guides were climbing that day were already high in the mountains. And any others who might have known and questioned him were back in the town or on their farms.

Rudi smiled at the passersby. *"Grüss Gott,"* he said —"God's Greetings"—in the ancient salutation of the Alps. *"Grüss Gott,"* they said in reply.

He was no longer hurrying. He walked with the

slow, rhythmic pace of the mountain people, and, though the path was now steepening sharply, he felt no strain. His legs, his lungs, all of his slight wiry body, were doing what they did best; what they had been born to do. His feet, through the soles of his shoes, molded themselves to each hump and crevice of the path. Arms and shoulders swung in easy balance. His breathing was steady, his heartbeat strong and even.

"A typical mountain boy," one would have said, seeing him at a distance. But then, coming closer, one would have seen that he was not typical at all. Partly, this was because of his slimness, his lightness of muscle and bone; but even more it was in his small, almost delicate features and his fair, pink-and-white complexion. Rudi Matt hated his complexion. In summer he exposed his face for hours to the burning sun, in winter he scrubbed it violently with snow, trying to make it brown and tough and weatherstained, as a mountain man's should be. But no stain appeared. No whisker sprouted. "Angel-face," the other boys called him. Or, rather, *had* called him, until they learned that his fists, though small, were useful. Most of the men of Kurtal had black hair. Rudi's was blond. Most of them had dark eyes. Rudi's were light—though exactly what color no one was quite sure. His mother called them hazel, but she saw them only when he was at home or around the village. When he left the village, when he climbed above it, they seemed to change, as the light changed. Looking up at the great peaks above the valley, they seemed to hold within themselves the gray of mountain rock, the blue of mountain sky.

Rudi Matt climbed on. Now that he was no longer afraid of being stopped, his heart was filled with peace and joy. Just why he had run off on this particular day he could not have said. He had had to—that was all. He had looked from the window of the hotel kitchen and seen the peaks that rimmed the valley rising vast and shining in the morning sun; and he could no more have stopped himself than he could have stopped breathing. A few minutes before, he had been a prisoner. Now he was free. He no longer looked backward—only up—as slowly the great mountain world unfolded before him.

The path bore away from the brook, zigzagged up the highest of the meadows and entered a forest. And here Rudi stopped. Beside the path, at the forest's edge, was a shrine. It was a tiny thing, no more than a rough wooden box nailed to one of the trees, and inside was a cross and a chipped image of the Virgin. Carved in the wood near the Virgin's feet was the name JOSEF MATT, and beneath it the dates, *1821–1850*.

Rudi had never known his father. It had been fifteen years since he had died. But every time in his life that the boy had come to this place he had stopped and prayed. He prayed now, kneeling in the soft moss before the shrine. Then he arose, crossed himself and climbed on through the forest.

A few minutes later he made a second stop. Leaving the path, he made his way between the trees to a large blue spruce and reached for the stout stick that was concealed in its branches. This was his *alpenstock*, the climber's staff he had made for himself, as a substitute for an ice-ax, which he did not own; and he kept it hidden here because he was afraid that if he took it home his mother or uncle might find it. It was a strong staff, almost five feet long, with a sharp point on one end and a crook on the other. And if it

4

was nothing like the real *alpenstocks* and axes that Kronig, the smith, made at his forge in the village, at least it was better than nothing. As he hefted it now in his hand, feeling its familiar weight and balance, it was no longer merely a stick, but a part of himself.

He climbed on. For a while, still thinking of his father, he walked slowly and somberly, with his eyes on the ground. But this did not last long, for he was young and the sun was shining and he was doing what he most loved to do in all the world. He tilted his stick before him like a lance. He picked up stones and threw them at the trees. He threw back his head and yodeled and the high wild YOOOO—LEEEE—OOOOO—LAAAY—EEEEE rode the still air like a soaring bird.

The path twisted upward. Always upward. The forest was close around him; then a little less close; then not close at all. The great firs and spruces fell away, and he came out onto a slope of dwarf pine and scraggly, moss-hugging shrubs. Sitting on a boulder, he ate a bite of lunch. He had no knapsack, any more than he had an ice-ax, but he had managed to stuff a piece of bread and another of cheese into a pocket before bolting from the hotel kitchen, and, plain and crumbled though they were, they tasted better than any food he had ever eaten in the hotel or in his home.

His eyes moved down across the treetops to the valley. There was the white thread of the brook dividing it; on either side the meadows and farms; in the valley's center the town of Kurtal. He could see the main street, the square, the church, the Beau Site Hotel, where he worked, and the two other hotels beyond it. All three buildings were new; even Rudi could remember when they had not been there at all. Ten or twelve years before, Kurtal had been no more than a tiny farming village, lost in a deep Swiss valley. But while Rudi had grown, it had grown too. It had become what the *Ausländer* called a "resort." Each year, during the summer months, there were more and more visitors—people from the cities, people from England, France, Germany, and even from faraway America—coming up in the coaches from the lowlands. In the last few summers there had been so many of them that there was even talk of building a railway.

It was the mountains that brought them, of course: the tall white glorious mountains of the Alps. In the old days the people of the outside world had not been interested in the Alps; they had left them to those who had been born and lived there. But in Rudi's own lifetime all that had changed. The *Ausländer* had come: first in trickles, then in droves. They had moved up into the villages, into the high valleys, onto the glaciers, onto the peaks themselves. The sport, the craft, the adventure of mountaineering had been born. In every village, men whose ancestors through all history had been farmers and herdsmen were now farmers and herdsmen no longer, but Alpine guides. And the profession of guide was the proudest in the land. To be a member of the Company of Guides of Kurtal was the highest honor that a man could attain.

Men had not only come to the mountains. They had conquered them. A generation before, only a handful of peaks in the Alps had been climbed to the top, but now, in 1865, there were scarcely any that had *not* been. One by one, year after year, they had been attacked, besieged and taken. Mont Blanc, Monte Rosa, the Dom, the Weisshorn, the Schreckhorn, the Eiger, the Dent Blanche, the Lyskamm—all these and a hundred more, the whole great white host of the most

6

famous mountains of Europe—had felt the boot nails of their conquerors in their summit snows.

All of them . . . *except one.*

Rudi Matt was no longer looking down into the valley. He was looking up and beyond it, and now slowly his eyes moved across the wide circle of the ranges. They moved over the meadows and forests, the glaciers and snowfields, the gorges and precipices, the ridges and peaks. They rested on the snowdome of Monte Rosa, the spire of the Wunderhorn (his father had first climbed it), the Rotalp (his uncle Franz), the soaring crest of the Weisshorn. Now at last he had turned completely; he was looking in the direction in which he had been climbing. And still his eyes moved on—and up—and up. The other mountains fell away. There was a gap, a deep gorge, a glacier. The earth seemed almost to be gathering itself together. It leaped upward.

And there it was. . . .

The Citadel!

It stood up like a monument: great, terrible—and alone. The other mountains were as nothing beside it. It rose in cliff upon cliff, ridge upon ridge, tower upon tower, until the sharp, curving wedge of its summit seemed to pierce the very heart of the sky. It was a pyramid built up out of a thousand parts—out of granite and limestone and snow and ice, out of glaciers, precipices, crags, ledges, spires, cornices—but so perfect was its vast shape, so harmonious the blending of its elements, that it appeared a single, an organic, almost a living thing. Rudi Matt had been born in its shadow. He had seen it every day of his life. He had stared up at it from the village, from the forests, from the glaciers on every side, until its every detail was fixed indelibly in his mind. But familiarity had not

7

bred indifference. The years had not paled its magic. Instead, that magic had grown stronger, deeper. And on this day, as on every day in his life when he had looked up at it, Rudi Matt felt again the catch in his breath and the wild surging of his heart.

There it stood. The Citadel. The last unconquered summit of the Alps.

"It cannot be climbed," said the people of the valleys. In the past fifteen years no one had even tried to climb it. "It will never be climbed," they said.

No?

Now he was moving on again. He came to a stream, stopped and drank. A furry marmot watched him from a nearby boulder, whistled shrilly and disappeared. High above, a giant hawk whirled slowly through the still, blue air.

Beyond the stream was a fork in the path. The right-hand branch, plain and well trodden, led off toward the Dornelberg and the Wunderhorn, two of the most popular peaks for climbing in the district. But it was not this branch that Rudi followed. Bearing left, he moved on along a barely visible trail that climbed upward toward the base of the Citadel. He was above treeline now. Even the dwarf pine and shrubs were gone—all grass and moss were gone—and the earth was a bare sweep of gravel and tumbled boulders. Among the boulders the going was tricky, for he had no proper nailed mountainboots; but his feet were nimble, his balance true, and, making deft use of his self-made staff, he climbed quickly and easily. When, after an hour, he turned and looked back, the rocky point where he had stopped to eat seemed almost as far below him as the village.

The world into which he had now come was one of

stillness and desolation. There was the gray of rock, the white of snow, the blue of sky—and that was all there was. The only movement, anywhere, was that of his own body; the only sound the scraping of his own feet against the boulders. Yet Rudi was not conscious of loneliness. He was too used to being alone for that. Every one of the perhaps fifty times during the past two years that he had climbed up to the Citadel's glaciers, he had been alone, and he was now as familiar with this world, and as at home in it, as in the valley below. Pausing now and then, he stared at the mountain that towered gray and monstrous above him. Most of the people in the town believed it was the home of demons, who would destroy anyone who ventured onto its forbidden slopes. . . . Well, maybe. . . . But he, Rudi, was not yet within a mile of the mountain itself. And if any demons did, indeed, come down into the foothills, they would do so, he was certain, only under cover of night.

He looked up, and the sun was bright and golden in the zenith. The thin finger of cold, that for an instant had touched him, dwindled and was gone.

The slope steepened. The boulders grew larger. He had come to the terminal moraine of the Citadel's glacier—the great mass of tumbled, broken rock which all ice-sheets push and grind before them in their slow descent. Ten more minutes brought him to the top of the moraine, and now the glacier spread before him. Or, more accurately, two glaciers; for he had come out at a point, facing the Kurtal ridge of the Citadel, where its northern and eastern ice-streams met and joined. The one on the north, which was broader, rose to the pass between the Citadel and the Dornelberg and was known as the Dornel Glacier. The eastern one, called the Blue Glacier, was the steeper and

9

climbed like a giant stairway to the saddle—or col—
near the base of the Citadel's southeastern ridge. Beyond this col, invisible from where he stood, still another glacier dropped away on the south side of the
mountain, toward the valley and village of Broli.

Rudi had ascended both glaciers. He had been to
Broli. No less than five times, indeed, he had completely circled the base of the Citadel, climbing up
one glacier and down another, traversing the cols and
lower ridges, threading his way through the deep, trackless gorges beneath the mountain's western face. He
had stared upward until his neck ached and his eyes
swam. He had studied every ridge and cliff and ice-
wall and ledge and chimney that could be seen from
below. He knew more about the approaches to the
Citadel than any guide in Kurtal. And yet he still
did not know enough. Still he kept coming up to
the glaciers to stare again, to study, to measure. To
do this, he had played truant from school—even from
church. Now he was running out on his job. Always it
meant tears and pleas from his mother, often harsh
words from his Uncle Franz. But he did not care. He
kept coming back. Nothing in heaven or earth could
have held him from coming back.

This time he went up the Blue Glacier. He had not
particularly planned to, and just why he picked the
Blue, rather than the Dornel, he could not have said.
Later, thinking back to that day, he racked his memory
for some sign, some motive or portent, that had been
the reason for his choice. But he could never find one.
He simply crossed the junction of the two ice-streams,
bore left, and climbed on toward the south . . . and his
destiny.

Like all glaciers, the Blue was cut through by crevasses: deep splits and chasms caused by the pressures

of the slow-moving ice. When hidden by snow these could be a great hazard to climbers; but on this midsummer day no snow had fallen in some time, the crevasses were plain to view, and there was no danger if one kept his eyes open and paid attention. Rudi zigzagged his way carefully upward. On the ice, of course, his smooth-soled shoes were even worse than on the boulders, but by skillful balancing and use of his stick he kept himself from slipping.

As he climbed, a black dot came into view on the high col ahead. This was an old hut, built many years before by the first explorers of the mountain, but now abandoned and all but forgotten by the people of the valleys. Rudi had twice spent nights there during his circuits of the Citadel, and he knew it well. But it was not there, specifically, that he was going now. He was not going anywhere, specifically, but only climbing, watching, studying. Every few paces now, he would stop and stare upward, motionless.

The east face of the Citadel rose above him like a battlement. Cliff upon cliff, it soared up from the glacier, its rock bulging and bristling, its walls veined with long streaks of ice. Far overhead, he could see a band of snow, which marked the mountain's first setback. Beyond it, the sloping walls disappeared for a space, only to bulge out again higher up—incredibly higher up—in a great gray thrust against the empty sky. So vast was it, so steep, so mighty, that it seemed more than a mere mass of rock and ice. More than a mere mountain. It seemed a new world rising up out of the old world that was its mother; a world with a life and a meaning of its own; beautiful and menacing, beckoning and unknown.

But it was not of beauty or terror that Rudi Matt was thinking as he gazed up at it now from the Blue Gla-

11

cier. It was of a deep cleft, wide enough for a man's body, that slanted up the rock wall before him—and ended. Of a series of ledges, broad enough for a man's feet, that rose one above another toward the high belt of snow—and petered out. His eyes searched up and down, to the right and the left. He climbed on, stopped, and studied the next section of the face. Then he climbed on again.

He moved through absolute silence. Later in the day, when sun and melting snow had done their work, great rock-and-ice masses would break loose from the heights above and come roaring down the mountainside. But it was still too early for this. The Citadel rose up like a tower of iron. There was no movement anywhere. No stirring. No sound.

And then there was a sound. . . .

Rudi stood motionless. It was not the sound of the mountain, of falling rock and ice. It was a voice. He waited; he looked around him; every sense was straining. But he saw nothing. Nothing moved. It was his imagination, he thought: a trick of his mind, or of the stillness. Or was it—and now the cold finger of fear touched him again—was it the voice of a mountain demon?

He stood without breathing. And the sound came again. It seemed at the same time to come from nearby and far away. He waited. Once more it came. And then suddenly he knew *where* it came from. It was from beneath the ice. From a crevasse in the glacier.

He approached the nearest crevasse and called out. But there was no answer. He went on to a second. No answer. Again he waited and listened. Again the voice came, faintly. Straight ahead was a third chasm in the ice, and, advancing cautiously, he peered over the edge.

CHAPTER 2

A Boy and a Man

THE CREVASSE was about six feet wide at the top and narrowed gradually as it went down. But how deep it was Rudi could not tell. After a few feet the blue walls of ice curved away at a sharp slant, and what was below the curve was hidden from sight.

"Hello!" Rudi called.

"Hello—" a voice answered from the depths.

"How far down are you?"

"I'm not sure. About twenty feet, I'd guess."

"On the bottom?"

"No. I can't even see the bottom. I was lucky and hit a ledge."

The voice spoke in German, but with a strange accent. Whoever was down there, Rudi knew, it was not one of the men of the valley.

"Are you hurt?" he called.

"Nothing broken—no," said the voice. "Just shaken up some. And cold."

"How long have you been there?"

"About three hours."

"Do you have a rope?" asked the voice.

Rudi looked up and down the crevasse. He was thinking desperately of what he could do.

"No."

"How many of you are there?"

"Only me."

There was a silence. When the voice spoke again, it was still quiet and under strict control. "Then you'll have to get help," it said.

Rudi didn't answer. To get down to Kurtal would take at least two hours, and for a party to climb back up would take three. By that time it would be night, and the man would have been in the crevasse for eight hours. He would be frozen to death.

"No," said Rudi, "it would take too long."

"What else is there to do?"

Rudi's eyes moved over the ice-walls: almost vertical, smooth as glass. "Have you an ax?" he asked.

"No. I lost it when I fell. It dropped to the bottom."

"Have you tried to climb?"

"Yes. But I can't get a hold."

There was another silence. Rudi's lips tightened, and when he spoke again his voice was strained. "I'll think of something," he cried. "I'll think of *something!*"

"Don't lose your head," the voice said. "The only way is to go down for help."

"But you'll—"

"Maybe. And maybe not. That's a chance we'll have to take."

The voice was as quiet as ever. And, hearing it, Rudi was suddenly ashamed. Here was he, safe on the glacier's surface, showing fear and despair, while the one below, facing almost certain death, remained calm and controlled. Whoever it was down there, it was a real man. A brave man.

14

Rudi drew in a long, slow breath. With his climbing-staff he felt down along the smooth surface of the ice-walls.

"Are you still there?" said the voice.

"Yes," he said.

"You had better go."

"Wait—"

Lying flat on the glacier, he leaned over the rim of the crevasse and lowered the staff as far as it would go. Its end came almost to the curve in the walls.

"Can you see it?" he asked.

"See what?" said the man.

Obviously he couldn't. Standing up, Rudi removed his jacket and tied it by one sleeve to the curved end of the staff. Then, holding the other end, he again lay prone and lowered his staff and jacket.

"Can you see it now?" he asked.

"Yes," said the man.

"How far above you is it?"

"About ten feet."

Again the staff came up. Rudi took off his shirt and tied one of its sleeves to the dangling sleeve of the jacket. This time, as he lay down, the ice bit, cold and rough, into his bare chest; but he scarcely noticed it. With his arms extended, all the shirt and half the jacket were out of sight beneath the curve in the cre-vasse.

"How near you now?" he called.

"Not far," said the voice.

"Can you reach it?"

"I'm trying."

There was the sound of scraping boot-nails; of la-bored breathing. But no pull on the shirtsleeve down below.

"I can't make it," said the voice. It was fainter than before.

"Wait," said Rudi.

For the third time he raised the staff. He took off his trousers. He tied a trouser-leg to the loose sleeve of the shirt. Then he pulled, one by one, at all the knots he had made: between staff and jacket, jacket and shirt, shirt and trousers. He pulled until the blood pounded in his head and the knots were as tight as his strength could make them. This done, he stepped back from the crevasse to the point where his toes had rested when he lay flat. With feet and hands he kicked and scraped the ice until he had made two holes. Then, lying down as before, he dug his toes deep into them. He was naked now, except for his shoes, stockings and underpants. The cold rose from the ice into his blood and bones. He lowered the staff and knotted clothes like a sort of crazy fishing line.

The trousers, the shirt and half of the jacket passed out of sight. He was leaning over as far as he could.

"Can you reach it now?" he called.

"Yes," the voice answered.

"All right. Come on."

"You won't be able to hold me. I'll pull you in."

"No you won't."

He braced himself. The pull came. His toes went taut in their ice-holds and his hands tightened on the staff until the knuckles showed white. Again he could hear a scraping sound below, and he knew that the man was clawing his boots against the ice-wall, trying both to lever himself up and to take as much weight as possible off the improvised lifeline. But the wall obviously offered little help. Almost all his weight was on the lifeline. Suddenly there was a jerk, as one of the knots in the clothing slipped, and the staff was almost

16

wrenched from Rudi's hands. But the knot held. And his hands held. He tried to call down, "All right?" but he had no breath for words. From below, the only sound was the scraping of boots on ice.

How long it went on Rudi could never have said. Perhaps only for a minute or so. But it seemed like hours. And then at last—at last—it happened. A hand came into view around the curve of the crevasse wall: a hand gripping the twisted fabric of his jacket, and then a second hand rising slowly above it. A head appeared. A pair of shoulders. A face was raised for an instant and then lowered. Again one hand moved slowly up past the other.

But Rudi no longer saw it, for now his eyes were shut tight with the strain. His teeth were clamped, the cords of his neck bulged, the muscles of his arm felt as if they were being drawn one by one from the bones that held them. He began to lose his toeholds. He was being dragged forward. Desperately, frantically, he dug in with his feet, pressed his whole body down, as if he could make it part of the glacier. Though all but naked on the ice, he was pouring with sweat. Somehow he stopped the slipping. Somehow he held on. But now suddenly the strain was even worse, for the man had reached the lower end of the staff. The slight "give" of the stretched clothing was gone, and in its place was rigid deadweight on a length of wood. The climber was close now. But heavy. Indescribably heavy. Rudi's hands ached and burned, as if it were a rod of hot lead that they clung to. It was not a mere man he was holding, but a giant; or a block of granite. The pull was unendurable. The pain unendurable. He could hold on no longer. His hands were opening. It was all over.

And then it *was* over. The weight was gone. There was a scraping sound close beneath him; a hand on the rim of ice; a figure pulling itself up onto the lip of the crevasse. The man was beside Rudi, turning to him, staring at him.

"Why—you're just a boy!" he said in astonishment.

Rudi was too numb to move or speak. Taking the staff from him, the man pulled up the line of clothes, untied the knots and shook them out.

"Come on now. Quickly!" he said.

Pulling the boy to his feet, he helped him dress. Then he rubbed and pummeled him until at last Rudi felt the warmth of returning circulation.

"Better?" the man asked, smiling.

Rudi nodded, And finally he was able to speak again. "And you, sir," he said, "you are all right?"

The man nodded. He was warming himself now: flapping his arms and kicking his feet together. "A few minutes of sun and I'll be as good as new."

Nearby, a black boulder lay embedded in the glacial ice, and, going over to it, they sat down. The sunlight poured over them like a warm bath. Rudi slowly flexed his aching fingers and saw that the man was doing the same. And then the man had raised his eyes and was looking at him.

"It's a miracle how you did it," he said. "A boy of your size. All alone."

"It was nothing," Rudi murmured.

"Nothing?"

"I—I only—"

"Only saved my life," said the man.

For the first time, now, Rudi was really seeing him. He was a man of perhaps thirty, very tall and thin,

18

and his face, too, was thin, with a big hawklike nose and a strong jutting chin. His weather-browned cheeks were clean-shaven, his hair black, his eyes deep-set and gray. And when he spoke, his voice was still almost as quiet as when it had been muffled by the ice-walls of the crevasse. He is—what?—Rudi thought. Not Swiss, he knew. Not French or German. English, perhaps? Yes, English. . . . And then suddenly a deep excitement filled him, for he knew who the man was.

"You are Captain Winter?" he murmured.

"That's right."

"And I—I have saved—I mean—"

Rudi stopped in confusion, and the Englishman grinned. "You've saved," he said, smiling, "one of the worst imbeciles that ever walked on a glacier. An imbecile who was so busy looking up at a mountain that he couldn't even see what was at his feet."

Rudi was wordless—almost stunned. He looked at the man, and then away in embarrassment, and he could scarcely believe what had happened. The name of Captain John Winter was known through the length and breadth of the Alps. He was the foremost mountaineer of his day, and during the past ten years had made more first ascents of great peaks than any other man alive. Rudi had heard that he had come to Kurtal a few days before. He had hoped that at least he would see him in the hotel or walking by in the street. But actually to meet him—and in this way! To pull him from a crevasse—save him. . . . It was incredible!

Captain Winter was watching him. "And you, son," he asked. "What is your name?"

Somehow the boy got his voice back. "Rudi," he said. "Rudi Matt."

"Matt?" Now it was the man's turn to be impressed. "Not of the family of the great Josef Matt?"

"He was my father," Rudi said.

Captain Winter studied him with his gray eyes. Then he smiled again. "I should have known," he said. "A boy who could do what you've done—"

"Did you know my father, sir?"

"No, unfortunately I didn't. He was before my day. But ever since I was a boy I have heard of him. In twenty years no one has come to the Alps and not heard of the great guide, Josef Matt."

Rudi's heart swelled. He looked away. His eyes fixed on the vast mountain that rose before them, and then he saw that Captain Winter was watching it too.

Unconsciously the Englishman spoke his thoughts. "Your father was—" He caught himself and stopped.

"Yes," said Rudi softly, "he was killed on the Citadel."

There was a silence. Captain Winter reached into a pocket and brought out an unbroken bar of chocolate. "Lucky I fell on the other side," he grinned.

He broke the bar in two and handed half to Rudi.

"Oh no, sir, thank you. I couldn't."

"When I meet a boy your age who can't eat chocolate," said Winter, "I'll be glad to stay in a crevasse for good."

Rudi took it, and they sat munching. The sun was warm on their thawing bodies. Far above, it struck the cliffs and snowfields of the Citadel, so brightly that they had to squint against the glare.

Then there was Winter's quiet voice again. "What do you think, Rudi?"

"Think, sir?"

"Can it be climbed?"

"Climbed? The Citadel?"

"Your father thought so. Alone among all the guides of Switzerland, he thought so." There was another pause. "And I think so too," said Captain Winter.

The boy was peering again at the shining heights. And suddenly his heart was pounding so hard that he was sure the Englishman must be able to hear it. "Is—is that why you have come here, sir?" he asked. "To try to climb the Citadel?"

"Well, now—" Winter smiled. "It's not so simple, you know. For one thing, there's not a guide in the valley who would go with me."

"I have an uncle, sir. He is—"

"Yes, I know your uncle. Franz Lerner. He is the best in Kurtal, and I've spoken to him. But he would not go. Anything but that, he said. Any other peak, any route, any venture. But not *that,* he said. Not the Citadel."

"He remembers my father—"

"Yes, he remembers your father. They all remember him. And while they love and respect his memory, they all think he was crazy." Winter chuckled softly. "Now they think *I'm* crazy," he added. "And maybe they're right too," he said.

"What will you do, sir?" asked Rudi. "Not try it alone?"

"No, that crazy I'm not." Winter slowly stroked his long jaw. "I'm not certain what I'll do," he went on. "Perhaps I'll go over to the next valley. To Broli. I've been told there is a guide there—a man called Saxo. Do you know him?"

"Yes—Emil Saxo. I have never met him, but I have heard of him. They say he is a very great guide."

"Well, I thought perhaps I'd go and talk with him.

After a while. But first I must reconnoitre some more. Make my plans. Pick the route. If there *is* a route."

"Yes, there is! Of course there is!"

Rudi had not thought the words. They simply burst out from him. And now again he was embarrassed as the man looked at him curiously.

"So?" said Captain Winter. "That is interesting, Rudi. Tell me why you think so."

"I have studied the Citadel many times, sir."

"Why?"

"Because—because—" He stopped. He couldn't say it.

"Because you want to climb it yourself?"

"I am not yet a grown man, sir. I know I cannot expect—"

"I wasn't a grown man either," said the Captain, "when I first saw the Citadel. I was younger than you— only twelve—and my parents had brought me here for a summer holiday. But I can still remember how I felt when I looked up at it, and the promise I made myself that some day I was going to climb it." He paused. His eyes moved slowly upward. "Youth is the time for dreams, boy," he murmured. "The trick is, when you get older, not to forget them."

Rudi listened, spellbound. He had never heard anyone speak like that. He had not known a grown man could think and feel like that.

Then Winter asked:

"This east face, Rudi—what do you think of it?"

"Think of it, sir?"

"Could it be climbed?"

Rudi shook his head. "No, it is no good. The long chimney there—you sce. It looks all right; it could be done. And to the left, the ledges"—he pointed—"they could be done too. But higher up, no. They stop. The chimney stops, and there is only smooth rock."

"What about the northeast ridge?"

"That is not good either."

"It's not so steep."

"No, it is not so steep," said Rudi. "But the rocks are bad. They slope out, with few places for holds."

"And the north face?"

Rudi talked on. About the north face, the west ridge, the southwest ridge. He talked quietly and thoughtfully, but with deep inner excitement, for this was the first time in his life that he had been able to speak to anyone of these things which he had thought and studied for so long. . . . And then suddenly he stopped, for he realized what he was doing. He, Rudi Matt, a boy of sixteen who worked in the kitchen of the Beau Site Hotel, was presuming to give his opinions to one of the greatest climbers in the world.

But Captain Winter had been listening intently. Sometimes he nodded. "Go on," he said now, as Rudi paused.

"But I am only—"

"Go on."

And Rudi went on. . . .

"That doesn't leave much," said the captain a little later.

"No sir," said the boy.

"Only the southeast ridge."

"Yes sir."

"That was the way your father tried, wasn't it?"

"Yes sir."

"And you believe it's the *only* way?"

"Yes sir."

Captain Winter rubbed his jaw for a moment before speaking again. Then—"That also is very interesting to me, Rudi," he said quietly, "because it is what I believe too."

Later, they threaded their way down the Blue Glacier. For a while they moved in silence. Then Captain Winter asked:

"What do you do, Rudi?"

"Do, sir?"

"Are you an apprentice guide? A porter?"

Rudi swallowed. "No sir."

"What then?"

He could hardly say it. "A—a dishwasher."

"A dishwasher?"

"In the Beau Site Hotel. It is my mother, sir. Since my father died, you see, she is afraid—she does not want—" Rudi swallowed again. "I am to go into the hotel business," he murmured.

"Oh."

Again they moved on without speaking. It was now late afternoon, and behind them the stillness was broken by a great roaring, as sun-loosened rock and ice broke off from the heights of the Citadel.

When they reached the path Rudi spoke again, hesitantly. "Will you please do me a favor, sir?" he asked.

"Of course," said Winter.

"Before we come to the town we will separate. And you will please not tell anyone that I have been up here today?"

The Englishman looked at him in astonishment. "Not tell anyone? You save my life, boy, and you want me to keep it a secret?"

"It was nothing, sir. Truly. And if you say that I have been in the mountains, my mother and uncle will hear, and I will be in trouble." Rudi's voice took on a note of urgency. "You will not do it, sir? You will promise—please?"

Winter put a hand on his shoulder. "Don't worry," he said. "I won't get you in trouble." Then he smiled and added: "Master Rudi Matt—dishwasher."

They walked down the path. The sun sank. Behind them, the mountain roared.

CHAPTER 3

Two Hundred Dirty Dishes

IN THE KITCHEN of the Beau Site Hotel old Teo Zurbriggen went about his work. He had long since finished up the breakfast dishes that Rudi had left half-washed, but meanwhile lunch had come and gone and a hundred new ones stood waiting for the suds. And for these Teo had no time, because he was busy cooking dinner.

Gretchen, the waitress, moved back and forth from the dining room. "The boy is a good-for-nothing," she snorted. "Running out and leaving his work."

"He did not run out," said Teo. "I have told you: his mother, Frau Matt, is sick and needs him. And besides," he added, "there are enough clean dishes for dinner."

Gretchen went back to the dining room, and Teo looked out the window. "The sun is low," he thought, "and he should be back soon. Even if he went all the way to the glaciers, he should be back soon."

Old Teo, they called him. He was not really so old; not more than perhaps fifty-five. But his brown skin was wrinkled, his hair almost white, his eyes pale and watery behind craggy brows. And also, he was a cripple. Fifteen years before, in the prime of his life, he

26

had been one of the foremost guides of Kurtal—and the only one willing to accompany Josef Matt and his employer, Sir Edward Stephenson, on their famous attempt on the Citadel. Unlike the other two, he had been brought down alive, but so badly injured from a thirty-foot fall that his career as a mountain man was over. Even now, he walked with a deep limp. His left arm was half paralyzed and his shoulder hunched up against his neck. He had tried farming, until his wife died and he grew too lonely. Then he had worked at odd jobs around the town. And when the Beau Site was built he became its cook.

He was a good cook—but not a happy one. If it had not made it too dark for his work, he would have put blinds on the kitchen windows to shut out the sight of the soaring mountains.

There were footsteps in the alley outside. "Ah, there's the runaway," thought old Teo. But it wasn't. It was Rudi's uncle, Franz Lerner.

He was a big man—not tall, but broad and stoutly built—and his shoulders filled the doorway as he entered. His face, too, was broad, strong and square-cut, with weathered skin, a short fringe of beard and dark, slow-moving eyes. Indeed, everything about him was slow: his gait, his gestures, his speech. Slow and deliberate. Slow and powerful. He was dressed in rough guide's clothing and held a pipe between his teeth.

"*Grüss Gott,*" he said to Teo.

"*Grüss Gott,*" said the cook.

Franz looked around. "Where is the boy?"

"He is out. I—I sent him to the market."

"His mother wants him to do an errand before he comes home. She asked me to tell him."

"I will tell him when he comes back."

At that moment Gretchen the waitress reappeared. "Good evening," she said to Franz. "It is too bad your sister, the Widow Matt, is ill."

"Ill?"

"Why yes. Is she not? Old Teo said the boy had gone to—"

She looked questioningly at the cook. Franz looked at the cook. Then his eyes moved to the stacks of dirty dishes.

"So," he said. "It is *that* again."

Teo said nothing.

Franz took a step forward. "Is it not?" he demanded. "He has sneaked off again to the mountains."

Teo cleared his throat. "There were not many dishes," he murmured. "And besides, the day was so fine—"

"It is not a question of how many dishes. Or of the weather. It is that here is where he works. Where he belongs. Not wandering around in the mountains."

"I am not sure you are right," said Teo.

"What do you mean by that?"

Teo shrugged his twisted shoulders. "You cannot put out a fire by wishing it out. You cannot bottle the wind."

The two men stood facing each other. Gretchen went back into the dining room.

"If you cannot control him," said Franz, "I shall have to speak to Herr Hempel, the proprietor. Perhaps he should work in another part of the hotel."

"And perhaps he should not work in the hotel at all," said Teo.

"He *must* work in the hotel. It is his mother's wish. He is to be trained for the business."

"He is not a child any more. He cannot be made to do what he does not want to."

"And what he *does* want to—"

"—is to be a guide, of course. If not a full guide yet, at least a porter—an apprentice."

Franz shook his head. "He is not strong enough to be a guide. He is too small. And also too irresponsible." He pointed at the dirty dishes. "Look how he leaves things. How he shirks his work. What would he do in the mountains, where there are real problems and responsibilities?"

"At least he should have the chance to learn." Old Teo came closer and his voice grew lower. "You are a guide, Franz," he said. "When I was young, I too was a guide, and we know how such things are. He cannot stand to see the other boys going out as porters and helpers, learning to be guides, while he works in a kitchen like a girl or an old man. He is Josef Matt's son, and the mountains are in his blood."

"And what do you think is in my sister's blood?" Franz demanded. "A widow at twenty-three, with her husband killed on the Citadel. A widow left with a single child. Do you expect her to let him do as his father did? To die as his father died?" He brought a big hand down heavily on the table. "No. There have been enough guides in the family. And enough sorrow for one woman. This boy will learn a trade, a profession. Soon now he will go for training to a big hotel in Zurich. When he comes back he will be a clerk, then a manager; one day he may even be a proprietor. Something the family can be proud of."

Teo studied him with his pale old eyes. "It is for your sister that you speak now, Franz," he said quietly. "Not for yourself."

"What I speak is sense. And what I speak is what will be." Franz turned abruptly to the door. "I will go now and tell her about this thing."

He went out. Teo stood for a while at the window, watching the mountains and the setting sun. Then he went back to his oven. . . . "Whatever they do, it will be no use," he thought. "They will see. They will find out. You cannot bottle the wind. . . ."

Frau Matt's house was small and neat. And so was Frau Matt. As a young girl, when she married Josef Matt, she had been one of the beauties of Kurtal, and though the years of her widowhood had faded her, she was still, in her late thirties, an attractive, almost a pretty woman. She had not grown fat, as did so many of the village women as they neared middle age. She had the same fine features and light complexion as her son. She was known for the sweetness of her smile. But there was no smile on her face this summer evening, as she sat listening to her brother Franz.

"No," she said sadly, "Old Teo does not seem able to control Rudi at all."

"He does not even *want* to control him," said Franz.

"When this summer is over it will be all right, I think. Now, at sixteen, he is wild and willful. But in the fall he will go to Zurich for his training. He will be away from the mountains. And when he comes back he will have interest and pride in his work."

Her brother nodded without speaking.

"You know what I want for him," she said. "How I have hoped and planned for him. You do not think I am wrong, Franz?"

"I think you must do as your heart tells you, Ilse."

"My heart—yes. But it is not just that. It is not of myself that I want to think, but of Rudi. So that he may have a good life. So that he may grow up and marry and have children, and not destroy it all by—"

30

She broke off. When she spoke again it was with a great effort to be calm and reasonable.

"If he were a different sort of boy—bigger and stronger—perhaps I would feel differently. But he is so small, so delicate."

"Yes," Franz agreed, "he is not built for the mountains."

"And he is so quick and bright. His manners are good. In the hotel business he can make a great success. If only he will stop wanting to be what he is not."

"It is when he thinks of his father that he wants to be a guide."

"Yes, of course—when he thinks of his father. . . . And then when *I* think of him. Of my own Josef. Of how young he was, how gay and proud. How he used to laugh when I worried about him—"

Frau Matt closed her eyes, and there was a silence in the room. Then the door opened and Rudi came in.

"Good evening, Mother," he said. "Good evening, Uncle."

The two looked at him without answering.

"Is something wrong?" he asked.

"Only that we were wondering," said Franz grimly, "if you were coming home at all tonight."

"It was very busy at the hotel today. There were many dirty dishes."

"Yes, I know. I saw them."

"You—you—" Rudi swallowed. "You mean you were there? It must have been while I was out on an errand."

"No doubt. And it must have been a very hard errand, considering what it did to your feet."

Rudi looked down at his shoes, scuffed by rocks and coated with the dust of the trail.

"Did—did old Teo say—"

"Your crony Teo told one lie after another. First to the waitress. Then to me. And now you are taking up where he left off."

Rudi was silent. His uncle stood up. "I am getting sick of these lies, boy," he said. "Good and sick of all this nonsense!"

Still Rudi said nothing.

"Well, what do you have to say for yourself?"

"I am sorry, Uncle."

"Sorry? Is that all? Sorry until the next time, when you do the same thing again."

"You promised me, Rudi," said Frau Matt gently.

The boy couldn't look at her. "Yes, Mother," he murmured.

"Why didn't you keep your promise?"

"I don't know."

"You don't know?"

"It—it is hard to explain. I did not mean to go— truly. I did not think of going at all. But when I stand there at the kitchen window, when I see the sun and the mountains—"

"I do not want to scold," his mother told him. "In all other things you are a good boy. Only in this do you disobey me and lie to me." She paused, studying her son's face. "I want you to be happy," she went on. "I want only to do what is right and good for you. In the hotel, and with Herr Hempel so interested in you, you will have such a fine future—the best of any boy in Kurtal. Can't you see how much better it is than the other? Than only climbing around on rocks and ice?"

"I have been a guide for twenty years," his uncle put in, "and look what it has got me. I do not have enough education even to speak to the fine visitors who now come here to Kurtal. I have not yet saved enough money to buy a dozen cows.

"Look what it has done for Teo Zurbriggen. He is crippled. He is poor. Soon you will have a fine career. You will be a business man, a gentleman. But he must work all his life in a kitchen."

There was a silence, and Rudi stared at the floor. "I will go now to the hotel," he murmured, "and finish the dishes."

But as he turned to leave there was a knock on the door.

"Come in," said his uncle.

And Captain Winter appeared.

"Ah—Franz," he said. "They told me at your house that I could find you here."

"It is an honor, my Captain. Sit down, please. This is my sister, Frau Matt."

Winter bowed respectfully. "The honor is mine, madam," he said, "to meet the widow of the great Josef Matt."

"And this is her son, Rudi," Franz said, as an afterthought.

The Englishman turned and looked at the boy, but he remembered his promise, and no sign of recognition showed on his face. "Hello, son," he said pleasantly. Then he turned back to Franz. "I just wanted to ask," he said, "if you're available for a climb tomorrow."

"Tomorrow? Yes, my Captain." Franz hesitated. "That is, if you do not mean—"

Winter smiled. "No, I don't mean the Citadel. I was thinking of the Wunderhorn. I know you've been on it often, and they say it's a good climb."

"Yes, it is good," Franz agreed.

"And that it gives a clear view of the Citadel."

"Yes, that is good too."

"Excellent. Suppose we leave tomorrow about noon. We can spend the night at the Blausee Hut and go on up the next morning. We'll need food and blankets, of course. It will probably be best to have a porter." He turned, as if struck by a sudden thought. "How about the youngster here?" he suggested, indicating Rudi. "He should do fine as a helper."

"No," said Franz. "No, my Captain. The boy is not available; he works elsewhere. But I will find a good man who—"

Rudi's voice cut suddenly across his uncle's. "Please!" The word was as if wrenched from his flesh. "Please! Just this once let me come, and I will show you what I can do!"

Franz shook his head. "It is not possible. Only now we have just talked of these things, and your mother does not—"

"But this is different, Uncle—with Captain Winter." Rudi's voice, his eyes, his whole body was pleading. "Captain Winter knows I can do it. He will tell you. Up on the glacier today he saw what I can do."

"On the glacier?" The guide's eyes moved to Winter. "You mean that he was with you, my Captain?"

"Oh, then they know—?" Winter glanced at Rudi.

"All we know," said Franz, "is that he went up into the mountains today. Leaving his work and defying his mother."

"But he told you nothing of what happened?"

"Happened?" Frau Matt repeated.

"No," said Franz, "he told us nothing."

"In that case," said Captain Winter quietly, "it will be my pleasure to tell you. Today, on the Blue Glacier, this boy saved my life."

"Saved—your—life?" breathed Frau Matt.

Franz stared at him. "What are you saying, my Captain?"

Winter told the story, and they listened in silence. Rudi listened too, feeling the blood slowly seeping into his cheeks and forehead, until it seemed to him that his whole face was on fire. Now and then he raised his eyes, but dropped them again almost instantly. And at last the Captain came to the end of the story.

Then he said: "What your son did, Frau Matt, was a very skillful and a very brave thing. There is no question but that I would be dead right now if he had not done it. I think his father, if he were alive today, would be proud of him."

Now the pounding in Rudi's head was so strong that he thought at any moment it might split right open. Through it, dimly, he was aware that his mother and uncle were no longer looking at Captain Winter, but at him. Indeed, Franz was staring, almost as if he had never seen him before.

"When did you learn these things?" the guide asked.

"I—I didn't." The boy's voice was no more than a whisper. "I just did what seemed best."

"And you held the Captain while he climbed up? All alone? With your own strength?"

"Yes, Uncle."

Winter crossed the room and put a hand on Rudi's shoulder. "Rudi told me," he said, "that he should not have been up in the mountains. But, as you see, it was very lucky for me that he was, and I beg you not to be angry with him. A boy who has done what he did deserves a reward, and I shall see that he gets it. But there's a reward *you* can give him that would be better than anything else." He paused and smiled at Frau Matt. "Let him come with us tomorrow on the Wunderhorn."

35

Franz started to speak, stopped, and looked at his sister. And now Captain Winter went over to her. "I think I know how you feel, Frau Matt," he said gently. "But, I promise you, there would be no danger. Your brother and I will be right there with him. And the Wunderhorn is not a difficult mountain."

Frau Matt looked at her hands. Then at last she looked up. . . . *"Please—please"* . . . Rudi murmured.

"What you have just told us—" his mother said to Winter. "What my boy has done—I am proud of him, of course. But—" she hesitated, "but there are things, my Captain, that perhaps you do not understand. Rudi is not a mountain boy, you see. He is not to be a guide, but a hotel man. For years we have planned his career, and now he is serving his apprenticeship in the kitchen at the Beau Site." Casting about for straws, she found one and clutched it. "Every day he works there. The cook needs him. He cannot be spared."

Rudi leapt forward and knelt by his mother's chair. "Yes—yes, I can—truly, Mother." The words tumbled over one another. "Old Teo will let me go—I know he will—he has said so. And besides there is Toni Hassler—he spoke to me last week—he would work as my substitute—"

He had seized her hands and was looking pleadingly into her face. Frau Matt looked back at him for a moment, and then past him, at the two men who stood watching. "I know that Captain Winter is a great climber," she said at last. "If he asks this for you— if he feels it is all right—"

Winter nodded reassuringly.

"And if your uncle—"

"It is up to you, Ilse," said Franz.

Frau Matt was beaten. "Then—then," she said "—this time—this once—"

But when she tried to go on, she couldn't, because Rudi was covering her face with kisses.

When he reached the hotel kitchen there were two hundred dirty dishes waiting for him beside the tub. But for all he cared there could have been two thousand.

During the whole evening he broke only three.

CHAPTER 4

Trial—

WHILE HE SLEPT, he dreamt *the dream*. The setting was the same as always: a thin ridge of rock, a dome of snow, and, beyond the dome, the blue and gleaming emptiness of the sky. But whereas, before, he had invariably been alone, there were now others with him: Captain Winter and his Uncle Franz, a few paces back, and behind them a small shadowy figure—perhaps his mother?—who seemed to be calling him.

All the rest, though, was exactly as in the other dreams. He, Rudi, stepped up from the rock onto the snow. He stood on the very crest of the snow, and all the mountain, all Switzerland, all the world, was beneath him. For a moment he knelt. Then, rising, he unstrapped a pole he had been carrying on his back, took a red flannel shirt from his knapsack, and tied the shirt to the pole by its sleeves. He set the pole into the snow—the magical, shining snow upon which no man had ever stood before; and now a wind was blowing, and the shirt flapped like a flame on the white summit of the Citadel. . . .

Later he awoke, and it was dawn. But the dream was still with him. Getting up, he went to the chest where he kept his few clothes and from the very bottom, where it lay carefully folded, took out—the red shirt. It was old and tattered and moth-eaten, and on the inside of the neck, in barely decipherable letters, was written the name *Josef Matt*. But the dye in the flannel must have been the best, for, in all the years Rudi had had it, its deep crimson had not faded. Spreading the shirt on his bed, Rudi examined it to see if the moths had been recently at work. They had. A new cluster of holes gaped from one of the armpits, and he must remember to patch them up soon, if the sleeve were not to fall off altogether. For a while he stood looking down at it. Once more, quickly, lightly, he bent and touched it. Then, refolding it, he put it back in the chest.

At the hotel there were of course the breakfast dishes to clean, but he did them in an hour. Excitedly he told Teo of what had happened, and, as he had been sure, the old cook was not only willing, but delighted, that he should go. The dishes done, he went out and found Toni Hassler and told him to report for work at noon.

When he returned, Old Teo pointed at a table. "There is a note for you," he said.

"A note?"

In all his life Rudi had never received a written message. He stared, unbelieving, at the folded sheet of paper, but when he picked it up he saw that, sure enough, it bore his own name. Opening it, he read:

If you will go to Alex Burgner's shop, you will find ordered for you some things that may be useful. They are only a small token of the admiration and gratitude of your friend and fellow-climber, John Winter.

A shout rose into his throat and stuck there. Teo was watching him, and he thrust the note into the old man's hand. Then, remembering that he couldn't read, he snatched it back and read it aloud; and, even now, he could scarcely control his voice.

The cook's pale eyes twinkled. "Well—" he said. "Well, things are getting interesting." And when Rudi still stood motionless: "So, what are you waiting for?"

"You mean I may go now?" Rudi hesitated. "But there is still the silver to be polished. And Toni Hassler is not coming until twelve."

"Good. That means I will have two hours of peace." Old Teo waved a hand at him. "Go on—off with you! *Lausbube!* And if you do not climb like your father's son you need not bother to come back!"

By the time he had finished Rudi was in the alley. Two minutes later he was in the shop of Alex Burgner. On a shelf, waiting for him, were a gleaming ice-ax and a knapsack, and Herr Burgner brought him a pair of boots to try on for size.

"But these—these are the finest—"

"Yes, the finest," said Herr Burgner. "That is what the Captain ordered."

For an hour he tramped the streets, breaking in the boots. Then he went home—and at the last minute remembered to take them off before walking on his mother's polished floors. He went to his room, changed his clothes, and came out again. And this time his mother was there. She stared at the things he was carrying, and he explained how he had come by them.

"Such fine gifts!" she exclaimed. "So generous!" And then, as an afterthought: "But what a waste, too, since you will be using them only once."

Rudi started to speak, but thought better of it.

"Ah well," said Frau Matt, "your Uncle Franz can

use a new ax and pack, and the shoes we can perhaps sell to a guide with small feet."

Sitting on the stoop, he again put on the boots. He adjusted the straps of the pack. He hefted the ax. At a quarter of twelve his uncle appeared, in his rough climbing clothes, and once more Rudi explained about his new equipment. Franz eyed the articles with grudging admiration. "Why is it that for twenty years I have been climbing on glaciers," he muttered, "and for me there has never been a rich Englishman waiting in a crevasse?"

As they started off, Frau Matt appeared in the doorway. "Franz—" she said.

They turned, and she looked up at her brother. "You will watch out for him?" she murmured.

"There is no need to worry, Ilse," he told her. "The Wunderhorn, it is nothing."

She looked at Rudi. "And you— you, my boy—you will do always as your uncle says—"

"Yes, Mother."

To his relief, she did not cry or cling to him. She did not even kiss him. She simply looked at him for another moment and then went quickly back into the house, while Rudi stared after her in surprise. What he did not know was that on another day, fifteen summers past, she had stood at that same door with his father, crying and kissing and clinging to him, as he set out to climb the Citadel. And that was a thing she could never do again, as long as she lived.

Captain Winter was waiting for them on the porch of the hotel. Fumblingly Rudi tried to express his gratitude, but the Englishman merely waved a hand, and they set about sorting their gear. Soon every-

41

thing was in its proper place: food, utensils, blankets, extra clothing, and a hundred feet of stout hempen rope. Then they shouldered their packs.

"All right, son?" asked Winter, smiling.

"Yes, sir."

"Pack not too heavy?"

"Oh no, sir."

The hotel fronted on the main square of the town, and as they walked across it Rudi's head was high and his step was proud. He knew almost everyone they passed, of course, and many greeted him and then turned and stared. Around the central fountain, where the guides gathered when they were not working, there was a rustle of interest and a row of brown-bearded faces raised from conversations and card games. "So you have a helper at last, Franz," called one of the Tauglich brothers. "It is good to see at last another Matt going to the mountains," said Andreas Krickel. A little farther on, a particularly wonderful thing happened: Klaus Wesselhoft came sauntering down the street. Klaus was eighteen and an apprentice guide. He was big and strong and loudmouthed, and he made a favorite sport of taunting Rudi by calling him "Plate-scraper" and "Angel-face." He didn't taunt him now, though. Instead, he walked past as if he had not seen him. But Rudi knew that he *had* seen him—seen the ax and the pack and the boots and the two men striding beside him—and suddenly his heart was singing and he wanted to shout in his joy.

Then the town was behind them. They crossed the brook and wound up through the meadows. They went in single file—Captain Winter first, his uncle second, himself third—and their pace was slow, but strong and steady. Soon they came to the forest's edge

42

and the wayside shrine. Winter bared his head as he passed. Franz crossed himself. More than any time before, Rudi wanted to kneel and pray, but with the two men there ahead of him he could not bring himself to do it and, instead, merely crossed himself, too, and said his prayer under his breath.

Soon after, they passed the blue spruce in which his staff was hidden, but there was no need for him to stop there today. As they climbed on, his fingers lovingly stroked the smooth haft of his ice-ax.

In two hours they had come up out of the forest onto the gray boulder-slopes above. So far, so good, Rudi thought. The one thing he had been worried about was his boots, for new boots were supposed to hurt. But these felt as if he had been born wearing them. Near treeline they stopped briefly for a bite of food and a drink of cold mountain water. Then, moving on, they came to the fork in the path which Rudi had passed the day before. This time, however, their route did not bear to the left, toward the Citadel, but right, in the direction of the Wunderhorn. They trudged up steep mounds of gravel, crossed a moraine and a small glacier, wound through a maze of tumbled rocks on the far side. And here Rudi had his first difficulties.

For it had grown warmer. Much warmer. In the forest they had been protected from the sun, but now it beat down on them, unobstructed, and soon Rudi's body was bathed in sweat. His pack seemed to grow heavier. Now and then he stumbled. With every step he was learning that it was one thing to roam the mountains, free and unencumbered, and quite another to be a porter carrying a thirty-pound load. But he would have bitten his tongue off before he complained; crawled on hands and knees before falling behind. He sweated. He strained. He kept going. And after another hour they came out onto a level stretch near the base of the Wunderhorn, and there before them was the small mountain lake called the Blausee and, on its far side, the overnight hut.

By the standards of a later time it was perhaps not much of a place. In years to come many Alpine cabins would be almost like small hotels, complete with cots or bunks, piped-in water, a cook and helpers, finally even telephones; and the Blausee Hut in 1865 had, to be sure, none of these. But it was nevertheless the pride of Kurtal. Built only a few seasons before, to accommodate the new crowds of tourists and climbers, it was strong and snug and had space for the night for as many as thirty people. There was a great hearth and firewood, brought up on muleback, for cooking. There was a plank table, benches and oil lamps, and in the loft above, reached by a ladder, piles of fresh straw on which to spread one's blankets. Once inside, the surrounding peaks and glaciers seemed as remote as the town itself, four thousand feet below.

The hut, that evening, was almost full, with guides and their employers. Some had merely come up for the walk and view and would go down in the morning. Some would set out for one or another of the nearby peaks. All the guides, of course, were known to Franz and Rudi, and again, as in the town square, there were glances and comments that made the boy's heart swell with satisfaction. Soon all trace of his tiredness was gone. The fire crackled cheerfully, and when dusk came the oil lamps gleamed. He and Franz and Captain Winter had their supper of meat and cheese, fruit and chocolate, and his uncle made no objection when he drank with them from their jug of wine. Later, he squatted by the fire, while the others, at the table, smoked their pipes, talked and occasionally threw a word to him over their shoulders.

A warm glow filled his body. He was where he belonged. He was a man among men.

CHAPTER 5

—and Error

IT WAS STILL DARK when Franz woke him. As in all mountain climbing, they were to make an early start, so that they could already be high on the peak by the best hours of the morning and back down to safety before the afternoon thaw.

Some of the others in the loft were also stirring. Some were still asleep. They ate a quick breakfast, and then put on their outer clothing, laced up their boots and went out. The cold cut at them like a blade, and it was hard for Rudi to believe that they were in the selfsame place in which, twelve hours before, he had been panting and sweating. Skirting the little lake, they began the ascent of a ridge that rose from its farther end, and it was good to be moving and to feel the blood slowly coming to life in the body. Apparently they would be the only climbers on the Wunderhorn that day, for there was no one ahead of them and no one behind.

It was still night, with no moon, but the stars gave enough light for them to find the way, and Franz did not bother to light his lantern. Nor did they need the rope yet, for the angle of ascent, though steady, was gentle. Franz went first, Captain Winter second, with Rudi—as befitted a porter—again last. And this morn-

46

ing he had no trouble at all in keeping up with them. For an hour their pace continued unbroken, while the stars paled and dawn showed in the east. The only sound between earth and sky was the clinking of axes against the rock.

Then they left the ridge and worked obliquely upward across a slope of frozen snow. But this, too, was not steep, and only once or twice was it necessary for Franz to pause and chop out footholds with his ax. In another half-hour they reached a second ridge: the main southern buttress of the Wunderhorn. Here the real climbing would begin, and they stopped and roped up.

"All right, boy?" asked Winter, smiling.

"All right, sir," Rudi grinned back.

Up they went then. And up. They followed the ridge for a while, worked out onto a face, returned to the ridge. They followed a deep cleft, then a series of ledges, then what seemed like a great curving stairway of granite slabs. The going was steep now. The mountain walls rose almost vertically. But Rudi felt no dizziness, and everywhere he was able to find good holds for hands and feet. Now and then, at a particularly tricky stretch, Franz and Captain Winter stopped up above and stood braced with the rope while he came after them; but not once did he need to put his weight on it, nor would he have slipped without it.

For a long time the air had been gray with dawnlight. And now suddenly it was golden, as the sun came up over the eastern ranges. The glaciers and snowfields below seemed almost to leap up at them in a dazzling glare. The mica in the rock around them glittered like diamonds. Quickly the day grew warmer, and soon they paused to strip off their sweaters and

47

stow them in their packs. Then up they went again. And up. And up.

Franz and Captain Winter alternated in the lead; and this, Rudi knew, was the greatest compliment a guide could pay to his employer, for no professional would dream of allowing an amateur to go first, unless he was certain that that amateur was as capable as himself. Watching from below, the boy noted the differences between them. His uncle climbed as he did everything else: slowly, carefully, deliberately. His big body inched over a bulge or around a cornice as if it were a moving part of the mountain itself. The Englishman, on the other hand, was all quickness, lightness and grace. He took no chances; all his movements were measured and sure. But he accomplished them with a dash and brilliance that made Rudi think of a fencer or jousting warrior, rather than of a man struggling with inanimate rock. Now that he was in his natural element on a mountainside, it was easy to see why John Winter was ranked as one of the finest climbers in the world.

The two men led. Rudi followed. And he followed easily. Not once did he need the rope; not once did he delay them by slipping or fumbling; and now a great exhilaration filled him, as he realized that what they could do, he could do too. Indeed, there were times when he could have gone faster. There were times when, peering up, he was certain that he could see better routes and holds and stances than the ones they were using. But this, of course, he kept to himself. It was enough to know that where they could go, he could go. Where *anyone* could go, he, Rudi Matt, could go too.

They were climbing on the south side of the Wunderhorn. When they turned they could see the valley and the town far below, and, all around, a high host of peaks. But one peak was missing. *The* peak was missing. For an hour they climbed, and then another, but the great tower of the Citadel remained hidden behind the shoulder of the Wunderhorn. Then at last they reached the shoulder. They came out onto an almost level stretch beneath the mountain's summit cone, followed it around to a point above the west face . . . *and there it was.* Finding a sunny ledge, they took off their packs, unroped and sat down to rest. Franz brought out cheese, sausage and a jug of tea. While they ate and drank they stared silently at the Citadel.

As on every other time that he had ever looked at it, something that was half thrill and half shiver passed through Rudi's body. High though they were—at perhaps 11,000 feet on the Wunderhorn—the Citadel appeared still to soar as far above them as it had from the valley. A monster of rock and ice, it seemed to blot out half the sky, rising in great sweeps and thrusts and jagged edges to the remote white crest that was its mighty summit. The other mountains, roundabout it, looked like foothills. It towered above them like a giant among pygmies. Preëminent. The King.

For a long time no one spoke. Captain Winter ate his lunch almost without noticing it, his eyes squinting out across the gulf of blue space. And now Rudi knew why the Englishman had wanted to see the Citadel from high up on the Wunderhorn, for much that was hidden from below was now plain and clear before them in the brilliant sunlight. Not only the lower slopes were visible, but the upper as well: the whole intricate maze of ridges and precipices, clefts and gullies, towers and battlements that formed the vast eastern side of the mountain. Plainest of all, in sharp profile against the sky, was the great twisting spine of the southeast ridge, and along it Rudi's eyes now moved slowly upward. Perhaps a third of the way from the bottom they stopped and fixed on the dark outthrust of rock known as the Fortress, which marked the highest point reached by his father and Sir Edward Stephenson, fifteen years before. Since then, no one had climbed even that far. And no one had ever climbed higher.

Captain Winter was studying the ridge too. Occasionally he moved a finger slowly through the air, as if tracing an imaginary route. Suddenly he spoke to Franz. "On your brother-in-law's attempt," he asked "—did he get to the top of the Fortress?"

"No," said Franz. "Only to the base."

"But he believed there was a way over it?"

"Over, or around it—yes."

"What do *you* believe?"

"I have no belief. I know nothing about the Citadel."

Winter's eyes met the guide's. "Wouldn't you *like* to know?" he asked.

"No, my Captain, I would not." Franz looked away. "It is an evil mountain, that. A killer mountain. It has been left alone now for fifteen years, and it is best that it be left alone forever."

The Englishman relapsed into silence. Again his eyes squinted and his finger traced slow patterns in the air. Several times Rudi was on the point of speaking —of giving his opinion, of pointing out this or that. But each time he stopped himself, because he did not want to seem forward. And because he was afraid of what his uncle would say. Presently Winter took a pad and pencil from his pack and began drawing detailed sketches of the Citadel. He worked on them for a long time and with great concentration. Franz, leaning back against a rock, seemed to be dozing. After a while Rudi grew restless and began exploring the shoulder of the Wunderhorn.

It had been decided that they would not go on to the summit. Winter had had what he wanted—an unobstructed high-up view of the southeast ridge of the Citadel—and he was not interested in laboring up to the top of a peak that had been climbed many times before. It was therefore not up but down that Rudi looked, as he moved across the high shoulder: along the route they had come up and now would soon be descending. Unless—an idea struck him—unless there was a better route. And suddenly he was convinced that there must be. While the others still rested, he would spy out a better, more direct way down from the shoulder, and that would be his contribution to the day's climbing.

Edging along the rim of rocks, he peered down, searching. A few yards along, there was a possible starting-off place, but investigation quickly showed that it led nowhere. Beyond it, however, was a second break in the rim that really promised a route. It began with a deep cleft, or chimney, and down this Rudi lowered himself with ease. At the bottom was a broad ledge and beyond it, to the left, a narrower, sloping ledge, leading diagonally downward to a jutting platform. What was directly beyond the platform he could not see; but about ten yards farther on the whole side of the mountain angled out in a fine craggy ridge that would obviously be easy going the whole way down. Rudi grinned with satisfaction. The mountainside below the ledge and platform was steep—almost vertical; there was nothing but thin air for three thousand feet to the glacier below. But mere steepness did not bother a real climber, so long as there were sound

51

holds for hands and feet. He would cross over to the platform, see if there was a way from its far side to the ridge, and, if so, hurry back and tell the others of his discovery.

He moved from the broad ledge to the narrow one. The granite wall above it was smooth, with no support for the hands, but he did not need any, for the two- or three-inch width of the ledge was enough for stance and balance. He took a careful step—a second step—a third. One more would bring him to the jutting platform. But before he could take it there was a soft tremor beneath his feet. One moment, his footing was a seemingly solid band of mountain granite; in the next, it was a crumbling mass of loose fragments. With a violent leap he thrust himself clear, lunged forward and landed on the platform, and in the same instant, behind him, the whole ledge on which he had been standing disintegrated and plunged in spinning fragments into space below.

For perhaps a minute he stood motionless. Leaning in against the rock, he struggled to control the rasp of his breathing and the pounding of his heart. Then, when he had half succeeded, he turned and took stock of his position. First he looked ahead, toward the ridge, and saw—nothing. The mountain wall beyond his platform was marble-smooth, without foot- or handholds of any kind, and no climber in the world could have crossed it. Then he looked back along the way he had come, and this was little better. Where the narrow ledge had been were now only a few crumbled edges of broken rock. He looked up—at a vertical cliff-face. He looked down—into space.

How long a time passed before he moved again he did not know. And then it was only a matter of inches, to the edge of the platform. Very slowly and cautiously he extended one foot until it rested on the crumbled rock where the ledge had been. He put part of his weight on it—a little more—and the foot slipped. A moment later he tried again. And slipped again. Suddenly something happened to him that had never happened before in his life. He was dizzy. The glacier far below him began to spin like a great white wheel. Sky and mountain spun, and a reeling, sickening darkness closed in on his body and brain. Back on the platform, he clung to the rock with all his strength, until at last the darkness lightened, the spinning slowed. He looked around again. His face was drawn, his lips white. "I must call for help," he thought. But he couldn't call. He had no breath left. And he was too ashamed.

Then, in the next instant, he saw that there was no need to call. Captain Winter and his uncle were climbing down the cleft from the shoulder and in a moment were on the broad ledge beneath it, looking across at him.

They did not have to ask questions. Their experienced eyes told them what had happened. "Stay where you are. Don't move," said Winter. And though he spoke quietly, his voice, in the still air, was as clear as if he had been at Rudi's side.

Even while he spoke, Franz was uncoiling his rope; and now, for the next ten minutes, he and Winter took turns in trying to throw one end across to the boy. But it was no good. The curve of the mountainside was such that, each time, the rope missed the platform by a few feet, and on the fifth or sixth try Rudi all but lost his balance in reaching for it.

"All right," said Winter finally, "I'm coming over to you."

But Franz shook his head. "No," he said. "It is I who will go."

"I am lighter," the Englishman protested. "It will be safer for me."

"He is my nephew, sir—not yours. And my responsibility."

Franz laid down his ice-ax and unslung his pack. Then he tied one end of the rope around his waist and handed the other to Winter.

"Wait—I will try again, Uncle," Rudi called. "I am lighter than either of you."

But Franz paid no attention. Advancing to the rim of the ledge, he studied the stretch ahead with grim face and narrowed eyes. "You will please hold me as best you can," he said to Winter. Then he started across.

Winter realized there was no use in further argument. He searched for a projection of rock around which he could secure the rope, found none, and coiled it, instead, around his own body. It was at best, however, a poor support. If Franz had been directly below him it would have been all right; a slip could have been caught before it gained momentum. But the guide was not below. He was off to the side. And if he lost his hold his body would swing back unchecked, like a pendulum, and almost surely pull Winter off the ledge.

Still there was no other way. The Englishman braced himself. The guide moved forward. He put a foot on the crumbled rock, tested it, put his weight on it. The fragments shifted a little, but held, and cautiously he brought his other foot forward. His fingers groped over the smooth wall above him, searching for the tiniest bump or crevice that would give him a hold. His progress was so slow that he scarcely seemed to be moving at all; yet presently he had taken a second step, and a third. Only two more were now needed to bring him to the platform, but the first would be to the spot where Rudi had tried to stand and slipped.

Franz's boot-nails scraped softly on the broken rock. There was no other sound. On either side of him Rudi and Winter stood as motionless as if they were part of the mountain, and for a long moment Franz was motionless too. Then he moved again. One foot moved. It inched slowly along the loose gravel, probed it, dug into it; and the other foot came after. For an instant Franz teetered above empty space, supported only by a half-inch of toe on the crumbling mountainside. Then he leaned forward—lunged—and was standing beside Rudi on the solid platform.

"By God," said Winter quietly from across the void. "That was climbing!"

But Franz was wasting no time on words. Pulling in the rope that trailed behind him, he made a loop near its middle and tied Rudi into it. "All right. Go on," he said.

The boy started across. Twice he slipped on the loose rock, but, with the rope held taut on either side of him, he did not fall, and in less than a minute he was beside Winter on the broad ledge. Then Franz, now alone on the platform, untied the rope from his own waist and secured it around a knob of rock. Winter pulled in his end; again the rope was drawn taut; and, using it as a sort of handrail, Franz came quickly and easily across.

"So," he said. "That is done."

There was of course no way of pulling in the length of rope that was tied to the knob. Cutting it loose with his knife, Franz fastened himself to the new, shortened end and picked up his ax and pack. Once—only once

—he glanced at Rudi, but his dark bearded face was expressionless.

They descended almost in silence. Occasionally Winter made a comment or suggestion about the route, but Franz merely grunted his replies; and to Rudi he did not speak at all. The boy was now tied onto the middle of the rope, with the Englishman ahead of him and his uncle behind. The latter scarcely let him climb at all, but simply lowered him down the mountain, as he would have done with a novice tourist. The guides of Kurtal had a contemptuous phrase for it—"Like a bundle of firewood."

Later, on the easy ridge above the hut, Winter walked beside him and put a hand on his shoulder. "Don't worry about it, son," he said gently.

Rudi couldn't answer.

"All of us make mistakes. Look at me, yesterday—walking straight into a crevasse."

The hand was warm, the words were kind; but Rudi scarcely felt or heard them. All he could hear was the slow, measured rhythm of his uncle's tread. All he could feel was the cold grimness in his uncle's face. Clearer than words, that face told him its message: that this, his first trial as a mountain porter, would also be his last. A wave of hopelessness engulfed him. And of bitter shame. For his, he well knew, had been the worst of all sins that a mountaineer can commit. He had made others risk their lives to save his.

CHAPTER 6

Master and Pupil

IT RAINED. For three days sun and mountains alike disappeared, and the valley of Kurtal was wrapped in a cloak of gray mist.

On the morning of the second day Captain Winter had asked Franz to meet him at the hotel. "Climbing will be impossible for a while," he told him. "So I am going on a short trip to Geneva."

"Then you will come back, sir?"

"Yes, then I'll come back." The Englishman paused, and his gray eyes studied the guide's face. "And I don't have to tell you, do I," he asked, *"why* I'm coming back?"

Franz said nothing.

"We could do it, you know. You and I, together. You're the best guide in the valley, Franz, and I'd rather do it with you than any man in the world."

Franz was shaking his head slowly.

"All right," said Winter, "you're still not convinced, and I'm not going to argue. . . . Let's leave it this way. I'll be gone only a few days. Think it over while I'm away; decide what's really in your heart; and when I come back—"

57

The sound of a horn came from the coach in the square outside. Winter shook hands and made ready to leave. "One other thing," he said, turning. "About the boy. Don't be too hard on him."

"The boy is all right," said Franz gruffly. "He is back where he belongs."

"Back where he belonged," Rudi scraped the dishes. He soaked them, scrubbed them, dried them, stacked them and put them on the shelves. A few hours later he did it all over again. And that evening. And the next morning.

The rain beat against the kitchen windows. Mist filled the streets beyond. And he was glad of the mist and the rain, because they shut out the mountains. He did not want to see the mountains: reminding him, mocking him.

His Uncle Franz had told no one of what had happened on the Wunderhorn, but whether from kindness or from family pride Rudi didn't know. When his mother had asked how things had gone, Franz had merely shrugged and said, "He is back all in one piece. Now he can return to his proper work." And the next day she had told Rudi to take his ax, pack and boots over to Franz's house. "If he can sell them, you will of course get the money," she said. "But it is a shame that they should lie idle in a cupboard when you have no more use for them."

In the hotel kitchen, Teo Zurbriggen watched him and said nothing. But he knew that something had gone wrong, and Rudi knew that he knew, and on the third morning he could keep his misery to himself no longer and told the old man the whole story. When he had finished the cook shook his head and muttered, "Yes,

58

that was bad. Bad. That is the trouble with you young ones. Once you have learned a little, then you think that you know it all."

Rudi worked. He ate and slept and got up and worked again. He did not see his uncle. He avoided his friends. His mind felt numb—frozen—and in it was only one small light, one corner of warmth. This was the thought of Captain Winter's return. Just how it would affect him, or for what he could hope from it, he could not have said. But still it was there. The waiting. The hope. Without it, he thought, he could never have faced each dreary day as it stretched before him.

On the fourth day the weather cleared. First the rain stopped. Then the mist lifted slowly, disclosing the high world above the valley: the meadows, the forests, the boulder-slopes, the glaciers, and finally the great circle of the peaks. Up on the peaks, of course, it had not been rain that had fallen, but snow, and the host stood white and gleaming in the returning sun. High above all the rest rose the Citadel, its summit a vast, blinding dazzle in the cloudless sky.

Teo stood at the open window and sniffed the air like an old bloodhound. Then he turned and looked at Rudi, who was at his usual place at the dishpan.

"Tomorrow is your day off?" he asked.

"Yes," said Rudi listlessly.

"I will make it my day off too. Gretchen can manage. Meet me at my house at eight o'clock."

The boy stared at him, uncomprehending. "Your house, sir?" he repeated.

"Yes, we will start from there."

"Start? What do you mean? Where are we going?"

"You are going to school," said Old Teo.

Leaving the town, they followed a twisting path up through the pastures. It was not the path that led toward the Citadel and Wunderhorn, but another one, on the opposite side of the valley. Old Teo went first and, in spite of his limp, kept up a strong and steady pace; and in two hours they were out of the forest and on the boulder-slope above. Directly in front of them now was a small peak known as the Felsberg. Dwarfed by the greater peaks around it, it was scarcely noticeable from the valley, and its summit was not even high enough to have caught snow in the recent storm. But, though small, it was steep and rugged, and it was often used as a "practice mountain" by guides and visiting climbers.

"Well," said Teo, peering up at its crags, "now we will see if you are a climber or a dishwasher."

Skirting the base of the Felsberg, they came to the foot of a tall cliff, and Teo sat down on a boulder. "All right," he said. "To the top and back, please. I will watch."

"Yes sir," said Rudi.

For a few minutes he studied the cliff, picking out his route. Then he started off. He did not, of course, have his fine new boots, and with smooth-soled shoes he had to be extra careful; but he concentrated closely and made good progress. He did not hug the rock, as an amateur would, but leaned well out from it, so that he could see what he was doing. He tested each hand and foothold before he trusted his weight to it and made sure that, whenever possible, he had three sound points of support. After each section of the climb he paused and again studied the rocks above him, so that he would not, by haphazard climbing, get himself into some impossible position from which he could neither go on nor descend. Reaching the top of the cliff, he rested briefly. Then, with equal care and concentration, he climbed back down to where Teo was waiting.

"Was it all right?" he asked.

"Yes, of course it was all right," said the cook. "And how else should it be? On such a little thing a cow could go all right—with three legs."

They moved to another point, and he had Rudi climb again. He had him climb a cliff face, on slabs, in a steep chimney, on a knife-edged ridge. "That was a little harder," he conceded, when the boy returned to him again. "For that it would take a four-legged cow."

They circled to another side of the peak, and Teo looked up at it. "Can you do this one?" he asked.

"Yes, I think so," said Rudi.

"All right—do it with this." Unslinging his pack from his shoulders, Teo emptied out the few things that were in it and refilled it with heavy stones.

"But—but that will throw me off balance—"

"Of course it will throw you off balance. On a real mountain, what would you rather be: a little off balance or dead from cold or starvation?"

Rudi slung on the load, and it almost buckled his knees. As he climbed, it swung maddeningly from side to side; it caught on projections and got wedged into clefts; on the steeper pitches it seemed to claw at his back like a live thing, trying to pull him loose from his delicate holds in the rock. But he made it. Up and down again. His shoulders ached, his knees shook, his body poured out sweat—but he made it.

"You want to be a guide," said Old Teo, as he rested. "A guide carries a pack. When he is a real guide he does not think of it as a load or a burden. It is as much a part of him as his rope or his boots or his

61

clothing. It is like part of his body. Do you understand?"

Rudi nodded.

"All right, do it again."

Rudi did it again.

Then Teo uncoiled his rope. "Show me your knots," he said.

The boy tied and untied knots, and the old man told him what was wrong with them. He had him practice until they were right. Next they turned to belaying—the technique of holding another person on a rope. First they worked on the rock belay, in which the rope is hitched around a projection in the mountain, to take the pull if a climber should fall; then on the body belay, used when there is no such projection, in which the rope is supported by the climber's own shoulders and arms. "Now let us see you rappel," said Teo, when that was over. And for a half-hour, while he watched and criticized, Rudi practiced lowering himself down unclimbable cliffs by means of the doubled rope wound around his body.

By now it was past midday. Teo squinted up at the sun. "Let us eat lunch," he said. "Afterward we will do the more important things."

Rudi had no idea what "the more important things" were; but he let it go. He would find out soon enough. Side by side, he and the old man sat on a flat rock at the foot of the Felsberg, munching their bread and sausage and looking out over the valley.

"Do you think I will ever learn, Teo?" he asked.

"Learn? To climb?" Teo rubbed a gnarled hand slowly along his jaw. "If by climbing," he said, "you mean putting one foot in front of the other and going up and down a mountain, you have learned already. Or perhaps you did not need to learn, but were born knowing." He paused, searching for the words for his thoughts. "But if you mean more than that—if you mean climbing as a guide climbs, as a true mountaineer climbs—then the answer is still to be seen."

"I want to learn, Teo. Teach me. Please teach me."

"I am not sure it is a thing that can be taught. Rather does it come with living—with growing. These climbs you have made just now: you did well on them, yes. But it is not important. It does not really matter. Do you know why it does not matter? It is because you made them alone."

Rudi started to speak, but the old man went on: "To climb alone, as one person—to find a way up steep places and not fall off: that is a part of mountaineering, of course. But only a small part. On a big mountain one does not climb alone. A guide does not climb alone. What does the word *guide* mean? It means to lead others. To help others. The other day, with that foolishness on the Wunderhorn. How did it happen? Why did it happen? Was it not, perhaps, because you had not yet learned this? Because you were thinking, not of others, but only of yourself?"

Teo was looking at Rudi, and the old eyes were not unkindly. But the boy could not meet them.

"Yes," he murmured.

"And so you did a thing to be ashamed of."

"Yes."

They were silent a while. The sun gleamed on the mountains. High in the sky across the valley, it struck with white fire on the crest of the Citadel, untouched and inviolate since the beginning of time.

"You did not know your father—" said Old Teo quietly.

Rudi shook his head.

"So I will tell you something about him. Your father

was the best climber there has ever been in Kurtal. He was strong. He was sure. He could go places on a mountain that other men would not even dream of. But it was not only this that made him the best. It was that—how shall I say it?—that he had a flame in him; a thing inside; not of the body but of the heart. Alone of all the guides in the valley, he believed that the Citadel could be climbed, and it was the hope of his life that he would be the one to do it."

Teo paused and smiled a little. "Perhaps you have heard," he said, "that your father, when he climbed, always wore a red shirt?"

"Yes, I have heard," Rudi murmured.

"And do you know why he wore it? He wore it, he said, because he knew that someday he would stand on the summit of the Citadel. He would stand there and put a pole in the snow, and then he would take off the shirt and tie it to the pole like a flag, and the red flag in the sky would be seen from all the valleys and cities of Switzerland. When your father said this, he smiled. He pretended he was making a joke. But, inside, it was not a joke. It was what he dreamed of; what he lived for."

Teo stared out at the great mountain. "Then at last," he said, "he had his chance. There came to Kurtal the great English climber, Sir Edward Stephenson, and he too believed the Citadel could be climbed, and wanted to do it. He and your father talked. They made their plans. They searched and explored. And then they set out. I was the only man in the valley who would go with them, and they took me along as assistant guide and porter."

Again he paused. He looked at Rudi's face. "Yes, you know the story. And you do not want to hear it again. But now you must hear it again, because it is

64

the story of what I have been saying to you. It is a story that any boy who would be a guide must know and never forget as long as he lives."

Rudi did not speak.

"We started out," said Old Teo. "They had decided that the southeast ridge gave the best chance for success, so we went up the Blue Glacier and spent the night at the old hut at the top. The next morning we began climbing the ridge. It was hard, but not too hard. It went. By midday we had gained perhaps two thousand feet and an hour later were at the base of the big cliff that is called the Fortress. Here it was much harder; perhaps impossible." He pointed out across the blue miles of space. "Even from here you can see how the walls stand up. There was no way over them, so we looked for a way around. First we went to the right, then to the left, and on the left, far out, almost overhanging the south face, we saw what looked like an opening. We started up for it; we were nearly there. And then the accident happened. High up on the Fortress there was a great roar, and we knew that rocks were falling. We tried to run for shelter. We almost made it. But not quite. Suddenly the great rocks were crashing around us, and, though your father and I were not hit, Sir Edward was. A rock fell beside him and rolled against him, and his leg was broken.

"For an hour we stayed there. We did what we could for him, but it was not much. And of course two men alone could not get him down. Others would have to be brought up from the village, with slings and a stretcher. Your father decided that I should go down. 'And you?' I asked. 'I will stay here,' he said. It was getting late, and soon it would be dark. At the best it would be noon the next day before help

65

could arrive. But there was nothing else to do. One of us had to stay with Sir Edward, and your father, who was chief guide, insisted that it be he. So I left them there and started down. Night came, and I lost my way. I slipped and fell." Teo paused and looked down at his misshapen body. "I fell, not all the way, but thirty feet, onto my left side. And since then I have been what you see now.

"But I was not dead. I was able to crawl on to the hut, and in the hut were two chamois hunters, and they hurried down to Kurtal. In the morning the rescue party arrived. But meanwhile a storm had come up. For two days no one could set foot on the mountain, and on the third, when they started up, they already knew what they would find. Sir Edward and your father were in a little cave beneath the Fortress, where I had left them. They were dead. Frozen."

During his recital the old man had kept his eyes fixed on the mountain, but now once more he turned and looked at Rudi. "Now do you understand," he said, "why I have again made you hear this story? Your father did not die because a mountain was too steep. He did not die for conquest or for glory. Waiting there on that ridge, he himself was strong enough to go on up, or to go down. But he would not go, because he would not leave his client. He was thinking, not of himself, but of another. His red shirt—the flag that was to fly from the top of the Citadel—do you know where they found it? On Sir Edward Stephenson. While he himself was freezing to death, your father had taken it from his own back to try to keep another man warm."

There was a long silence.

Then Teo stood up. "Well, it is getting late," he said. "And there is still one more climb to be made."

He picked up his rope and handed one end to Rudi. Then, to the boy's astonishment, he tied the other end around himself.

"You—you will climb too?" asked Rudi.

"Yes, I will climb too."

Rudi looked up at the sheer cliffs rising above them. Then back at Teo. He looked at the crippled leg, the hunched shoulder, the withered arm. "But—but you cannot—" he protested.

"I know I cannot," said the cook. "Not alone, without help. . . . But I will not be alone. And you will help me."

Rudi stared at him.

"You will be my guide," said Teo.

"You mean—you would trust yourself—"

"To the son of Josef Matt? Yes, of course I will trust myself."

Seconds passed; perhaps a minute. Man and boy stood motionless, facing each other. Then they turned and walked together to the base of the cliff.

"So, up with you," said Teo.

Rudi began climbing. He climbed watchfully and carefully, while Teo payed out the rope, and presently a call from below told him that it had almost reached its full length. When he came to a good stance he turned and looked about him, and, finding a sound knob of rock, he passed the rope around it for a belay. "All right, come on!" he called. And Teo came. Rudi pulled the rope in smoothly and firmly around the rock, his body tensed for any pull or jerk. But there was none. The old man climbed slowly—very slowly— but he did not slip or stumble, and in a few minutes he was standing beside the boy on the ledge.

They went on to the next pitch. And the next. Each time Rudi went first, climbing as far as the rope would

67

let him, and then stopped and secured it while Teo came after. Sometimes the belay was around rock, sometimes, when no rock was available, around Rudi's own body. But still Teo made no use of the support. Peering down at him from his perches, the boy marveled at how he maneuvered his crippled body on the delicate hand- and footholds: keeping his strong side always in toward the rock-face, turning his handicaps into assets, moving always at a strange lopsided angle in order the better to keep his balance. And when he came up beside Rudi it was only to nod and say, "All right—go on."

But by now they were high on the cliff. And the going grew harder. Rudi had to climb one stretch, first by jamming an elbow and knee into a crevice in the rock, then by reaching up with his free hand and pulling himself onto a ledge above. Here there was no rock projection, and he used the body belay, bracing himself as best he could. There will be trouble this time, he thought. And there was. Teo got his good elbow and knee into the crevice and somehow managed to hoist himself up, but when it came to grasping the rim of the ledge, his crippled arm could not make it. He reached out and missed. Reached again and missed. Then his body made a lunge. His hand touched the ledge. It clawed at it—but could not hold it. At the same instant his voice came up to Rudi, as quietly as if he were talking to him from the stove in the hotel kitchen. "Steady now," he said. "Hold me."

There was a slight scratching sound: that was all. Then the pull came. Teo's hand slipped down from the rim, his elbow and knee lost their hold in the crevice, and he dangled free against the mountainside. The rope bit into Rudi's body like a circular knife. It would cut through him, he thought. But it did not cut through him. Nor did it pull him from the ledge. Braced and straining, he held fast. Then he pulled. He pulled in a foot of rope and hitched it around him; pulled again, hitched again; and again. He could hear Teo's feet scraping for support on the wall below. His hand reappeared on the rim, and then his other hand: the good hand. Rudi pulled and hitched, pulled and hitched. And then suddenly it was over; the strain and bite and tearing pressure were gone, and Teo crawled up onto the ledge beside him.

"That was not bad, boy," the old man said to him. "For a young *Lausbube,* not bad at all."

Twice more he slipped before they reached the top of the Felsberg. And three times on the way down. But each time Rudi held him; and each time, though he sweated and strained, the shock and the fear were less. Where did *he* come off to be afraid, he thought grimly, when Old Teo, struggling and dangling below, was trusting his life to him without a murmur?

At the bottom, they untied themselves from the rope. Teo coiled it carefully and stowed it in his pack.

"Not bad," he said again.

And that was all he said.

But on the way down through the forest Rudi's heart sang like the birds in the berry bushes. He had done all right, he thought, over and over. He had learned to climb as a guide climbs and atoned for the disgrace of the Wunderhorn. He had done all right—and things would be all right. Teo would tell his uncle; he himself would tell him, plead with him, show him what he could now do. And when Captain Winter came back— his mind raced forward—yes, when the Captain came back: that was when everything would really change. The Captain was on his side. He would persuade his uncle, convince his uncle. And then—the boy raised his eyes. He held them, fixed and shining, on the great shape that filled the sky on the far side of the valley. Yes, yes, he thought exultantly—*when Captain Winter came* . . .

Then they were in the town, in the streets, back at last in the hotel kitchen. As he was tying on his apron, Gretchen, the waitress, came in from the dining room.

"There was a gentleman here looking for you," she said in a bored voice. "He looked like an Englishman. He said he wanted to tell you goodbye."

"Goodbye?" Rudi's voice was a whisper.

"He said he had come back here this morning but was leaving again on the afternoon coach. There was something about talking to your uncle—I don't know. Anyhow he left."

"Left? Left Kurtal? You mean for good—"

Gretchen took a stack of dishes from a shelf and yawned. "That's right," she said. "For good."

CHAPTER 7

A Prisoner Escapes

FRANZ LERNER sat in his sister's parlor and slowly shook his head.

"He is a strange man, this Captain Winter," he said. "As a climber, he is the best *Herr* I have ever had. He can do things that some of the best guides cannot do. But he is too ambitious. He is like a man possessed."

"He thinks only of the Citadel?" said Frau Matt.

"Yes, only of the Citadel. Do you know what he did, Ilse? He offered to pay me twice the usual guide's fee if I would go with him. *Twice,* mind you! For four days it would have been enough to buy a calf or two shoats. Only what good would calves and shoats do me if—" He broke off, shrugged and puffed thoughtfully on his pipe.

"You did right, brother," said Frau Matt.

"Yes, I did right." Then he said it again, almost angrily. "I did right! . . . I said to him, 'My Captain, it is a privilege to climb with you. It is not like climbing with other clients, who must be pushed and pulled up a mountain; but like with another guide, a companion, an equal. Do you know what I will do, my Captain? I said to him. 'I will climb with you not for twice the

71

usual fee, but for *half*. We will climb all the mountains you like, by whatever routes you like. The Dornelberg by the west ridge. The Täschhorn by the north face. Anything. Any peak from Mont Blanc to Austria.' " Franz shook his head again. "But no, he does not want that. All he wants is one peak. That accursed peak. . . ."

His eyes moved to the window. He gazed up past the rooftops, past the sloping meadows, the forests, the boulder-slopes, the glaciers, to where the great fang of the Citadel pierced the shining sky. " 'There are some things, my Captain,' I said, 'that God intended for men; and there are some things that He did not. He did not intend men to swim the oceans, or to reach the center of the earth, or to fly. And He did not intend them to climb the Citadel. The Citadel He is keeping for Himself, untouched—forever. And I do not believe,' I told him, 'that men should set themselves against the will of God.' "

Frau Matt, too, was looking from the window. Then, suddenly, she turned away and hid her face in her hands. After a moment her brother got up and came over and stood beside her. "I am sorry, Ilse," he murmured, putting a big hand gently on her shoulder. "I will not talk of these things again."

Rudi listened and did not speak. He went about his work and did not speak. In the hotel kitchen, he soaked and scrubbed and dried and stacked the endless heaps of china and pewter, and, like his mother, he kept his eyes from the windows.

He wished that it would rain. He wished that the mist would close in over the village streets, shutting out everything beyond. But it did not rain. The sky remained flawlessly clear. Even though he kept turned away from the window, the great image beyond it filled the kitchen with its presence, and when at night he went home and to bed it followed him relentlessly into his dreams.

"Cheer up, boy. Be patient," Old Teo told him. "You're young, and all the world's before you."

But it was cold comfort. What good did it do to have the world before him, when he couldn't get to it? When he was like a prisoner staring at it from behind the bars of a cell?

One day he broke five dishes. The next day, seven. Then old Teo left him to watch a cheese fondue that was simmering on the stove, and he forgot about it and let it burn. And this time even the patient cook lost his temper. "By the Virgin and three hundred saints!" he shouted angrily. "You are like some silly girl in love— that's what you are. You are a nincompoop—a *dummer Esel*—"

His mother spoke to Herr Hempel, and the proprietor gave him a lecture. "Yes sir," he answered. "No sir," he answered. But it had no effect. Nothing had any effect. He did what he was told to do, spoke when he was spoken to, moved like a sleepwalker through the blankness of the days.

The worst ordeal was walking back and forth from his home to the hotel, for it was then that he would meet the other boys of the town. Even with his friends it was hard enough—with their questions about what had happened and why his uncle had not taken him climbing again. And with those who were not his friends it was unendurable. "Hey, here comes the master guide!" they would taunt him. "All hail the conqueror of Mount Dishpan! Where's your apron, guide? Where's your mop?"

Then it was Sunday and his mother was off visiting, and he was sitting alone in his room. Going to his

73

clothes chest, he took from the bottom his father's old red flannel shirt, spread it on the bed, and once again examined the moth holes. . . . Well, there was nothing else to do. . . . Downstairs he found his mother's sewing basket, and, taking it and the shirt outside, he sat down on the front steps and set to work on the bigger holes in the armpits. The afternoon sun was bright, the little sidestreet quiet and empty.

And then, suddenly, not empty; for, looking up, startled, he saw that Klaus Wesselhoft had come by and had stopped, staring at him. Klaus stood with his legs widespread and his hands on his hips, and his thick lips were spread in a mocking grin.

"Well, now," he said, "if it isn't the young ladies' Sunday sewing circle."

Rudi said nothing.

"Fawncy finding Master Rudi Matt, the famous boy guide, busy doing his crocheting."

Still Rudi said nothing.

"Or is it embroidery, Angel-face? Do tell now? Some lovely Swiss lace, maybe?"

Rudi put down the shirt and pushed the basket aside. Then he stood up and rushed him. Klaus was eighteen. He was taller and broader than Franz Lerner and had hands like two hams at the butcher's. But Rudi rushed him just the same, arms flailing. With one fist he hit Klaus on the chest and with the other on the shoulder, and then something big and hard exploded between his eyes, and he was sitting in the street with blood gushing from his nose.

"Naughty naughty," said Klaus, wagging a finger. "The great guide Angel-face had better stick to his embroidery."

Then, while Rudi got to his feet, he sauntered off, whistling, down the street.

The weather held fine. The town was full of visiting climbers, and the guides were busy: climbing all day, sleeping up in the huts, returning home every second or third night, only to start off for another climb the next morning. As the foremost guide of Kurtal, Franz Lerner was the busiest of all. In one week he made an ascent of the Wunderhorn with a client from Zurich, one of the Rotalp with two Americans, and a traverse of the Dornel Glacier with a young couple from England. Twice he used Toni Hassler as porter; once—and this filled Rudi's cup of bitterness—Klaus Wesselhoft. Each time his uncle returned to the town Rudi resolved to speak to him, reason and plead with him, take him to Old Teo, who would tell him how well he had done on the Felsberg. But each time something held him back. Pride? Fear of rebuff? He wasn't sure. Or perhaps it was neither of these, but rather that where his uncle would take him, if he consented, was not where he wanted to go. He did not want any mountain, but only one mountain. *The* mountain. And the chance for that was gone.

Then, late one afternoon, he came home from the hotel and found Franz, back from the Rotalp, talking with his mother on the steps of the house.

"There are more climbers this summer," he was saying, "than I have ever seen before in Kurtal."

"Yes, I have noticed," said Frau Matt. "Not only the hotels but the huts must all be full."

"So full there is hardly room to sleep. . . . Even the old hut—you know, the one beneath the southeast ridge of the Citadel that has not been used for years—even that now has someone in it. Today I passed near the foot of the Blue Glacier and looked up, and there was smoke coming from its chimney."

They continued talking, but Rudi went on in. He

went up to his room and sat on his bed and for a long time he remained there, motionless, while his uncle's words repeated themselves over and over in his mind. For if his uncle did not know what those words had meant, he, Rudi, did. As clearly as if it stood before him, he could see the old hut, bleak and lonely against the evening sky. He could see the thread of smoke above it. And within the hut, *Captain John Winter.* . . . Yes, Winter: that he knew. . . . Perhaps alone. Perhaps with a guide from Broli, on the far side of the mountain. For that, of course, was what had happened. Captain Winter had not really left at all. He had merely gone around the mountain and up the valley beyond, to Broli. He had seen the famous Broli guide, Emil Saxo, whom he had talked about that first day on the glacier, and they had gone up to the hut together. Or, if Saxo had refused, he had gone alone. One or the other. But he himself had gone. That was certain. He was there because he had to be; because he could not leave the Citadel; because it was *his* mountain.

As it was Rudi's mountain. . . .

The boy ate his supper in silence, then returned to the hotel for his evening chores. Later, in the darkness, he came back home, kissed his mother goodnight, went up to his room again and lay on his bed. But he did not undress, and he did not fall asleep. He lay quietly through the hours until the clock reached exactly two, and then he rose and, going to the chest, took out his heaviest clothes and, from the bottom, his father's flannel shirt. These he wrapped into a tight bundle. Then, finding a pencil and scrap of paper, he wrote a brief note: *Dear Mother, do not worry. I will be all right. Love, Rudi.* Without light and in stockinged feet, he left the room. He slid the note under his mother's door.

Then he descended the stairs. In the kitchen he found a piece of sausage and another of cheese and stuffed them in his pockets. A moment later he was out the front door. He did not pause to put on his shoes until the house was out of sight around a corner.

The next step was the dangerous one. Rounding a second corner, he came to his Uncle Franz's house and stopped. He looked sharply, but there was no light; listened, but there was no sound. Now his shoes came off again, and, putting down the bundle of clothing, he approached softly and tried the door. In the memory of the oldest inhabitant, there had never been a burglary in Kurtal, and few houses had locked doors. This one was not locked. Lifting the latch, Rudi stepped inside.

It was pitch dark, but he knew what he was looking for, and where it was: the large cupboard in the hallway where his uncle kept his mountain gear. In a few moments he had found and opened it. But now for the first time he needed light, and cautiously he struck a match. The contents of the cupboard showed in a dim yellow glow: lengths of coiled rope on a row of hooks; on other hooks, knapsacks and clothing; against the wall, ice-axes; on the floor, boots and crampons. One match was enough. What he was looking for was there. Quickly he took the ax, the boots and the pack that Captain Winter had given him; then, closing the cupboard, moved through the blackness toward the door.

A plank creaked under his foot. He stopped and listened. There was no other sound. But now suddenly his heart was pounding, his hands were damp, and where his stomach had been was a cold hollow emptiness. Now at last there *was* a thief in Kurtal, he thought. And it was he. A thief in the night. In his mind's eye he could see his uncle asleep in his room upstairs; his mother asleep, the whole village asleep; only himself awake in the darkness, sneaking, prowling. Suddenly he wrenched his mind away. He must not think like that, for to think would be to end it all. He clutched the things he carried in his hands. "They are mine," he thought fiercely. "I am not a thief. They were given to me. They are mine!"

Now he was out of the house. He closed the door gently. Once again he rounded a corner and stopped, and this time he sat down and put on his boots. He stuffed the bundle of clothing in his pack; his father's shirt, the sausage and cheese. Grasping the ax, he started off. When he had gone about a block he remembered that he had forgotten his regular shoes. He had left them where he had taken them off, beside the stoop of his uncle's house. For an instant he hesitated; and then he went on again. Where he was going he would not need them. And besides, it was too dangerous to turn back.

The streets were deserted. There was no sound anywhere except the tread of his own boots on the hard-packed earth. Once he was startled by a moving shadow, but it proved to be only a foraging dog. In five minutes he was at the edge of the town, and a few minutes later across the stream and following the path on the far side. He needed no light. The stars were enough, and the path showed ghostly gray between the dark slopes of the meadows. A cow lowed. The stream roared and faded and was gone. His boot nails clinked against the gravel. Strongly and steadily he pushed on.

Then a thicker darkness loomed ahead. The forest. And at the forest's edge, the shrine. Here, as he had done so often before, he paused and kneeled; and this time he remained kneeling for a long while, his head bowed, his lips murmuring the ancient prayer of the mountain guides.

Rising, he stood looking at the shrine, but the cross and the Virgin were the merest shadows within it, and the name carved in the wood beneath them could not be seen at all. Why Rudi did what he did next he could not have said, except that he needed to do it. Lighting a match, he held it up to the shrine, and there in the flickering light was the old lettering: JOSEF MATT, *1821–1850*. He touched the letters lightly with his finger. Then the match went out, and he climbed on.

A little later he made his second stop. In the forest it was far darker than on the meadows, but, even so, he had no difficulty in finding the blue spruce and the stout stick that lay hidden in its branches. This time, though, he did not carry it in his hand but fastened it on his back into the straps of his pack. With his new ice-ax, he no longer needed it as a staff. It was for something else that he needed it; something he scarcely dared dream of. . . .

The path steepened.

He climbed on.

CHAPTER 8

White Fury

IT WAS STILL NIGHT when he came out onto the
boulder-slopes above the treeline. Far below and behind him the lights of the village glinted like motes in
a well of darkness. But by the time he reached the
junction of the Blue and Dornel Glaciers the eastern
sky had begun to pale, and as he worked his way to the
left, up the Blue, the world around him emerged slowly
into gray dawnlight.

As often happens in the high mountains, dawn
brought, not warmth, but increased cold, and for the
first time Rudi paused to put on one of the extra sweaters that he carried in his pack. Even with its protection, however, the chill gnawed through to his bones.
An icy breath rose from the white waste of the glacier. High above him, the ramparts of the Citadel rose
into the twilight like the outposts of a lost and frozen
planet.

But it was not on the Citadel that the boy's eyes
were fixed. It was on the crest of the glacier beyond him;
on the black dot of the old hut that stood there; on
the thin plume of smoke that rose up from the hut
into the still, windless air. . . . Yes, he had been right,

he thought exultantly. Captain Winter was there. He was surely there. . . . Plodding on, he zigzagged his way between the great crevasses. No snow had fallen for several days, and there was little danger of his breaking through into a hidden chasm; but still he moved watchfully and carefully. Two lessons—one from Old Teo and one from his own stupidity—had been enough. Never again was he going to risk either his own life or another's by blundering first and thinking afterward.

Halfway up the glacier he passed the crevasse from which he had rescued the Englishman. The holes dug by his toes were still visible in the blue ice of its lip. Beyond it, the glacier narrowed and steepened between huge converging walls of rock, and here his progress was slower, as, for perhaps half an hour he had to chop steps with his ax in the smooth slanting surface. As he climbed, the sky grew brighter. Already the heights of the Citadel, far above him, were gleaming in the first rays of the sun. But he moved on steadily, and the sun had not yet struck the glacier when its containing walls fell abruptly away and he came out on the broad saddle of its upper snowfield.

Here, for a moment, he stopped. He stared at the hut that now lay close before him: no longer a minute dark speck, but a solid mass of stone and timber, perched on a rocky ledge above the highest level of the snow. It was an ancient hut—weathered, bleak and gray—and although the thread of smoke still rose from its chimney, there was no other sign of life about it. Rudi tramped across the snowfield and clambered up a few boulders to the ledge. Approaching the door of the hut, he stopped and listened, but heard only the crackling of a fire. Then he opened the door and went in.

Directly before him was the fireplace and a small

blaze. And bending over them with his back turned—
a man. As Rudi entered the man looked around and
rose; at full height, his head almost touched the beams
of the low-ceilinged room. He was a man the boy
had never seen before: a giant of a man, with massive
shoulders, a broad red face and small, piercing eyes, as
blue and cold as glacier ice. He wore a guide's feathered
hat, tipped back on his head, and held a steaming pot
in one of his huge hands.

He looked at Rudi without speaking.

"Is—is not Captain John Winter here?" asked the
boy.

"What do you want of Captain Winter?"

"I have come to find him."

"So?" The giant looked him up and down slowly,
then turned his back and set the pot on a table.

"You are Herr Saxo?" asked Rudi.

"That is right," said the man. "I am Emil Saxo."
Again he turned and eyed Rudi. "And who are you,
boy? You are not from Broli?"

"No sir, I am from Kurtal. And I—"

"From Kurtal, hey?" Saxo grunted. "I thought all
Kurtalers were too afraid of their skins to come so close
to the Citadel."

Rudi started to answer, but stopped himself. There
was a moment's silence. Then he said. "I am looking
for Captain Winter, Herr Saxo, and if you would
please—"

But there was no need to go on, for at that moment
the door opened and Winter came in. He wore boots
and climbing clothes and was stowing a small telescope into a case slung over his shoulder. "The sun is
up, Emil," he said. "I had a good look at the ridge, and
I think—"

Seeing the boy, he broke off and for a moment sim-

82

ply stared. Then he stepped forward with hand outstretched. "Rudi! My old friend, Rudi!" he exclaimed. "What on earth are you doing here?"

"I have come to join you, sir," said the boy.

"Join me?"

"To—to make the ascent of the Citadel."

Again Winter stared. But the guide Saxo guffawed loudly. "Yo ho, that's a good one!" he said. "To make the ascent of the Citadel—that's really a good one!"

Winter looked at him briefly, and then back at the boy. He was still struggling with surprise and trying to marshal his thoughts. "Well," he murmured. "Well, I'll be—" Something that was half a smile touched his lips, and he put his hand on Rudi's shoulder. "Anyhow, first things first, boy. You must be tired and hungry. Sit down. We're just ready for breakfast."

He took three tin cups from a shelf and set them beside the pot on the table. From a pack Saxo produced bread, preserves and a slab of dried meat. "You have met Emil Saxo, of Broli?" Winter asked, as they sat down. "This is Rudi Matt," he told the guide. "Son of the great Josef Matt, of Kurtal."

"So?" Saxo's thick eyebrows went up a little. "He was a good man, Josef Matt," he conceded grudgingly. "The best of the Kurtalers."

"And his son here is going to be a good man too," said Winter. "Already he has done some fine climbing. Not to mention saving my life."

He told briefly of what had happened on the glacier, and the guide listened in silence. They ate and drank steaming tea, and Rudi glanced around the interior of the hut. It was a tiny and decrepit place, far different from the other, newer huts, like the Blausee. There was no loft; only the one room. For furnishing, there was the warped table, a bench and a lopsided shelf. In a corner was a thin layer of moldy straw, on which Winter's and Saxo's blankets were spread. High on one wall, the mortar between two stones had fallen away, and the hole was stuffed with old sacks and shreds of clothing.

"We had to spend the first hour," said Winter, "clearing away the cobwebs."

"When did you come up, sir?" asked Rudi.

"Yesterday—during the afternoon." Winter looked at the boy curiously. "And you?" he said. "You must have climbed half the night."

"I left early this morning."

"Ummm. . . . And what about your mother and uncle? What did they say about your coming?"

Rudi swallowed. He was prepared, but still he swallowed. "They said it was all right, sir."

"You mean they gave you permission?"

"Yes sir."

Winter was still watching him with a curious expression. Rudi could not tell if he believed him or not.

"With you—if I was with you, sir," he murmured, "they said I could go."

Silence filled the room. His lie seemed to fill the room. "First I was a thief," he thought. "Now I am a liar. Dear God," he prayed—"dear Jesus and loving Mary—forgive me. I am wicked. I am evil. But I cannot help it. Forgive me."

"How did you know I was here?" asked Winter.

"I was sure that you could not leave the Citadel, my Captain, and I remembered what you once said about perhaps going to Broli. Then we heard there was someone in the hut, and I was sure that it was you."

"And your uncle?"

"My uncle?"

84

"He still wouldn't come?"

"No sir."

"But he allowed you to?"

"Yes sir."

There was another silence, and Captain Winter sipped his tea.

Then Saxo spoke. "Perhaps it is good to have the boy here," he said. "He can keep the hut clean and have food ready for our return."

Rudi's heart sank. He looked from the guide to Winter. "But, sir, that is not why—" He fumbled. "I mean, I came to—"

"I know why you came, son," said Winter quietly.

He finished his breakfast without speaking again. Saxo had risen and was coiling a length of rope.

"It is time we got going," he said.

"You are starting today, sir?" asked Rudi.

Winter nodded and rose too.

"For the actual climb—no. Today we're just going to reconnoitre. Up to the base of the ridge, and then following it for a way. As far as the Fortress, perhaps, if we can make it. Then, if it looks all right and the weather holds, we'll make our real try in a couple of days. But first we'll have to go down to the valley for more food and equipment."

"And I—I may—please—?"

"Come outside," said Winter. "I'll show you what we're planning."

They went out, and the sun was up, and it was much warmer. Standing side by side, they peered up at the great mountain that tiered above them into the cloudless sky. The southeast ridge seemed to loom almost directly overhead; and yet, Rudi knew, it was not so close as it looked. In terms of time and human effort it was not close at all, for its base was separated from them by

85

a savage slanting wilderness of ice- and snowslopes, slag and boulders, cliffs and chasms.

"I think the best way," said Winter, pointing, "is across the col above the Blue Glacier and then up that smaller glacier, on the left until we reach the icefall. Through the telescope there looked to be a good enough route up the icefall, and beyond it we'll have our choice of a snowslope—you see it?—or of climbing the cliffs along its side. Either way would bring us out close to the foot of the ridge, and from there on it will be simply a matter of following it. We know it can be climbed at least as far as the Fortress—thanks to your father and Sir Edward Stephenson."

Emil Saxo had come from the hut and stood beside them, squinting upward. "I think maybe we will not stay on the ridge all the time," he said. "There are places where it may be better on the south face."

"Perhaps," said Winter. "That we can decide when we get there." He turned away from the mountain. "Well, are we ready?" he asked.

"We," he had said.

Rudi watched. . . .

"Come on, boy. What are you dawdling for?"

Rudi's heart swelled. He could hear it thumping in the stillness. But then there was another sound, and it was Saxo's voice.

"Boy?" he said. "You do not mean the boy is coming?"

"Why not?" asked Winter.

"The Citadel is a great and fierce mountain. It is no child's play."

"And Rudi here is no child. Wait until you see how he climbs."

"You have told me yourself there is no guide in Kurtal who would venture on the Citadel. And now this boy comes—not even a grown man—"

"We're not climbing the Citadel today," said Winter quietly, "but only reconnoitering. The boy is his father's son. Josef Matt's son. Remember that. Let him come with us, and we'll see what he can do."

Saxo hesitated. His sharp blue eyes studied Rudi as if he were some sort of unfamiliar insect. Then he looked back at Winter and shrugged. "You are the *Herr*," he said. "If it is what you want—very well. . . . But only for today," he added, "only for reconnaissance. I am not going to pull some young *Lausbube* six thousand feet to the top of the Citadel."

"Truly, sir—" Rudi began. But Winter interrupted him.

"All right," he said. "We won't plan beyond today." He turned and gazed steadily at the boy. "But one thing must be understood, Rudi," he added. "There will not be any experiments, any individual climbing, any route-finding on your own. You will be an apprentice porter, that is all. And you will do exactly as Emil and I tell you to."

"Yes sir," Rudi murmured.

Winter stood watching him for another moment; then turned away. "Well then, let's go," he said.

Re-entering the hut, they got their axes, and Saxo slung his rope over his shoulder. Since they would return that same evening, there was no need to carry packs, and they merely stuffed a few pieces of cheese and chocolate into their pockets. They put out what was left of the fire. Then they started off.

For the first hour or so the going was easy. Following the route Winter had pointed out, they moved along the crest of the Blue Glacier, cut across a slope of tumbled boulders, and came out on the smaller tributary glacier that descended from the east face of the Citadel. Here, however, the gradient steepened sharply, and they paused to rope up. And for the next two hours they zigzagged slowly up the long incline of ice.

As he had done with Franz on the Wunderhorn, Winter alternated with Saxo in the lead, but this time Rudi's position was in the middle of the rope. On such a slope the work of the leader was arduous, for almost every move required the cutting of a step before their feet could gain a hold in the smooth surface. The bright prong of the ax rose and fell. Chips of ice flew out and slithered down the white chute beneath them. The leader cleared the step, tested it, moved up and chopped again. The others followed him.

Rudi would have been glad to take his turn in the lead; indeed, he was burning with desire to show the two men what he could do. But he was mindful of what Winter had said to him. He did not volunteer, or even speak at all, but concentrated on each step, on his balance, on making no move that would disturb the climber above or below him. He took particular care to keep his body well out from the slope, so that there would be no outward pressure of his feet that might result in a slip.

The gradient increased from forty degrees to forty-five, from forty-five to more than fifty. It seemed no longer a slope they were ascending, but an immense white wall, to which they clung like ants. But still the bright ax-head rose and fell. Still they stepped up, waited, stepped up again. And at last the steepness eased off before them and they came out on the uppermost level of the glacier.

Here was what is called a *bergschrund:* the great final crevasse that separated the main section from the icefall above. Standing on its lip, they looked down into a bottomless cavern of blue ice; then set about the next step of finding a way to pass it. A quick glance showed that there was no way around to the side. Here at its apex the glacier was no more than a hundred yards wide, and the *bergschrund* extended the whole way across it, ending against smooth and vertical rock-walls. Nor could it be jumped, because its farther rim was much higher than the one on which they stood. The only possible way was across a natural snow-bridge that spanned the crevasse near its center . . . *if* the bridge would hold them.

Edging out to the last inch of solid ice, Saxo drove his ax down into the snow. It went through, unchecked, for perhaps a foot; then struck firmer snow underneath and held fast. The guide moved to another position and tried again. Winter moved up beside him and drove in his own ax. The results were the same.

"It should go," said Saxo.

And the Englishman nodded.

Then he hitched the rope around his ax and payed it out slowly, while Saxo moved out onto the bridge. The guide put out one foot and rested it on the snow. It sank in for an inch or two. Then the snow tightened and held. He took a second step, and a third. On the third his leg went in almost to the knee—but then stopped. And with the fourth he reached the upper rim of the crevasse. Winter nodded to Rudi; and now the boy went across, while the two men belayed him from either side. And finally he and Saxo held the rope on the upper rim, as Winter followed in their tracks.

"So far, so good," said the Englishman.

The *bergschrund* was behind them.

Next came the icefall, or upper glacier: a steep, tumbled labyrinth of ice that cascaded down the flank of the mountain. Here they were no longer on a smooth open surface, but in a wilderness of towers, ridges and deep gullies, through which they had to grope their way as if through a trackless forest. For a while Saxo led, then Winter, then Saxo again, threading the maze like bloodhounds on a spoor. Sometimes they followed a blind alley that ended in a deep chasm or unclimbable wall, and they had to retrace their steps. But always, in the end, they found a way up and over, and their progress, though slow, was steady and sure. When, after an hour or so, Rudi turned to look back, the glacier was a mere streak of white, flattened and remote. The *bergschrund,* at its apex, showed only as a thin bluish line, almost directly below.

It was close to noon. The sun was high and warm. It shone in dazzling prisms on the ice-towers, or seracs, that rose around them, and they moved on as quickly as they could, knowing that this was the time of day when these towers might melt and fall. None fell nearby, however. Occasionally they would hear a hollow rumbling off to the right or left, but the frozen pinnacles around them loomed massive and motionless, as if made of stone. They climbed on, steadily and in silence.

And at last they came out on the upper margin of the icefall. The bristling white forest of seracs fell away behind, and before them, instead of cliffs and gullies, was a long smooth slope of snow. It was the slope, Rudi recognized, toward which Winter had pointed from in front of the hut. At its crest, now not more than an hour's climbing above them, was the southeast ridge of the Citadel, thrusting jagged and immense into the sky.

They rested briefly and ate their cheese and chocolate.

"All right, son?" asked Winter, smiling.

"All right, sir," said Rudi.

"Not tired?"

"No, not tired."

And it was true. Even though he had had no sleep the previous night—and had climbed through half of it —it was still true. In part, perhaps, it was simply because he was young and strong; in part, because there was no pack to carry. But mostly it was because the joy and excitement within him left no room for tiredness. Now, on this day, after years of hoping and dreaming, he was to set foot on the Citadel at last. He felt as if he could climb to the foot of the ridge in a few easy bounds; as if he could go on and on, without resting, without pausing, until he stood at last on the summit itself.

The two men were studying the terrain above them: the snowslope that lay directly ahead and the rocky cliffs on either side.

"It will have to be the slope," said Winter.

Saxo nodded. *"Ja,* the rocks are too steep."

"It's not a good time of day for steep snow, of course. But if we keep well in toward the southern cliff, where it's shaded—"

"It should be all right," said the guide. "It should go."

They got up and started off again. Saxo went first, Rudi second, Winter third, and they were still on the rope, though on the stretch ahead there seemed no real need for it. For the slope was not nearly so steep as that of the glacier below. And its surface was not ice, but soft, powdery snow. True, it called for considerable effort in kicking and scuffing, particularly for Saxo, who was breaking trail; but there was no step-cutting, no long waits, no slippery toeholds, no danger of falling. Reaching the lee of the southern cliffs, they turned parallel to them and plodded upward.

They climbed in absolute silence. On the ice there had been the steady rhythmic clink of axes and boot-nails, but here in the white drifts there was no sound at all. Up they went. . . . And up. And up. . . . Each step was the same as the last; and as the next. The snow churned up by their feet hung in the windless air like a shroud of crystal. Beyond the shroud, ahead of Rudi, were Saxo's shoulders, swinging slowly to his powerful stride. Beyond them, and above, the vast ridge of the Citadel seemed to swim in stillness against the gleaming sky.

Then for a moment the sky was gone. The ridge, Saxo, the snow crystals, they were all gone, and where the brightness had been was darkness. Rudi's head jerked up. He forced his eyes open. Perhaps he was tired after all, he thought, if they could close that way without his willing it. Or if not tired, sleepy. Yes, that was it—sleepy. The slow measured pace, the warm air, the soundless snow: all of them seemed to be drawing him softly into an embrace of sleep. His eyes closed again—opened again. He watched the snow gliding slowly past beneath him. And that was all there was in the world. The snow, the gliding, the stillness.

Then, beyond the stillness, a sound. A rumbling.

And a second sound: a shout from Saxo.

He stopped. He looked up. And what rose above them was no longer a slope, but a wave. A white wave, tumbling and plunging; a wave so huge that it seemed the whole mountainside had peeled off in foaming whiteness and was descending directly upon their heads. The rumbling swelled to a roar. Through the roar he could hear Winter, behind him, calling out: "To the left! Up on the rocks! Quick!" Then the voice was gone. There was only the roar. The thunder. He tried to turn—to run. He saw Saxo's form lunging before him. He felt the jerk of the rope, and he *was* running. He was running, stumbling, falling, rising, running again. And then the avalanche hit him. It lifted him gently up, then flung him fiercely down. The rope jerked again—agonizingly. His feet flew from under him. The sky spun and was gone. Everything was gone, except the white thundering fury of the Citadel that bore him on and on, down and down. . . .

CHAPTER 9

The Challenge

FRANZ LERNER, that day, had taken a novice client for a practice climb on the Felsberg. By midafternoon they were back in town, the client had been deposited at his hotel, and Franz, as was his custom, walked on down the main street to the Edelweiss Tavern.

The Edelweiss was the favorite resort of the guides of Kurtal. Indeed, it was almost a club; for few visitors came there—and no wives—and a man could enjoy his beer and pipe quietly in the company of his own kind. On this particular afternoon there were perhaps a dozen men there. Some had not climbed that day; others, like Franz, had returned early from short excursions. At one of the tables was a group of older men: Andreas Krickel, the Tauglich brothers, Johann Feiniger, Hans Andermass. At another sat several younger guides and porters—Klaus Wesselhoft and his like—who patronized the Edelweiss because it made them feel important and who hoped someday to be promoted to the senior table.

It was all the same as usual. And yet, somehow, not the same. As Franz came in, he was aware of a tenseness in the atmosphere; of an absorbed conversation suddenly interrupted while all the men looked up at him.

"Well, here you are," said Peter Tauglich. "Have you heard the news?"

"News? What news?"

"Your friend the Englishman is climbing the Citadel."

For a moment Franz simply stared at him. "Climbing—the—Citadel?" he repeated slowly. Then he shook his head. "No, you must be mistaken. It is not possible."

"Very likely not possible," said Andreas Krickel. "But he is nevertheless trying."

"No," said Franz again. "He is ambitious, Captain Winter. About the Citadel he is perhaps a little crazy. But not so crazy that he would try it alone."

"He is not alone."

"What? You mean he is with a guide? What guide?"

"He is with Emil Saxo."

"Saxo? Of Broli?" Franz looked from one to another of his fellow-guides. "How do you know?" he demanded. "Who told you this?"

"Hans here told us." Krickel nodded at Andermass.

"Hans?"

"I was in Broli today," said Andermass. "I had to go there on a matter of business, but no one would talk business. All they would talk about was this Captain Winter and Saxo. How they had left yesterday to go up to the Citadel."

There was a silence. All eyes were fixed on Franz. Franz ordered a beer, sat down at the senior table, and filled and lighted his pipe. When his beer was brought he sipped it slowly.

"They are fools!" he said suddenly.

"Yes, of course they are fools," agreed Johann Feiniger.

"They will be killed," said Paul Tauglich.

"They will be destroyed before they even set foot on the mountain."

"Have they been seen?" asked Franz.

"Seen?"

"Through the telescope at the Beau Site. Have you looked for them?"

"Yes, we have looked," said Krickel. "Since Hans returned from Broli we have taken turns looking. But we have seen nothing. Teo Zurbriggen is now at the telescope, and he will come and tell us if he sees them."

"But he will not see them," said Peter Tauglich.

"Because they are already dead."

"Because the demons of the Citadel have destroyed them."

The man who had last spoken crossed himself, and a few others did the same. At the next table the younger guides listened tensely, eager to enter the conversation; but not daring to break in on the older men.

Franz drank from his beer glass and set it down with a thump. His face was dark, his eyes filled with smouldering anger.

"Saxo!" he said. "One might have known it. Emil Saxo!"

"He is a bad one, that Saxo," said Krickel.

"He is proud and treacherous."

"And a boaster."

"But the best of the guides in Broli."

Klaus Wesselhoft, at the other table, could contain himself no longer. "There are *no* good guides in Broli!" he shouted. "They are *Lumpen*—no-goods! There are twenty guides in Kurtal who can climb better than this Saxo—"

The older men paid no attention to him. Or at least they pretended not to.

Again there was silence in the tavern. Beyond the window, people went by along the street, and then one of them stopped and looked in. Someone nudged Franz, and, glancing up, he saw that it was his sister, Frau Matt. At first he merely nodded and expected that she would move on. But, instead, she gestured to him, and, rising, he crossed to the door and went out.

"You are back early," she said.

"Yes. Today I went only to the Felsberg."

"But Rudi is not yet home."

"Rudi? Why should he be home?"

"If he came back with you—"

"Back with me?" Franz stared at her. "What are you talking about?"

"You mean—" said Frau Matt—"You mean he was not with you today?"

"Of course not. He was at the hotel, the same as always."

Frau Matt shook her head. "No," she murmured. Her face had suddenly gone pale, and her brother took hold of her arm.

"What is it, Ilse?" he demanded. "What are you talking about?"

"He is not at the hotel. He has not been there all day. I thought he was with you."

"With me? On the Felsberg? Why should you think that?"

"Because he left me a note. When I woke up this morning there was a piece of paper under the door. It said he would be all right; that I should not worry. So I thought of course—"

Her voice faltered—stopped. She looked up at Franz with worried eyes.

"The fool!" he muttered. "The damned crazy young fool!"

"If he was not with you, then where—?"

"I'll tell you where. He has gone with—" Franz caught himself. When he continued, his voice was under control. "He has gone on another of his wanderings. Up to the glaciers or somewhere. It is the sheerest disobedience and defiance; we must be hard with him when he comes back. But—" Franz patted his sister's arm, "—but it is nothing to fret about. He will be all right. He has only gone to the glaciers, I tell you. At most to one of the huts."

He went on reassuring her, comforting her.

But when she had gone on and he went back into the tavern, his eyes were hard and his face drawn and grim. While the others continued talking about Winter and Saxo he sat silently with hunched shoulders, staring at the stained wood of the table.

Then there was the sound of footsteps outside. The door was flung open and Teo Zurbriggen burst in. "I have seen them!" he cried. "I have seen them!" Limp and all, he had obviously been running. His usually pale old eyes were glittering with excitement.

A spark of tension leapt through the room. Half the men got to their feet.

"You've seen them?"

"How?"

"Where?"

"A minute ago. Through the telescope. I had it trained on the icefall above the Blue Glacier, and suddenly there they were at the top of it, heading up the snowslope toward the ridge."

A few of the men started toward the door.

"No, it is no use looking now," said Teo. "I watched

as long as they were in sight, and then they moved in behind the cliffs."

The men stopped.

"You are sure of this?" someone asked. "You can swear you saw them?"

"Of course I can swear. Do you think they were spots in my eyes? For almost five minutes I watched as they climbed up in a row: one, two, three. . . ."

"Three?"

"Yes—three."

All eyes went to Hans Andermass.

"But you said—"

"That there were two, yes. The Englishman and Saxo. That is what they told me in Broli."

"They did not speak of another?"

"No."

"Then who is the third?"

"A friend of the Englishman's, perhaps?"

"Another guide? A porter?"

There was a silence. Up to this point Franz Lerner had sat motionless at the table, taking no part in the questioning. But now he raised his head and spoke quietly. "No, it is none of those," he said. "I will tell you who the third is. It is my nephew."

The others stared at him.

"Your nephew?"

"Rudi Matt?"

"Angel-face?"

"Yes," said Franz.

"It is ridiculous. Impossible."

"Ridiculous, yes. But impossible—no." Franz turned to Old Teo. "Was he at the hotel today?" he asked.

"No," said the cook.

"Where was he then?"

"His mother came and said that—"

"—that he was with me. But he was not with me. He is up there, I am telling you. Up on the Citadel with that madman!"

Old Teo looked at him. The others looked at him. For a long moment no one spoke or moved. Then Teo limped over to where the barmaid stood behind her counter. "A beer, please, Maria," he said.

The girl set one out for him. Teo turned and raised his glass, and his glance moved slowly over the men in the room. "I drink to Rudi Matt," he said, "—the only true mountaineer in Kurtal."

His words hung in the stillness. Then an angry murmur arose.

"What are you talking about?"

"A mountaineer?"

"Angel-face?"

"He is a crazy boy, that is all." Franz Lerner stepped forward. "A wild fool of a boy, who must be taught his place."

"I think perhaps," said Teo, "that he knows his place better than you do."

"Watch what you say, old man."

"I am watching what I say. And what I say is this. You call yourselves guides. You call yourselves mountain men. But you are not. You are like a herd of sheep, a crowd of old women. There is just one real mountain man in all the valley, and he is a boy of sixteen called Rudi Matt."

Franz glared at him. The others glared too. Every man in the room was on his feet, facing the angry little cripple who was mocking and defying them.

"You call him crazy," said Teo. "You call him a fool. But do you know what I call him? I call him the son of his father. Yes, I have seen it. I know. He has the blood of his father—the spirit and courage of his father

100

—and he is the only one in Kurtal, man or boy, who deserves to wear the badge of an Alpine guide."

A dozen voices tried to break in on him, but he went on relentlessly. "You are the great mountaineers—yes, of course. Each day you go out and climb peaks that have been climbed a hundred times before; that a mule could climb, or an old grandmother. And then you come back and drink your beer and tell yourselves how good you are. . . . Well, maybe now you will find out you are not so good. . . . While you sit and swill your beer three climbers are on the Citadel. An Englishman; a man from Broli; and from Kurtal—what? A man? No, a boy. A sixteen-year-old boy, who alone among you is not afraid—"

"Who's afraid?"

The voice was Klaus Wesselhoft's. Old Teo wheeled on him. "You are, you lout." He surveyed the others. "You all are. Since Josef Matt died, fifteen years ago, not one of you has dared set foot on the Citadel. It is too high, you say; too dangerous. It is impossible. . . . All right. Sit here in the Edelweiss. Swill your beer. And see how you feel when the 'impossible' summit is climbed by others. When the world no longer knows the Citadel as the mountain of Kurtal, but as the mountain of Broli. Of Emil Saxo . . ."

Again he raised his glass. He looked around the room. "Come, gentlemen," he said. "Let us drink to the success and fame of the great guide of Broli—Emil Saxo."

No one spoke. No one moved. And then, at last, one man moved. Franz Lerner came slowly forward, stood beside Old Teo and faced the others.

"You have heard what Zurbriggen has said," he told them quietly. "And there are not many men who can speak as he has without our raising our hands against him. I will tell you this: I am not a coward. No guide of

101

Kurtal is a coward. But neither are we fools who wish to throw our lives away. In years past many men have died on the Citadel. Josef Matt, who was the greatest among us, died on the Citadel. It has never been climbed, and I do not believe it ever will be. Neither by us, nor anyone else."

"Especially not by Emil Saxo," put in one of the guides.

"No, never by Saxo," said another.

"The showoff—the big mouth—"

"The boaster of Broli—"

"Tomorrow morning," Franz continued, "I shall start off for the Citadel. There is no use starting now, for one cannot get up the glacier in the darkness. I shall go on until I find the three who are up there. They will not have got far, I promise you that. And when I do, I shall bring down my nephew. I shall talk Captain Winter out of his foolishness."

"And Saxo?"

"Yes, what about Saxo?"

"We'll show him. We'll pull him down."

"Yes, we'll go with you. We'll pull him down together."

"Together—the guides of Kurtal!"

Suddenly everyone in the room was talking at once. The voices grew louder. Fists thumped on the table.

"Very well," said Franz. "The more the better. Those who are coming be in the square at five in the morning."

"I'll be there," said Andreas Krickel.

"And I," said Paul Tauglich.

"I too," his brother added.

"And I," said Klaus Wesselhoft.

"One—two—three—four—" Franz counted. "With myself, five."

"Six," said another voice.

All eyes went to Old Teo, who had been standing to one side, unnoticed and forgotten.

"Do not worry—I will not hold you back," he said. His pale eyes, which a few minutes before had been filled with anger, now seemed almost to be smiling. "It is my day off from the hotel, you see. And this is something, I think, that I would not like to miss."

CHAPTER 10

Three to Make Ready—

HIGH ON THE MOUNTAINSIDE, the avalanche poured down in white billows. The three climbers caught in its path were tossed like chips in a storming sea.

Instinctively Rudi struck out like a swimmer, struggling to keep near the surface of the flowing tide. But the tide was too strong. It threw him head over heels, flinging his arms and legs about as if he were no more than a rag doll. Its deep roaring drummed in his ears. He seemed to be spinning through space. . . .

And then, suddenly, the spinning had stopped. The roaring was gone. He lay still; and around him the snow was still. He lay motionless in a tomb of white silence.

Once again his mountaineer's instinct had come into play, and this time it probably saved his life. At the last instant before coming to rest he had thrown his bent arm over his face, and its protection left a tiny pocket of air for his nose and mouth. For the moment at least, he could breathe. When he opened his eyes the snow brushed the lids; but he was nevertheless able to see a little; and he could tell from the brightness of the light that he was not buried deeply.

Still there was danger. Great danger. For he knew that if he tried to dig out his movements might only sink him deeper in the drift; or, worse yet, might stir the delicately balanced snow into a fresh avalanche. For a while he lay motionless, listening for sounds of the others. But there was only the white silence. He thought of trying to cry out, but in the same instant knew that his strongest effort would be no more than a whisper.

There was nothing for it: he *had* to move. He was lying on his back, with his head down the slope at a lower level than his feet, and his first attempt was at least to get up even. This he managed at last, by a series of careful twists and wriggles. Then he set about raising himself still higher. Once again he used a swimmer's motions—this time a sort of backstroke, pushing the drifts down and away from him—and slowly he made progress. His body, though encased in snow, was soon wet with sweat from his efforts. No longer able to keep his arm over his face, he was sometimes close to suffocation. Now and then the snow shifted beneath him and he lost a few precious inches that he had gained. But it did not give way altogether. And it did not avalanche. Gradually he worked his way upward, until at last the great moment came when his head broke the snow's surface. A dazzle of light filled his eyes. A rush of air filled his lungs. In another few moments he had maneuvered himself into a standing position—still hip-deep in the snow, but upright, in control of himself, able to move and function. Looking down, he realized with astonishment that he still held his ax in his hand.

He rubbed the white veil from his eyes and gazed around at the tumbled drifts. The others? Where were the others? The two lengths of the rope that joined him to them disappeared into the snow in opposite directions, and there was no sign of where—or how deep—their ends might be. Grimly, almost desperately, Rudi pulled at one of the lengths and dug at the snow around it—and then in the next moment saw, with a flood of relief, that there was no further need to. For suddenly, a few yards off, there was a movement on the slope. A dark shape was materializing out of the whiteness: first an arm, then a head, then a broad pair of shoulders and a man's whole body. Before Rudi could reach him Emil Saxo was standing upright in the drift, brushing the snow from his face and swearing angrily under his breath.

The guide barely glanced at Rudi. His eyes went quickly to the other length of rope. And then the two of them were hauling, digging and probing, uncovering the buried strand foot by foot, following it diagonally across the slope toward the rock wall that bounded it, coming at last to the edge of the wall where Captain Winter lay buried under some four feet of snow. He was conscious. He had managed to keep breathing. But he had been thrown in such a position that he had been unable to work himself free, and, as they dug him out, they saw that he was bleeding from a gash in the head. He had been flung, he said, against one of the rocks of the wall, but luckily it had been only a glancing blow. It was nothing, he assured them. He would be all right.

But as they sat on a ledge of the wall, resting, the blood still dripped down across his forehead and cheek, and presently Saxo took a cloth from his pack and made it into a rough head-bandage. "It's nothing, I tell you. Nothing," Winter insisted. And after a few minutes he seemed wholly himself again. . . . Was Rudi all right? he asked. Yes, the boy assured him. . . . And Saxo? Yes, the guide was all right too.

"It was stupid, trying such a slope in the afternoon sun," the Englishman said ruefully.

"Ja, it was stupid," Saxo agreed.

"That old Citadel is a fierce one."

"Ja, it is a fierce one."

There was no question of going higher that day. Apart from their mishap, the sun was already low over the western ridges, and they had neither food nor shelter for a night out. Circling the avalanche area, they reached the bottom of the slope and then worked their way through the icefall and down the upper glacier. Though they moved far more swiftly than on the ascent, darkness had already fallen when they reached the hut.

They built a fire, and while their supper cooked Rudi sat watching the flames. Then, the next thing he knew, someone was speaking his name, his eyes jerked open, and Winter was standing before him smiling, as he held out a plate and cup.

"Tired—eh, boy?" he asked.

"No sir," Rudi assured him.

But he was tired. Bone tired. The previous sleepless night and the long day's climbing had at last caught up with him, and it was all he could do to keep his eyes open while he ate his food. Ten minutes later he was lying on the straw in a corner of the hut. Captain Winter and Saxo sat at the table, talking, and he wanted to join them—or at least listen to them. But his body could not move; his ears could not hear; his eyes could not see. Beyond his closed lids the fire flickered dimly. Then it was dark.

And then it was light. The sun was shining. Again a fire was blazing in the hearth and Winter and Saxo were sitting at the table. I have overslept, Rudi thought, as he bounded up.

The two men glanced at him, and Winter smiled. "Good sleep?" he asked.

"Yes sir."

"Rested?"

"Yes sir."

And this time it was the truth. All his tiredness was gone. He was ready for the day and the day's work. Ready for—anything.

Leaving the hut, he splashed his face and hands in the nearby stream. Then, back inside, he ate his breakfast. The two men were still at the table, talking; or rather, at the moment, Captain Winter was talking and Saxo was listening. The Englishman looked somewhat the worse for wear. Blood had soaked through the bandage which he still wore around his head, and his face appeared drawn, under its layers of stubble and windburn. But, if the flesh was a bit battered, nothing had happened to the bright flame of his spirit. His voice was strong and sure, his eyes gray and gleaming, as he spoke of the goals and problems that lay ahead.

"Even after what happened yesterday," he was saying, "I'm convinced that the snowslope is the best approach to the mountain. Now that we've cut the steps in the glacier and know the best route through the icefall, we can get up to it in half the time; and until afternoon there's no danger of avalanche. Once we reach the ridge it will be simply straight-forward rock-climbing for the next few hours. Perhaps there'll be a few tricky stretches, but they shouldn't bother us. We know it can be done because it's been done before."

His eyes shifted briefly to Rudi and then away again.

"It's at the base of the Fortress," he went on, "that things will get interesting, for from there on we're on our own. A lot of people, of course, think that there's no way past the Fortress; but there has to be—and it's up to us to find it. My own hunch is that it won't be straight up and over, but off to the left, to the south of the ridge. . . ."

Up to this point Saxo had listened silently, his broad face expressionless. But now suddenly, for the first time, he spoke.

"That is the way the first climbers thought to go."

"Yes, that was Josef Matt's way. The way he was about to try before," Winter hesitated, "—before the accident to Sir Edward Stephenson."

"I do not think Josef Matt was right," said Saxo. "I think the best way is either straight up along the line of the ridge or over to the other side, toward the east face."

"But Matt and Stephenson tried there first. And their porter said later that they could find no route."

Saxo shrugged. "Perhaps they did not look hard enough. Or did not have the skill."

Winter's face clouded. He started to speak, changed his mind and got up from the table. "Well, there's no use arguing about it," he said. "We'll see how it goes when we get up there. Now we'd better be on our way."

Rudi had risen, too, and stood expectantly beside him. "We will start today—?"

"For the Citadel? No." Winter turned to him. "Today Emil and I will go back down to Broli for more supplies. We'll have to spend at least one night on the mountain—maybe two—and we'll need tents, food and other things. Tonight we'll stay in Broli and come up again tomorrow morning. Then the next day, if the weather's good, we'll make our start."

"Emil and I," he had said. Rudi looked at him questioningly. "And I, sir? I will go down with you too?"

Winter shook his head. "No, there's no point in that. You will go down to Kurtal."

"To Kurtal?"

"Yes. There's not enough food here even for one person, and you can bring up some of your own. And also—also there's a thing that's been on my mind ever since you came up here. I'd like you to make one last try with your uncle."

"With—my—uncle?"

"Yes. To persuade him to come too. To join us."

"But—but—"

"If he allowed you to come he can no longer be so strongly against it. Tell him that we've found a way; or at least a beginning. That now at last is the the big chance—and that I ask him to come with us."

Rudi stood motionless, speechless. His body and mind seemed frozen. He was scarcely even aware of the movement beside him, as Saxo rose and faced Winter.

"Come with us?" the guide repeated. "Who is to come with us?"

"The boy's uncle—Franz Lerner."

"From Kurtal?"

"Yes, from Kurtal."

Saxo shook his head. "No, that cannot be. I cannot agree to that."

"Cannot agree to it? What do you mean?"

"I am a man of Broli. A man of Broli does not climb with a Kurtaler."

"Not climb with a Kurtaler? That's ridiculous. Franz Lerner is one of the best guides in Switzerland. I've

110

made dozens of climbs with him. On the Weisshorn, the Dom, the Dornelberg—"

"Yes, on the Weisshorn, the Dom, the Dornelberg. But now we are not speaking of these. We are speaking of the Citadel. And what happens when you ask him to go on the Citadel? He will not go, will he? He is afraid —as all the Kurtalers are afraid. You have to leave Kurtal and come to Broli to find a guide who will do it. All right, I said to you: I, Emil Saxo, am not afraid. I will climb the Citadel with you. I will climb for the honor and glory of my village. But I will not drag up with me some Kurtaler who has not the skill or courage to do it himself."

"Drag? Drag a guide like Lerner? What are you talking about?"

"I am—"

"You're talking nonsense, that's what." Winter's voice was sharp. His eyes were suddenly angry. "Like a stupid provincial villager who can't think beyond his own doorstep. . . . So Franz Lerner is not from Broli, but from Kurtal. What of it? Does that make him any the worse guide? Any the worse man? He's one of the best guides in the Alps, and you know it, and if he'll come with us he'll make us just that much the stronger. Give us just that much better chance of reaching the top."

He paused. Saxo didn't answer. The guide's broad face was set in stubborn lines and his small eyes were fixed on the floor.

When Winter spoke again his voice was no longer angry, but quiet and earnest. "Look, Emil," he said, "you want to climb the Citadel. You've dreamt of it for years—you've told me so. And so have I. Ever since I can remember I've said to myself: if there is one thing you must do in your life it is to climb this wonderful, terrible mountain that no man has ever conquered. . . . All right, I want to climb it. So do you. So does this boy here. And his uncle. Yes, I know Lerner refused to come. He's superstitious; full of old taboos and traditions. But in his heart he wants to, and now I think he'll come. . . . You're a big man, Saxo—big in body. Be big in mind too. Forget your prejudices, and if Lerner will come, accept him. Let's go after this mountain in the strongest way; the wisest way. Not as an Englishman and a Swiss. Not as a man from Broli and a man from Kurtal. Simply as human beings, working together. The Citadel is too great for anything else. Too important . . ."

Still the guide looked silently on the floor. Such ideas were obviously new to him, and his indecision showed on his face.

Winter put a hand on his arm. "Come on," he said, "it's time to go. We'll talk more about it on the way down."

He slung on his pack and picked up his ice-ax, and slowly Saxo followed suit. Rudi watched them as if from the depths of a dream. Ordinarily he would have been angry at what Saxo had said about his uncle and his village. He would have listened tensely to the conversation and perhaps even have joined in. But, as things stood, he had scarcely heard it. All he could hear were Winter's words: *"You will go down to Kurtal."*

He couldn't. . . . He couldn't.

Winter was halfway to the door when he stepped before him. "Please, sir—please—" he murmured.

The Englishman looked at him curiously.

"Do not send me down to Kurtal. It is no good."

"No good?"

"About my uncle. When he sees me—"

Winter smiled. "No, I think you're wrong," he said. "I think your uncle will come. Wait and see."

"I do not mean that. I mean—" He couldn't say it. "Please," he begged. "Let me come with you to Broli. I can be useful. I will carry a pack—"

"Emil and I can manage the packs." Winter shook his head. "No, Rudi—go down to Kurtal. Talk to your uncle and bring him back with you. Tell him that I want him, and need him. That climbing the Citadel wouldn't be the same without Franz Lerner."

He glanced at Saxo, nodded and went to the door. Then he looked back. "Better start down soon," he added, "so you'll arrive early and have a good rest. Tell your uncle to bring his high-climbing and bivouac equipment. We'll meet you back here at noon tomorrow."

He went out, and Saxo followed him. For a moment Rudi stood rooted, and when he reached the door the two men were already swinging down the path. He started to call, but no words came. He had a hundred things to say—and nothing to say. Silently he watched while the others moved down the boulder-slope toward the Broli Glacier. The last thing he saw was Winter's bandaged head bobbing whitely against the grayness of the rock.

The breakfast fire burned out. The sun climbed the sky. Down by the stream a marmot rose on its hind legs, shrilled and darted off. Then it was silent again. For a long time Rudi sat alone on the steps of the old hut.

He looked at the worn boulders beneath his feet. Raising his head, he looked at the great mountain that towered above him. At the stoneslope, the upper glacier, the icefall, the snowslope. At the southeast ridge slanting up to the grim walls of the Fortress.

Then he turned away. What was the use of looking? . . . His lie had caught up with him. His sneaking and thieving had caught up with him. There was nothing to do but start down. Down to the village. To his mother's tears and uncle's anger. To the mocking laughter of Klaus Wesselhoft. To the dirty dishes of the Beau Site Hotel.

He stood up. Going into the hut, he got his ax and pack. Slung through the pack-straps was his old handcut staff, and this he removed and stood in a corner, for he would not need it now. Nor would he need the old red flannel shirt that was inside the pack.

He went out and closed the door and climbed down through the boulders to the glacier. There was a thin covering of snow on the ice, and he could see the footprints of Captain Winter and Saxo bearing westward in the direction of Broli. He turned east, following the crest of the glacier. For perhaps half an hour he moved on with slow, mechanical steps; and then he stopped. For he had reached another turning-off place. Directly ahead, the main stream of the Blue Glacier dropped steeply downward: to the boulder-slopes, the lower hut, the treeline, the valley. To the left, climbing higher, was the upper tributary they had followed the previous day. At its apex was the *bergschrund;* beyond the *bergschrund,* the icefall; beyond the icefall, the snowslope; beyond the snowslope . . . the Citadel.

For several minutes Rudi stood there, motionless.

Then he turned left.

CHAPTER 11

Alone

THERE WAS THE SKY. There was rock and ice. There was a mountain thrusting upward into blue emptiness—and at the foot of the mountain a tiny speck. This speck was the only thing that lived or moved in all that world of silent majesty.

Rudi climbed the white slope of the upper glacier. He did not hurry. He looked neither up at the peak nor down at the valley, but only at the ice flowing slowly past beneath his feet. In the ice were the marks of their boot-nails from the previous day, and it was easy to follow the route. When the slope steepened, there were the steps cut by Winter and Saxo with their axes. He had only to step up, balance briefly, step up again—and again.

With the step-cutting, it had required two hours to reach the *bergschrund*. Today it took him perhaps a third of that time. Coming out on the rim of the great crevasse, he approached the snow-bridge, tested it, and crossed without mishap. Then, still following the trail of the day before, he threaded his way through the steep maze of the icefall.

The seracs rose around him in frozen stillness.

And Rudi's mind seemed frozen too. What he was doing was not a result of conscious choice or decision; it was simply what he *had* to do. He had not lost his senses. He knew that alone, and without food or a tent, there was no chance on earth of his reaching the top of the Citadel. And it was not hope for the top that pushed him on. It was simply—well, he wasn't sure— perhaps simply the hope to set foot on the mountain. Or more than the hope. The need. The need of his body, his mind, his heart, to come at last to the place of which he had dreamed so long; to stand on the southeast ridge; to follow where his father had led; to climb, perhaps, even as high as the Fortress, which was as high as any man had gone. That was what he wanted; what he *had to have*. That much. Before it all ended. Before descending to the village; to his uncle's anger, his mother's tears, Klaus Wesselhoft's laughter; to the soap and mops and dishpans of the Beau Site Hotel.

He climbed on. The seracs slid past like tall hooded ghosts. And then they dropped away behind him and he came out at the base of the snowslope. Above him he could see a trail of zigzagging footprints, extending perhaps halfway to the ridge and disappearing into smooth drifts where the avalanche had erased them. The drifts were huge, billowing, dazzling in the sunlight; but he knew that they had frozen overnight and that the sun was not yet strong enough to dislodge them. He shuffled his boots in the snow, and it was firm and dry. As Winter had said, the slope was safe in the morning.

Even so, he was cautious as he climbed upward, testing every step before trusting his weight to it. And when he came to the avalanche area he detoured to the left and kept as close as possible to the bordering

116

rock-wall, so that he would have something to cling to, just in case. . . . But nothing happened. The snow stayed as motionless as the rock. In all that spreading wilderness there was no movement except that of his own two legs plodding slowly on through the drifts.

And then—he stopped—then there was a movement. He felt it rather than saw it: the merest flicker or shadow, not on the slope, but on the cliff high above. He tensed, peering upward. . . . A stonefall? . . . No. There was no sound. And then again there was the flicker: a moving speck of reddish brown against the tall grayness of the rock. Suddenly it leapt into focus. It was a chamois. For an instant it stood outlined on a crag, motionless, staring down at him; and Rudi, motionless too, stared back. Then the animal moved again —wheeled—vanished. It was as if the cliff had opened and swallowed it. And the stillness closed in again, even more absolute than before.

Rudi moved on. Through the stillness. Up the white slope. Kick—step, he went. Kick—step. Kick—step. And though the going through the deep drifts was slow, it was neither steep nor slippery, and his progress was steady. He looked back—and the icefall was far below; ahead—and the ridge loomed nearer. . . . Nearer. . . . And then at last the great moment came, and the slope was beneath him. There was no longer snow under his feet, but solid rock. He took a step up —a second—a third . . . and stood on the southeast ridge of the Citadel.

Here he sat down and rested. He pressed his hands against the cold stone, as if to convince himself that he was really there. Not on its glaciers; not on its approaches; but on the mountain itself. He looked down along the way he had come, and there, beyond glacier and snowfield, forest and pasture, tiny and remote, lay the green valley of Kurtal. On the far side of the ridge he could now see all the way to the village of Broli. It was as if he were already on a mountaintop, with all the world below him. . . . Until he looked up. And then everything changed. . . . Then he was no longer on a mountain's summit, but at a mountain's base, and there was the whole great mass of the Citadel still towering above him into the sky.

His eyes moved slowly upward across the slanting wilderness of rock and ice. To the right was the east face, to the left, the south: two monstrous, almost vertical precipices soaring up out of the bounds of sight. Between them, and joining them, was the twisting spine of the southeast ridge; and while this, too, was steep, it was not so steep as the faces, and was broken up into a maze of towers, clefts and ledges that at least offered the possibility of being climbed. From where Rudi sat he could not see to the summit of the Citadel, nor even to its high shoulder. Some two thousand feet above him the ridge flared up into the bold broad promontory that was called the Fortress, and what lay beyond it was hidden from view. There remained, Rudi knew, fully two-thirds of the mountain —another four thousand feet of savage rock thrusting up and up to the final pyramid. But, in practical terms, it was still as remote from him as when he had stared up at it through the blue miles from the valley below. The Fortress was as far as he could see. And as far as he could go.

If he could go that far . . .

He looked at the sun and estimated it to be not quite noon. If he were to be down safely by dark, he could allow himself—what? Perhaps two hours for going up. That meant about another hour to get back where he was. Three o'clock. He figured the times down the snowslope, the icefall, the upper glacier. Yes—two hours up, and he could still be down to the hut by nightfall. Beyond the hut he did not figure. He could not force his mind to think of it.

He stood up. He grasped his ax.

Then he began the ascent of the ridge.

As he had judged from below, it was steep—but not too steep. Indeed, for the first few minutes the going was even easier than on the snowslope or glacier, and he was able to swing up from boulder to boulder with long easy strides.

This did not last long, however. Soon the gradient sharpened, the boulders gave way to solid rock, and, pausing, he slung his ax through his pack-straps to give himself the free use of both hands. From here on it would be real climbing. He worked up a series of slabs and gained fifty feet; along a shallow gully for another fifty. Then there was a bulge to be rounded and a wall to be scaled, but he chose his route carefully and negotiated both without trouble. Hand- and footholds were plentiful. The rock was sound and firm. At the rate he was going, he thought, he would reach the Fortress in nearer one hour than two.

But the rate, of course, did not continue. Presently he came to a pitch of almost smooth rock, on which he had to search and grope for every stance. And above this, faced with two possible ways around a crag, he chose the wrong one, came out at the base of an unclimbable wall, and was forced to backtrack and try again. The angle of the ridge itself remained fairly constant, but the two faces of the mountain, on either side of it, fell away with ever-increasing steepness, until his route was no more than a thin slanting line between two gulfs of space. Sheer height, as such, did not bother him, as it would have bothered a lowlander. He could look down without dizziness or panic. But, nevertheless, he looked down no more than he had to. He concentrated on what lay ahead and made absolutely certain of the soundness of his holds before each upward move.

There was an easy stretch. Then a harder one. For a distance of some thirty feet the ridge narrowed to knife-edged thinness, and he was forced to straddle it and push himself up with his hands. Then came a series of towers, or *gendarmes,* blocking the ridge completely, so that he had to leave it and work his way out onto the south face. Here the going was by far the hardest he had yet encountered. Behind and below him was a thousand feet of emptiness, and often as much as a minute passed while he clung motionless, searching for holds in the smooth granite above. Once or twice he came close to despair. "It is impossible," he thought. "I cannot do it." But no sooner had he thought it than he heard Winter's voice as he spoke to Saxo down in the hut. "It has been done before," Winter had said.

Rudi's lips tightened. His eyes narrowed. . . . Yes, he knew it had been done before. And he knew *who* had done it before. . . .

He found his hold, pulled himself up, climbed on. And on.

Beyond the *gendarmes* the going was again easier. The ridge broadened, buckled, and slanted skyward like a vast ruined staircase. He moved up through absolute stillness. There was no wind. Now and then a cold tide of air seemed to flow down from the heights above, pressing against his clothing and fingering through to the flesh. But the air made no sound. Earth and sky, mountain and valley—the whole world that spread above and beneath him—was as transfixed

120

as the world of a dream, and in all of it only he, Rudi, was awake and moving and alive.

He moved on. The stillness deepened. The cold, too, seemed to deepen, creeping through his clothing, through his flesh, into his blood and bones.

Suddenly he stopped and turned. He had felt a shadow behind him. But when he looked back there was only the empty ridge slanting down into gray distance. . . . He looked up. Was it the sun? . . . No, the sun seemed the same as ever: yellow and flaming in the dark blue of the sky.

And yet—

His eyes searched the cliffs on the far side of the snowfield. Perhaps he could find the chamois again; find something—anything—that lived and moved. But there was only rock and ice, space and stillness. Only the shadow that still hovered about him, and the coldness that seemed to touch his very heart. Suddenly fear gripped him. Fear far worse than that of falling; fear such as he had never known before in his life. "I cannot go on," he thought wildly. "It is the warning of the mountain. Of the demons."

He crossed himself. He dropped to his knees and closed his eyes. "I do not believe in demons," he murmured, "but only in my Father Who is in Heaven. Only in Him—and in my other father, who has climbed on this mountain before me."

He waited, motionless. As motionless as the rocks around him. And slowly, blessedly, he felt the fear draining from his body and heart. When he stood up again, the coldness was gone. The shadow was gone. He studied the ridge above him, hitched up his pack, and began to climb. He climbed through the vast stillness, alone . . . and yet somehow, he knew, no longer alone. For now his two fathers climbed with him.

He stepped up, balanced himself. Stepped once more —and stopped. Before him the ridge flared out into a curving, almost level platform, and beyond the platform rose a sheer wall of granite. As Rudi stared up at it his heart was pounding. For he had reached the Fortress.

If he was tired he did not know it. If it was growing late he did not know it. All he knew, all that mattered, was that he had gained his goal; that he was standing now on the highest point of the Citadel that any man had reached before him. A wave of emotion filled him, different from any he had ever known. It brought no need to exult, to yodel, to shout in triumph, as had always happened on his other, lesser mountain victories. What he felt was too deep for that; too strong for that. A shout would have been a blasphemy in that high secret place to which he had come at last.

Slowly his eyes moved upward over the great battlement before him, and he saw that it was indeed like the wall of a fortress: smooth, vertical and impregnable. With a fifty-foot ladder based on the platform, a man could have topped it, but without the ladder it might as well have been a wall of glass. He looked to the right, where it merged into the east face of the mountain; then to the left where it joined the south face. And from that moment on he looked nowhere else, for he had seen what he was looking for. . . . "To the left," Captain Winter had said, "—that was Josef Matt's way. . . ." And it would be his, Rudi Matt's, way as well.

He moved toward where the platform curved out of sight above the south face, and in a moment he was standing on the edge of an abyss. The platform still continued—or, rather, a narrow sloping ledge that formed an extension of the platform—and he carefully followed it around. He took four steps—five—six. And stopped. The ledge ended, petering out into the vertical walls of the Fortress. But from its farthest end he could see what he had hoped to see: the one break in the great cliff's defenses. No more than five yards beyond him, and starting at about the level at which he stood, a long cleft, or chimney, slanted upward through the otherwise unbroken rock.

This, he knew, was the way past the Fortress—the "key" to the upper mountain which his father had found fifteen years before. From where he stood he could not see the inside of the cleft, but its depth and angle were such that he was sure he could climb it. If—*if*—he could reach its base. . . .

Sidling to the very end of the ledge, he studied the gap beyond. There was no place to stand—he could see that at once; nor were there any cracks or knobs for handholds. But the wall, though vertical, was not altogether smooth. The rock between ledge and cleft protruded in a sort of wrinkled bulge, and if one could cling to the bulge for as much as a few seconds it would be possible to worm one's way across. For a long moment he remained where he was: gazing, measuring. Then suddenly he moved. Stepping out from the ledge, he inched out onto the bulge, using not only hands and feet, as in ordinary climbing, but all of his body that he could bring into play. He gripped the rock with arms and legs, pressed against it with chest and thighs, holding on not by any actual support but by the friction of his moving weight. Space wheeled beneath him. The remote glaciers glinted. But once committed, he could not stop, or even hesitate, for such a maneuver had to be made quickly and in perfect rhythm, or it could not be made at all. His clothing scraped against the granite; his knees and elbows churned; his fingers clawed and kneaded. Once he slipped—and once more—but both times the friction of his body held him, and a moment later, with a final twist and thrust, he swung off of the bulge into the base of the cleft.

His shirt and trousers were torn. His fingers were bleeding. But he scarcely noticed them. All he had eyes for was the long slanting shaft that now rose directly above him up the sheer wall of the Fortress. And yet, he thought suddenly with a great lift of the heart—he had been right; his father had been right. The cleft extended all the way to the top of the precipice. It was climbable. It was the way past the Fortress!

Instinctively he started up. . . . And in the next instant stopped. . . . For in that instant, for the first time since he had begun the ascent of the ridge, he thought of the hour. He glanced at the sun and saw that it was halfway between the zenith and the western horizon. Obviously he had been climbing more than two hours, but how much more he could not be sure. "It is time to go back," he thought. "You *have* to go back." But it was one thing to think it and another to do it. A hundred feet above him, within easy reach, were the upper slopes of the Citadel, which no man had ever trod—or even seen. He could not go on up and explore them: that he knew. There was no choice but soon to start down. But first he must have one glimpse, one moment's experience, of that high, hidden world above the Fortress.

He moved up again. Stopped again. . . . No, he thought—it was too late even for that. He must turn back here. He must start down. . . . But when he moved again it was still forward, still upward. The prudence that tried to hold him back was no match for the magic that drew him on.

The lower third of the cleft presented no difficulties. Then followed a stretch where it became a sort of narrow smooth-walled shaft, which at first glance appeared impassable; but, after some trial and error, he managed it by bracing his back against one wall, his feet against the other, and levering himself upward. Above this, in turn, was a chockstone—a huge boulder wedged across the cleft—but this, too, he climbed successfully. And the last third of the way, like the first, was easy. Perhaps twenty minutes after entering the cleft, he emerged at its top onto a flat shelf above the cliff-face—the first human being to have passed the grim barrier of the Fortress.

Now, standing there in awe, Rudi Matt looked up at what no man's eyes had ever seen before. Starting directly in front of him, the southeast ridge, which had been blocked off by the Fortress, continued its upward progress, twisting on and on until it at last merged into the great bulge of the mountain's shoulder. So great was the distance that it seemed he was again back at the foot of the peak, rather than a third of the way up its flank. But distance in itself was unimportant, compared to the other thing he saw—and this was that the ridge appeared climbable to its very end. How it would go from there to the top of the shoulder he was too far away to tell. Nor could he see beyond the shoulder, for the final summit was still hidden behind its jutting cliffs. But up the ridge, at least, the way was clear. There would be problems, of course. There would be obstacles. But no obstacles, so far as he could see, as formidable as the Fortress. Nothing that a skilled climber could not successfully surmount.

A deep, almost fierce joy welled in the boy's heart. Even though he must now turn back, he had already gone higher into the unknown than any man before him—including his father. He had proved that his father had been right: that there was a way past the Fortress, and that it was, indeed, the "key" to the mountain. With his own eyes he had seen the way ahead, leading upward and upward.

For another moment he stood there on the mountainside. Alone in the emptiness. Alone in the stillness. . . . And then—then, suddenly—no longer in stillness. For he had become aware of a sound. . . . He listened; and where silence had been there was now a low, deep humming. He looked up; and the sky was gray, the sun shrunken and remote. The shadow had returned—the shadow that he felt behind him earlier, as he climbed the ridge below the Fortress —only now it was not behind, but all around him. The coldness had returned: into his bones, into his blood. Moment by moment, it deepened. The shadow deepened. The humming deepened. From the shoulder of the Citadel, high above him, a plume of snow streamed out across the darkening sky.

CHAPTER 12

A Boy and a Ghost

THE FIRST BLAST of wind struck him as he made for the top of the cleft. It battered against his body and ripped at his clothing, and he had to cling to a projecting crag to keep from being flung from the mountainside. In the short lull that followed, however, he was able to lower himself into the cleft, and there he had some protection. The wind rose again, screaming through the upper air and moaning in the hollows of the rock. But only gusts and eddies penetrated the deep crack in the wall, and he was able to keep his hand- and footholds. In half the time it had taken him to go up, he worked his way down to the narrow ledge at its bottom.

Here he was again exposed to the gale. But fortunately it was blowing straight in against the mountainside, pinning him to it rather than pushing him away, and he was able to get across the bulge in the precipice with rather less difficulty than he had had before. That, however, was the end of his good luck. As he came around the curving shelf to the platform at the base of the Fortress, the storm struck him crosswise with such force that he had to throw himself flat on the rocks. And now it was not only wind that it hurled at him, but snow as well.

On hands and knees he crept forward—and stopped. Somewhere ahead of him the platform ended and fell away into the long spine of the ridge, but where that somewhere was he could not tell. All he could see were the rocks directly in front of him, and beyond the rocks the driving snow. Each time he moved it might be toward the ridge—or toward the two-thousand foot precipice of the south and east faces.

He peered up into the gray churning of the sky. Then, lowering his head, he covered it with his arms and waited. But, minute by minute, the storm grew in intensity, and when he looked up again the snow lashed into his eyes in blinding horizontal waves. The voice of the wind rose from a moan to a wail, from a wail to a high insane shrieking. . . . And then, through the shrieking, there was another sound: a deep rumbling sound, high above, that brought Rudi half to his feet in sudden terror. It was a rock-fall, he thought. Here in this exact spot, fifteen years before, the fateful avalanche of boulders had roared down upon his father and his companions; and now the same thing was happening to him. . . . He struggled to his feet, only to be knocked flat again by the wind. He looked about, desperately, for some sort of shelter, but there was only the blinding snow, streaming like white needles into his eyes. In a moment now the hail of rocks would be upon him. He waited, crouched and tense. But the rumbling was gone. And now he realized it was not a rock-fall he had heard, but thunder. In the next instant a fork of lightning split the sky, flooding the mountainside with a wild greenish glare. And the thunder rolled again . . . louder.

No—this time no rocks had fallen. But that did not

mean he was safe from them. Any moment the lightning might strike on a crag above and send its splintered fragments plunging down; or, worse yet, might hit directly at the exposed ledge on which he was trapped. Again crawling on hands and knees, Rudi worked his way in toward the wall of the Fortress. Groping along its base, he searched for some sort of shelter. And at last he found it: a hollowed-out section of rock, with its sides and top projecting outward, so that they formed, in effect, a small shallow cave. He crept into it, wedged himself back in the farthest corner, and murmured a brief prayer of thanksgiving. For here he was protected not only from falling rock and lightning, but also from the full fury of the wind. He wiped the caked snow from his eyes and nose. He beat his chilled hands together. He waited.

How long the storm continued, he did not know. On that battered mountainside time had ceased to exist, and there was only the storm: only the wind and snow, the thunder and lightning, the wild roar of sound that grew and grew until it seemed to come no longer from the churning air but from the deep roots of the mountain itself. If any stones fell on the platform before him, he could neither see nor hear them. On three sides his world was bounded by black walls of rock, on the fourth by an opaque screen of streaming white.

The wind slackened slightly . . . and he waited.

It rose . . . and he waited.

Again and again.

And then once more it slackened, but this time did not rise, and he knew that at last the storm was blowing itself out. Minute by minute the shrieking faded. The snow no longer blew in horizontal waves, but fell in a long slant—and then straight down—and then not at all. Far in the distance the wind still moaned across crags and icefields, but on the high flanks of the Citadel there was no sound or movement. The peak stood up, vast and white-mantled, frozen in silence and space.

But still Rudi sat motionless. The passing of the storm brought no shout to his lips or lift to his heart; for now, suddenly, he was aware of something he had forgotten during the hours past. Time had *not* ceased to exist. The sun had not stopped in its course. It had moved on above the tempest—steadily, inexorably—until now only its last light was gleaming above the white ranges to the west. The storm was gone; yes. But in its place was oncoming night.

Creeping from the cave, he got to his feet, crossed to the outer edge of the platform, and looked down. The ridge, now snow-covered, slanted away into gray dusk, and, even as he watched, he could see the shadows thickening, as they flowed up over it from the gulfs below. The snowslope, at the bottom, showed merely as a faint white gleaming. The icefall and glaciers, still farther down, were altogether hidden in darkness.

Sudden panic seized him. . . . He had to get down, he thought wildly. He had to get down, or die. . . . Lowering himself from the platform, he tried to follow the ridge. His eyes searched for invisible holds, and his feet slipped and stumbled on the snow-rimmed rocks. He lost his balance, fell and brought up with a thud against a heap of broken slag. Picking himself up, he went on—only to slip and fall again. On this second fall he landed only a few inches from the abyss of the south face, and the jolt was not only to his body but to his senses. Once more he pulled himself to his feet, but he descended no farther. To spend the night on the mountain was to die—

perhaps. But to try to go on was to kill himself surely. It had been on this very ridge, at night, that Teo Zurbriggen, coming down from the Fortress, had fallen and become a cripple for life. And on that night the rocks had not even been slippery with snow.

A tremor passed through him. For several minutes he remained where he was, while the darkness thickened around him. Then, slowly he worked his way back to the platform beneath the Fortress. Crossing the platform, he re-entered the shallow cave.

His body was bruised and aching. His head throbbed. He tried to force his mind to think, to plan, to decide what to do. But there was nothing to do—at least until morning. Nothing except to get through the night. To stay alive through the night. Fumbling in his pack, he got his extra sweater and put it on. He brought out a slice of bread and a small lump of chocolate, which was all the food he had with him; but even though he had not eaten for almost twelve hours, he had no appetite.

He sat in the darkness. In the stillness. He listened, but the last sounds of the storm were gone. From his hollow in the mountainside he looked out and down, but there was only white snow and gray rock; only the ridge falling away into space. He strained his eyes downward for a flicker of light, but there was none. The hut was hidden beneath the bulge of the ridge (tonight it was empty, anyhow), and the valley and town of Kurtal were shut off by the intervening mass of the Dornelberg. . . . Kurtal. . . . For the first time since early that morning he thought of the world below. Of his mother and his uncle. Of his disobedience, his defiance, his wilfulness, and the pass to which they had brought him. Far from comforting him, the image of home served only to remind him

131

of what he had done and where he was: to fill him with such loneliness and emptiness as he had never known in his life before.

He sat alone in the night—in the sky—high on the great mountain from which he might never come down. The darkness seemed to grow even thicker, the stillness even deeper. . . .

Then his head jerked up. His eyes opened. He realized that he must have slept, but for how long he didn't know. What he did know, however—instantly—was that something had changed. It was still night; but the night had changed. A thick mist had closed in. Beyond his hollow in the rocks the night was no longer black and empty, but a ghostly gray. The world below was gone. Everything beyond the edge of the platform was gone. There were only the great banks of vapor, weaving like shrouds in the windless air.

And it was cold. Far colder than it had been even in the wind and snow of the storm. Shreds of mist licked his face as if with icy tongues, and a chill rose from the black rock and gripped his bones. He shifted his weight and began rubbing his hands together—and then suddenly his hands were still, as if frozen in mid-air. His body tensed. His eyes strained into the night, but there was only the mist. As he watched, the mist seemed to shift and thicken, to be forming itself into gray moving shapes.

Night and mist: that was all there was. . . . And at the same time not all, for something else was there too. . . . Something that could neither be seen nor heard, but that nevertheless existed. A part of the mountain; a part of the darkness. In all that wilderness of rock and ice, Rudi knew, there was no single other living thing. But he knew, too, that he was no longer alone.

He shivered. Reaching into his pack, he brought out the one extra piece of clothing that it still contained: the old red flannel shirt. It was big enough to fit over his other clothing, and he pulled it on. Folding his arms, he held his hands tightly in the armpits and felt a slow stirring of blood in his frozen fingers. Yes, he thought—the shirt was old, but it was still warm. It might save him. His father's shirt would save him. The same shirt that he had worn, fifteen years before, on the Citadel; that he had taken from his own body to give to Sir Edward Stephenson, when—

The faint warmth vanished; his blood froze. For in that instant it came to him. . . . The terrible knowledge. The terrible truth. . . . *The cave in which he was sitting was the one in which his father and Sir Edward Stephenson had died.*

He tried to leap to his feet, but couldn't move. A scream formed in his throat, but made no sound. . . . Yes, of course it was the cave—it had to be—it was the only cave in the walls of the Fortress. He should have known it all along. . . . He sat rigid. Peering around him, he could almost see the two bodies, lying frozen and stiff in the darkness. Staring out into the weaving mist, he knew now, with cold terror, what thing it was that hid behind it. He knew what the shadow had been—the invisible finger that touched him as he climbed the ridge—the thing, the presence, that had followed him all that day up the desolate mountainside. The old dark legends of the Citadel rose up before him: the ghosts, the demons of the forbidden mountain crowding down upon him from the haunted heights. And among them, leading them, one ghost —the most terrible ghost—its face white and hollow, ice sheathing its sightless eyes. A ghost with a red shirt, moving gaunt and frozen through the mist.

Rudi crouched, motionless. In an instant the scream would burst from his lips. In an instant he would leap up and run, racing wildly from the cave, across the platform, down the ridge—stumbling, falling, plunging—over the rocks, over the cliffs, into the abyss —anywhere—so long as it was away from this accursed place. In an instant now. . . . But the instant did not come. Still he crouched, unmoving, still he crouched in silence, while the horror moved toward him out of the night and the mist; while the white face flickered and the dead eyes gleamed and the shirt hung from its bones like a bloody shroud. . . . And when at last a sound came from his lips it was not a scream but only a whisper:

"Father—Father—"

Then the strange thing happened: the incredible and wonderful thing. His heart was suddenly calm. His fear had vanished. And with it, the spectre vanished. There was only the mist and the night and himself alone in the night. And he thought: "Yes, of course—that is all it is—my father. My father who died here; who died proud and unafraid; who gave the shirt from his back to a man whose need was greater. As he has now given it to me. . . ."

He looked down at the shirt that covered him, and his body, beneath it, seemed no longer cold, but almost warm. He looked out past the walls of the cave, and the mist and darkness were still there, but the evil was gone from them. . . . "And I am not afraid either," he thought. "My father is not here to harm me, but to watch over me. To make me the guide that he was; the man that he was. My father—

—who art in heaven,
hallowed be thy name—"

134

He prayed. Then he slept. In his father's shirt; in his father's cave; on his father's mountain.

At the first light he awoke and rose. Crossing the platform, he peered down along the ridge; and though it was still covered with snow and mist still filled the air, he could at least see the form and pattern of the rocks. For a moment, turning, he looked up at the Fortress and the gray nothingness above it. Then he began the descent of the ridge.

He moved slowly, testing each hold and stance before he used it and scraping the snow away carefully with his hands and feet. But even so, he slipped constantly. His body felt drained and strengthless, and his arms and legs were like bars of lead. He stumbled, slipped, caught himself, moved on—and slipped again. Soon the slip would come, he thought dully, when he would not catch himself; when he would fall, as Old Teo had fallen, plunging and twisting through space.

No!

He had stopped. He kicked his numb feet against a rock. He held his hands under the red shirt until again he felt the stirring of blood. He looked down into the mist—up into the mist—and beyond it, at last, the sky was brightening.

No! He would not fall. He would not fall.

As he moved down again his lips were tight and grim. He was Rudi Matt, the son of Josef Matt. And he would make it.

He would make it. . . .

CHAPTER 13

—Four to Go

A FEW MINUTES after noon, John Winter and Emil Saxo reached the head of the Broli Glacier and moved up onto the rocks beneath the hut. They moved slowly, for their backs were heavily laden. A corner of white bandage showed under the brim of Winter's hat.

Reaching the rocks, he paused and looked up at the mountain. "The mist is lifting," he said.

Saxo nodded. *"Ja.* If the sun comes out it should be all right for tomorrow."

The Englishman's glance moved to the hut. Its door was closed and no smoke came from the chimney. "It doesn't look as if the boy's back yet," he commented.

"Of course he is not back. Nor will he be."

"I think he will."

Saxo shook his head. "No. The boy himself—perhaps he would come. But his uncle, or the other Kurtalers, they would not. Nor would they let him. It is as I have told you. The Kurtalers are no mountaineers. They are afraid of the Citadel."

Silently they moved on up over the boulders. In five

136

minutes they reached the hut, opened the door—and stopped, staring. No one was in it; but packs of food and equipment lay ranged along the walls, and both table and fireplace showed obvious signs of recent use.

Winter glanced at the guide, and a smile touched his lips. "So they wouldn't come?" he said.

Saxo's narrowed eyes moved over the row of packs. "The boy and his uncle," he said, "could not have carried all this."

Winter shook his head.

"There are more. Many more."

The two men unslung their own packs. Then Winter went to the door and looked up and down the slope. "Rudi!" he called. "Rudi!" And then, "Franz! Franz!"

There was no answer, no sound at all; and he re-entered the hut. Saxo was still staring at the row of packs.

"Six," he muttered. "There are at least six of them. But who? Why?" Suddenly he smashed fist into palm and almost shouted: "They have plotted something, these Kurtalers. There is scheming—trickery—"

"Trickery?" said Winter.

"That so many have come. And I ask you, why have they come? Not to climb the Citadel—no. The Kurtalers are afraid of the Citadel. I will tell you why. It is to keep us from climbing it!"

"Keep us—"

"Yes. They are afraid, but they are also jealous. What they cannot do themselves they do not want to be done by a man of Broli." Saxo was working himself into a dark rage. His huge hands opened and closed. "But I will show them," he went on. "They can bring six or sixty or their whole village, and still they will not stop me. They will see what a man of Broli can do."

"Emil!" Winter's voice was sharp. "Stop this nonsense!"

"It is not nonsense. It is what I tell you. A scheme; a Kurtaler trick——"

The guide relapsed into sullen silence. Winter sat down at the table, rubbing his jaw meditatively, and when he spoke again it was more to himself than to Saxo. "So six have come," he said. "The boy, his uncle and four others. And I am not surprised—no—for if Franz Lerner would come, others would come too. In their hearts the Kurtalers want to climb the Citadel as much as we do. . . . Rudi goes down to the village and speaks to his uncle. His uncle speaks to the other guides. And this morning they come up. They start early and arrive before us, and when they see we are not yet here, they decide to——" He broke off, puzzling.

"To what?" demanded Saxo. "Climb the mountain? In new snow? Without their packs?"

"To reconnoitre, perhaps."

"What should they reconnoitre? When the boy has already been up past the icefall. No, it is trickery, I tell you. They are hiding from us. Lying in wait for us."

"Rot!"

Winter jumped to his feet. He paced up and down. He went to the door, looked out and came back again. Several times he was on the point of speaking, but each time changed his mind. The more he tried to think it out, the more his confusion deepened.

If Rudi had told them——

No.

Or if the six planned to——

No.

None of the *ifs* made sense.

"All we can do is wait," he said.

Sitting down again, he opened his pack and sorted out its contents. Saxo stared moodily at the floor. Then, simultaneously, both men looked up. For from outside, at first faintly, then more and more plainly, came the sound of approaching footsteps. Once more Winter leapt up. "We won't have to wait," he exclaimed. "They're here!"

The next instant the door opened and Franz Lerner appeared. Behind him was the guide Andreas Krickel, and behind him, in turn, the two Tauglich brothers and Klaus Wesselhoft. Last of all was old Teo Zurbriggen, and as he entered the hut he closed the door behind him.

Franz looked at Winter—at Saxo—then back at the Englishman. His chin was thrust forward and his face was grim. "Where is the boy?" he asked.

"The boy?" said Winter.

"My nephew, Rudi Matt. Where is he?"

"Isn't he with *you?*"

"With us? How could he be with us?" Franz took a step forward. "Let us stop the pretense, my Captain. We know that the boy is up here. That he came to join you."

"Yes, of course he joined me. But he left yesterday morning. He went down to Kurtal."

"To Kurtal?"

"You mean—he didn't arrive?"

There was a pause. Franz looked at his companions and then back at Winter. "I do not know what you are talking about," he said. "Three nights ago the boy ran away—"

"Ran away?" repeated Winter.

"Yes, from his mother's house. And—"

"He didn't have permission?"

"Permission? To come here? Of course not." Franz's

139

eyes narrowed. "That is what he told you, eh? That he had permission."

Winter nodded. "Why, the little faker—"

For a moment a smile touched his lips. But only a moment. As the guide went on, his face grew tense and troubled.

"He sneaked away," said Franz. "He left a note that made it plain he was going to the mountains, and when we heard that you were here we were sure that he had come to you. Yesterday morning we started up to find him. To bring him back. We reached this hut at noon, but there was no one here. All afternoon we searched— on the glacier, on the moraines, up to the icefall— but we found nothing; so we returned and spent the night here. Today we searched again and still found nothing—until we saw you, an hour ago, coming up the Broli Glacier."

"Are you sure," Winter asked, "that you couldn't have missed him on the trail?"

"The trail?"

"Coming up yesterday from Kurtal. While he was going down."

Franz shook his head. "It is impossible. There is only the one way: along the glacier—along the path." He took another step forward and his eyes were dark and angry. "No, the boy did not come down," he said. "He is still here; you are hiding him from us; and I de- mand—"

Something in Winter's face made him stop. Slowly his own face changed, and when he spoke again his voice was low and strained. "You mean he is not here, my Captain? You give me your word?"

"No, he is not here."

"Where is he then?"

Winter sat down at one of the benches by the table

140

and stared silently at the floor. Then, raising his head, he told quietly of what had happened the day before. The guides stood motionless, listening. And when Winter had finished there was, for a few moments, no sound or movement in the room.

Then Andreas Krickel said: "We must go back down the glacier."

"And look in every crevasse," said Paul Tauglich.

"It is all we can do——"

"The only hope——"

They looked at Franz, who stood as if he were carved of stone. And at last his lips moved. "His mother," he murmured. "My sister. What shall I tell her? What will she do?" He spoke as if from the depths of a trance. His eyes moved, dull and unseeing about the room. Then they fixed on Emil Saxo, standing alone to one side, and suddenly the tide of pain and anger welled up in him. "And you——" he shouted. "You—man of Broli. What do *you* say to all this?"

Saxo stared back at him. "I?" he said. "What have I to do with it?"

"You have everything to do with it. If it were not for you, the Englishman would not be here; the boy would not have come. You call yourself a guide, hey? You think you are better than the guides of Kurtal? So tell me what kind of a guide is it who cannot take care of his party—who looks out only for himself—who stands like a dumb ox while a boy is in danger —is lost——"

Saxo took a step forward. "Watch your tongue, man," he said. "I do not take such talk from a Kurtaler."

"You will take more than talk. It is because of you this thing has happened, and you will pay for it!"

The two men glowered at each other. Then Franz,

too, stepped forward, and the other Kurtal guides moved up beside him.

"Yes, make him pay," said Peter Tauglich.

"We will show him," said Klaus Wesselhoft.

"The boaster from Broli—"

"The coward from Broli—"

"We'll see who's the coward," roared Saxo. "Come on, you Kurtal sheep, I'll take on the lot of you!"

He doubled his hamlike fists. Franz lowered his head like a bull. In another moment they would have been at each other, but John Winter leapt between them. "Stop it!" he commanded. Then he wheeled on the others. "Stop it—all of you!"

The guides looked at him sullenly, as with both hands he pushed Franz and Saxo away from each other. "I'm sick of this nonsense," he snapped. "Broli—Kurtal. Kurtal—Broli. One of you is as bad as the other; as stupid as the other. Fighting about your damned villages. Snarling like animals, while the boy is probably—"

His voice stopped, as if cut off by a knife. He was no longer looking at the men, but past them, at the door of the hut; and now, in the sudden stillness, the others turned and stared too.

"Mother of God!" someone murmured.

For in the doorway stood Rudi Matt.

His slight body was bent with tiredness. His clothing was in tatters. Dirt mixed with wet snow caked his face and hands, and streaks of blood showed on his fingers and cheeks. But as he faced the others he drew himself straight. His lips were smiling, and his eyes shone with the blue of the mountain sky. "I have found the way," he said to them. *"I have found the way!"*

Franz was the first to move. His anger forgotten—

Saxo forgotten—he hurried forward and grasped the boy by the arm. "You are alive!" he exclaimed. "You are alive, and all right—"

"Yes, I am all right," said Rudi. "And I have found the way."

"The way?"

"Past the Fortress. To the top of the Citadel."

Franz gaped at him. The others gaped. "You mean —you have been on the Citadel?" his uncle asked incredulously.

"Yes. Since yesterday. I was caught in a storm, and then it got dark and I had to spend the night. . . . But it doesn't matter. . . ." Rudi's voice was almost shaking with excitement. "Because I found it—truly. The way around the Fortress, that Father looked for. I found it and climbed it—"

"Climbed it?"

"Yes. To the left there was a chimney, and I climbed to the top of it. Above the Fortress there is the ridge again, and it is easy. I could not go on. The storm came, and it was late. But I could see from where I stood—it was easy all the way to the shoulder."

There was silence. And eight pairs of staring eyes. In Franz Lerner's eyes was a turmoil of conflicting emotions: relief and bewilderment, anger and uncertainty, and beneath these—deeper than these—something that was close to awe.

But it was not Franz who spoke next. It was Teo Zurbriggen, who now suddenly limped forward, his old face shining with excitement. "So, you have done it, boy! You have shown them!" he cried. "And I am proud of you. Your father would be proud of you."

"I—I—" Rudi stammered—stopped. He had no

more words. He looked from Old Teo to Franz, trying to read the expression in his uncle's face.

Captain Winter came up and put an arm around him. "You're tired, son," he said. "Come, sit down. Rest." He turned to the others. "The boy must be starving. Get him some food."

He and Teo led Rudi to the table. They took off his pack, his boots, his wet outer clothing, and wrapped a blanket around him. Some of the guides started a fire. Others got food from their packs. Only Franz Lerner still stood motionless, watching—as if in a trance from which he could not rouse himself.

"Here, now—"

They brought him hot tea. They brought him porridge and bread and cheese. And while he ate he told them the story of his solitary adventure.

"And the whole night," said Andreas Krickel, "—all of it you stayed up there, alone?"

"Yes sir," said Rudi.

"You were not afraid?" asked Paul Tauglich.

"Yes, I was afraid."

"But nothing happened?"

"No."

"There were no spirits?" said Klaus Wesselhoft. "No ghosts or demons?"

There was a pause. The men's eyes were fixed on Rudi.

"No," he told them. "No ghosts. No demons."

Captain Winter began asking him about the details of the route, and he described them as best he could. But his glance kept wandering to Franz Lerner, who still stood motionless and apart, until at last he could no longer bear the weight of his silence.

"Uncle—" he said.

"Yes?"

"You are angry?"

Franz shrugged. "What is the use of anger?"

"And—" He could scarcely speak the word. "And Mother—?"

"I had thought you had forgotten that you have a mother."

Rudi winced. "No," he murmured, "I have not forgotten."

"You simply do not care what you do to her?"

"Yes, I care. Only—only I—"

"Only you care more for your wild schemes. Yes, I know." Franz paused, and when he went on his voice was hard and flat. "It is because of your mother that I am here," he said. "For myself, it no longer matters what you do. You are crazy, like your father, and will probably kill yourself like your father. But if you do not think of your mother. I think of my sister. I said to her, I will come up after you. If you are still alive I will find you. . . . All right, you are alive. You have eaten and rested. Come on now—we shall go down."

Abruptly he turned and thumped across the hut to the doorway. The others watched him. Rudi did not move.

"Well?" said Franz, turning.

The boy hesitated. His eyes pleaded. Franz moved back into the room, as if to take him by the arm, but a small gnarled figure stepped quickly in front of him.

"No," said Teo Zurbriggen.

Franz looked at him without speaking.

"You cannot do this—no. You must not. It is not fair to him."

"Fair? What do you mean, not fair? The boy has disobeyed and defied me. He has defied his mother. He has thieved, connived, lied——"

"Yes, of course he has." Teo's voice was heated. "And do you know why? Because you have driven him to it, you and his mother. Because you have tried to make him into something he is not. . . . Of course he has done these things. And so would I, in his place. And so would anyone."

Franz's face was dark. "Keep out of this, old man," he said. "It is no business of yours."

"Yes, it is my business. I have climbed with Rudi's father on every mountain around Kurtal. And now I have climbed with the boy, on the Felsberg, and I know what he can do. To climb is in his blood, in his bones. Give him a chance, and he will become even a greater guide than his father."

Franz did not want to listen. He started to brush past. But now a new voice broke in—a quiet yet compelling voice—that made him stop and turn.

"He's right, Franz," said John Winter.

Franz was silent.

"He's right—and you know he's right." The Englishman came closer and stood before him. "You feel you owe loyalty to your sister, and I understand that," he said. "But there's also something you both owe to the boy, and that's the freedom to be himself. . . . He's a born mountaineer. For years now I've climbed all through the Alps, and I've never seen a better one. . . . Yes, he's young; he still has things to learn. But the most important things he doesn't need to learn, because he has them already. And most of all, he has the will to climb. He has the heart.

"Yes, he disobeyed you," Winter went on. "And he lied to me. But he meant no harm by it. As Teo says, he was only doing what he *had* to do. And on the Cita-

146

del: there, too, he was only doing what he had to, because he knew that if he went down to Kurtal he could not come up again. Yes, it was a risk. It was foolish and impetuous. But it was magnificent. He followed his father—went higher than his father—found what is probably the only way up the mountain. Don't make him go down now, Franz. Tomorrow we're going to try for the top. Let him come with us; give him the chance. It's his birthright. And he's earned it."

There was a long silence. Franz looked at Winter, then at Teo, then back to Winter.

"Franz—" said the Englishman.

"Yes?"

"Why have you come up from Kurtal?"

"I have told you. Because the boy was here."

"Yes, I know. But is that the *only* reason?"

"I do not—"

"Wasn't it also," said Winter, "because Saxo and I were here? Because you knew we were here to climb the Citadel?"

Franz did not answer. He was staring at the floor. But the eyes of the other guides moved to the man from Broli, who was sitting alone near the fireplace, splicing two lengths of rope.

"Yes," said Andreas Krickel suddenly. "Because of Saxo, too."

"Because he has no business here," said Paul Tauglich.

"This hut belongs to us of Kurtal."

"The Citadel is the mountain of Kurtal."

"And he is a trespasser."

Saxo looked up at them. Then he put his ropes aside and got slowly to his feet. "The mountain of Kurtal?" he repeated. "Or perhaps you mean the mountain of Broli? For ten years I have come to

147

this hut. I have circled the Citadel and explored the routes to it, and never once, up here, have I seen a Kurtaler. There has been no guide of Kurtal since Josef Matt who is not afraid even to look at it."

A murmur of anger rose around him, but the giant from Broli paid no attention. "Yes, you are the great mountaineers," he taunted them. "Captain Winter comes to Kurtal. For days he is there, trying to find a guide. And who will go with him? No one. So he comes then to Broli; he speaks to me; I say yes, I will go. And only then does it become *your* mountain. Because you are jealous. Because you do not want to see a better man do what you cannot do yourselves."

The murmur grew louder. The men of Kurtal edged forward. Only Franz Lerner still stood motionless, with his eyes on the floor.

"Watch what you say, Saxo—"

"Boaster—"

"Liar—"

"Yes, liar," said Teo Zurbriggen. "With all your talk, what have you done? I at least have been on the Citadel—reached the Fortress—"

"You—yes," conceded Saxo. "For you alone, old man, I make an exception. But your day is done now. And the rest of you—" His eyes moved arrogantly from one to another. "You are sheep—chickens. You are afraid to come even as far as this hut, until you are shamed into it by a boy."

The Kurtalers glared. Their hands were clenched tight. Once again it appeared only a matter of seconds before fists would be flying.

Then once again, something stopped them. . . . But this time it was not Winter. . . . Franz had at last raised his head. He was looking steadily at the man from

Broli. And now his voice, though low and controlled, seemed suddenly to fill the little room.

"You think we are cowards, Saxo?" he said.

"I think what I see."

"That we are afraid of the Citadel?"

"Well, aren't you?"

"No, I am not," said Franz. He paused. *"I have come here to climb it."*

There was a sound as if of a sharply caught breath. Then silence. Then a babble of voices. And, among them, Old Teo's was the first and the loudest.

"Yes! Yes!" he shouted, almost beside himself with excitement.

"Yes!" roared the others. "To climb it! To climb it!"

"That is why we have come—"

"The guides of Kurtal—"

"To the mountain of Kurtal—"

"For the glory of Kurtal—"

John Winter stepped forward and put his arm around Franz's shoulder. A smile wreathed his lean face, and his eyes were shining. "Of course that's why you've come," he said. "And I knew you would. I've known it all along."

Franz looked at him uncomprehendingly. He did not return the smile, and his expression was deeply troubled. "You are not angry, my Captain?"

"Angry? Good Lord, man, why should I be angry?"

"That we must do this. That I must be your rival." Winter started to speak, but he went on quickly. "I am sorry, sir. Truly sorry. Many times you asked me to go with you, and I refused; and now I am here and must climb without you. I am sorry—but I cannot help it. We of Kurtal cannot help it. We cannot stand by while this man of Broli mocks us; while he sets off with you to try to climb our mountain. . . . No. We have heard

149

the challenge and we accept it. And it will be a guide of Kurtal, not of Broli, who will be the first to the top."

Again the men around him were shouting and cheering. Then, above their voices came an even louder voice—like the bellow of a bull. "The first, hey?" roared Saxo. "We will see about that. We will see how you like it when I am on the summit rolling stones down at you, and you are running and bleating like sheep."

"Boaster!" said Franz.

"Coward!" answered Saxo.

"We will show you!"

"You will be shown!"

In their anger, momentarily, Winter had been forgotten. But he still stood between them. He was no longer smiling. He had said no word while they shouted at each other. But now suddenly, as the two guides looked at him, something in his face made them stop.

"No," he said quietly. "No, Franz. No, Emil. It won't be like that."

They stared at him.

"It won't be like that at all," said John Winter. "Because we are going together."

There was a stunned silence.

"Together?"

"On the Citadel?"

"No!" said Saxo.

"No!" said Franz.

"We are going together," Winter repeated. "Or I, for one, am not going at all."

"You expect me to climb with a Kurtaler?"

"And me with a man from Broli?"

"That is exactly what I expect," said the Englishman. "Here you stand—two of the best guides in Switzerland. Above you is the greatest mountain in Switzerland. For years, Emil, you say you've dreamed of climbing it. And you too, Franz: you've dreamed of it —in your heart. . . . Well, here you are now. Here's your chance. Are you going to take it or throw it away?"

His gray eyes fixed on one, then the other. "What are you?" he asked. "Men? Or children? Which means more to you: your stupid village prejudices—or climbing the Citadel? Together we can do it, I tell you. Together we'll be the strongest team that has ever climbed in the Alps. But separately, there's not a hope. Quarreling and competing—there's not a hope. The Citadel is too great for that. It will have none of that. Those who get to the top will never do it by fighting each other; only by helping each other. By working together."

He paused. There was not a sound in the hut.

"Franz—Emil—" he said. "I beg you. Forget about Kurtal and Broli. Forget your squabbles and your foolish pride. Here we are, ready to go. The weather is clearing, and tomorrow will be fine. In the morning we'll start off—as a team—pulling together. And the rest of you will stay here in support. It's the strongest possible combination. We'll have every chance of success. Take the chance—I beg you. Together. Together!"

He stood between them, motionless, waiting. His lean face, under its strip of bandage, was tense with emotion, and the flame of his spirit gleamed in his eyes.

"Will you?" he said.

There was another silence. It was now or never. In the minds of Franz Lerner and Emil Saxo the Englishman's appeal struggled with the pride and prejudices of generations.

Franz looked at the floor. He looked back at Winter. His very body seemed almost visibly to be swaying, and when at last he spoke his voice was no more than a whisper. "Of all the *Herren* I have ever had, my Captain," he said, "I respect you the most. As a climber, and as a man. For anyone else I would not do this—could not do this. No. But for you—"

Winter's eyes moved to Saxo.

"Emil?"

Again a pause. A wavering. The man from Broli drew in a long, slow breath. "If there is no other way—" he murmured.

Winter's face was shining. He shook Saxo's hand. Turning, he shook Franz's. "And now—" he said, standing between them.

The guides faced each other, motionless. The guide from Kurtal and the guide from Broli.

"Now, you—" said Winter.

Franz hesitated. Saxo hesitated. Then slowly their hands rose and met. Simultaneously, the others pressed forward around them, and the hut shook with the hubbub of their excitement.

"So, it is settled!"

"Tomorrow is the day!"

"On to the Citadel!"

"To victory!"

"The three of you—"

"No, not three," said Winter. "Four. . . ." In the sudden silence that followed he looked questioningly at Franz. "That is right, is it not?" he asked quietly. "There are *four* to go?"

Franz did not answer at once. For a moment he returned Winter's gaze; then his eyes moved slowly past him to the corner of the room where Rudi had sat, forgotten, during the long wrangle between the men.

"You are feeling all right, boy?" he asked.

Rudi had risen to his feet.

"Yes, Uncle."

"You think you could climb tomorrow?"

"Oh yes, Uncle."

"Hmmm—" Franz shrugged and turned back to Winter. "For you, my Captain, I am doing strange things," he said. "God grant I shall not live to regret it."

CHAPTER 14

First of All Men

THEY WERE UP before dawn. By the light of a few candles they ate a quick breakfast and made their final preparations. Into the four packs went their food, extra clothing, blankets, camping gear. To the outside of Franz's and Saxo's packs were strapped the two tents that had been brought up from Broli.

For long hours the previous evening the two guides and Winter had discussed the plan of attack. It was their hope that they would have to spend only one night on the mountain; for the route to the base of the southeast ridge had now been established, and Rudi had pioneered the way to the top of the Fortress and reported no major obstacles on the ridge above. If all went well, they would be able to pitch camp near the shoulder, make their bid for the top the next morning and descend all the way before dark. As old mountain hands, however, they knew that all might *not* go well. The weather might break. There might be difficulties and mishaps. And they were therefore taking enough food for a possible second night out. This would allow them three full days on the mountain, and if it could not be climbed up and down in that time it probably could not be climbed at all.

Four to go. Five to remain behind.

Of the five, Krickel, Peter Tauglich, Wesselhoft and Old Teo were to spend that day and night at the hut, and the next day the first three would start up toward the base of the ridge, to meet and help the climbers on their way down. Teo (too old and crippled for this) would remain at the hut and have a hot meal awaiting their return. And Paul Tauglich would descend this morning to Kurtal, to bring word to the waiting village of what was happening.

At first it had been assumed that Old Teo would be the one to go down. But he had flatly refused. "Fifteen years ago I did what I could on this mountain," he told them. "And now again I shall do what I can."

"But your work—" someone pointed out. "Won't they expect you at the hotel?"

"Yes, they will expect me. And a certain dishwasher as well." A smile deepened the creases of his leathery face. "But for a few days the tourists can eat sandwiches—while I am chef to the conquerors of the Citadel."

No one wanted to go down, and finally Paul Tauglich had been chosen by lot. He would report to the mayor, the Guides' Central Committee, the whole town.

"But first—first of all," Franz told him, "you must speak to my sister. She has now been waiting two days and must be almost out of her mind. You will go to her right away—yes?—and tell her we have found the boy."

Tauglich nodded.

"But not that he is climbing the mountain. Only that we have found him. That he is here at the hut and all right. For the love of God, *not* that he is on the mountain!"

"You need not worry," said Tauglich.

In a corner of the hut Rudi quietly packed his knapsack. He had slept long and well; the ordeal of his solitary climb seemed far behind him; he felt rested, strong and calm. . . . Yes, most of all—and most strangely—calm. For now at last the awful uncertainty had ended. The hoping and despairing had ended. The decision had been made, and there was a job to do. Gratitude filled his heart—to Captain Winter and Old Teo, who had championed him; to his uncle, who had finally accepted him—and, along with gratitude, a resolve as deep and inward as his very being. Whatever happened, he would not fail them. He would be worthy of their trust.

He packed his share of the food supply. It was not a full share; he had insisted he could carry more; but the men had said no, this was enough. He packed the utensils that had been assigned to him and a few items of clothing loaned by the guides (for his own had been hopelessly soaked and ripped during the two previous days). Snug in the middle of the sack he stowed the old red flannel shirt. And to its outer straps he lashed his four-foot pole.

There was a guffaw close beside him, and looking up, he saw Saxo. "Going fishing boy?" asked the man from Broli.

"No. No sir. It is only—"

"Come on, take it off. It will make the climbing harder."

Saxo reached out for it, but Rudi stopped him. "No," he said. "No—please—I must take it."

Franz and Winter had come up. "Take it? Why?" said his uncle. "What use is such a stick? You have a fine new ax."

156

"Yes, I know. But—but this is for—" He couldn't say it. "But I use this sometimes, too."

"Nonsense. Take it off."

"Please, Uncle—"

"If he wants it so much, why not let him take it?" said Winter. "I've seen him climb with it. In fact, he once saved my life with it. Maybe it will be useful again."

Rudi looked at him gratefully. Franz seemed about to argue, but changed his mind, and Saxo turned away with a shrug. "If he gets stuck in a chimney," he said, "don't say we didn't warn you."

Now they were ready. They slung on their packs, hefted their axes, stamped with their stiff boots on the old plank flooring. The others were going to go with them as far as the top of the Blue Glacier, and from there Paul Tauglich would start down toward Kurtal and the rest would return to the hut. One by one they filed out the door.

It was still night as they descended through the boulders beneath the hut, but by the time they were out on the glacier the darkness had begun to pale. It was a perfect dawn: clear, windless and dry. The peaks, emerging slowly from obscurity, had received no new snow during the night, and their ridges rose sharp and bare against the graying sky. Gazing up at the vast walls of the Citadel, the climbers knew, with a lift of their hearts, that if ever they could be scaled, it would be on a day like this.

In less than half an hour they reached the parting of the ways. Not a word had been spoken on the march. And now the farewells were brief. . . . A clasping of rough hands. *"Grüss Gott."* "Go with God. . . ." Then Paul Tauglich was on his way down the Blue Glacier, and those who were to wait at the hut turned to go back.

But for a moment, before he left, Teo Zurbriggen stood close beside Rudi. "Remember what you've learned, boy," he said.

Rudi nodded.

"And remember this, too. If there is trouble—if there are problems to face and you are in doubt what to do—ask yourself only one question: *'What would my father have done?'*"

"I will," said Rudi.

The others had already started off, and Teo limped after them. But after a few paces he looked around and shouted: "And come down quickly, *Lausbube,* or our kitchen will be full of dirty dishes."

. . . And now again, for the third time, Rudi was ascending the steep tributary glacier that slanted up toward the base of the Citadel. They were all on one rope—Saxo, Captain Winter, his uncle and himself, in that order—and, using the steps that had already been cut, they moved easily and steadily. When he first turned and looked back, the others were already out of sight below. And by sunrise they were at the crest of the glacier and crossing the snow-bridge over the *bergschrund.*

They threaded the steep maze of the icefall and moved up the snowslope beyond—by now as familiar to Rudi as the forest paths six thousand feet below. All traces of the avalanche were gone, obliterated by the snowfall during the recent storm. But in the cool of the morning the new snow was firm and sound, and they climbed straight upward, without fear of another slide. Instinctively the boy's eyes went up to the cliffs on the left, where he had seen the chamois two days before; but this time there was no hint of movement on the gray walls of rock. He bent his head to the slope. . . . Kick—step. Kick—step. Kick—step. . . . And when he next looked up they were at the base of the ridge.

Here, for the first time, they rested. They had a slab of bread each and a swallow of tea. Then they were on their feet again, peering upward. "You take the lead now, Rudi," Captain Winter suggested. "You're the one who knows the way."

Rudi hesitated. He glanced at his uncle, who seemed about to protest; but in the end Franz said nothing, and he moved out in front. His uncle was now directly behind him on the rope, with Winter and Saxo in the third and fourth positions.

He was well aware of the honor and responsibility that had been conferred on him, and he climbed with the utmost care. For the first long stretch of the ridge, however, the going was better than he had dared hope. Wind and sun had done their work well: blowing the snow away, melting the ice-patches, leaving the rock bare and dry. Even when they reached the steeper pitches, which had slowed him up on his first ascent, he now had no trouble at all. For, whereas before he had had to search for holds and stances, he now remembered them well and swung up surely and easily.

Best of all, he was no longer alone and afraid. He had confidence in himself. And the confidence of others.

There was no wind. The sun was brilliant. Soon they were sweating from their exertions and paused to take off their outer jackets. Then they were climbing again. Climbing. . . . Climbing. . . . Up the narrowing ridge, across the knife-edge, toward the towering *gendarmes*. Out onto the south face, past the *gendarmes,* back to the ridge. On and on, up the spine of the ridge, while the precipices on either side dropped away steeply and the glaciers and valleys receded slowly into distance.

An hour. . . . Two hours. . . .

Then at last the ridge broadened and flattened. They pulled themselves up onto the level platform of rock and stood facing the sheer wall of the Fortress. For a moment Rudi's eyes fixed on the shallow cave at its base. But for only a moment. Then he turned, moving along the platform toward the south face, and his uncle and Winter followed him.

Saxo, however, lingered behind, staring up at the granite battlements. "Wait!" he called after them.

The others looked back, and he gestured. "It can be climbed here," he said. "Here on the right."

"No, the way's around to the left," Winter said. "Josef Matt's way. The way Rudi climbed."

"If you come here to the ledge," said Rudi, "you will see the cleft and—"

"I do not need to see it," Saxo interrupted. "There is a route up the wall. It will go."

"But—"

"It will go, I tell you."

The three others returned to where he stood. "Perhaps it will," said Winter. "But since one way has already been found, why bother with—"

"Because I say there is a better way." Saxo's eyes were sullen and defiant. "You have employed me as guide, have you not, Herr Winter? That is what I am —a master guide of Broli. And I am getting tired of following these Kurtalers, as if I were some sort of tourist."

"But the boy's been here before—you know that. He's climbed the cleft and—"

"I do not care what the boy has done. As a guide, it is my professional opinion that this is the best route."

160

There was a silence. Winter bit his lip. Since the previous day, when by main force of will he had brought them together, he had had no trouble with the guides. True, they had scarcely exchanged a word. But at least they had worked together and come this far without argument, and he had hoped they could go the whole way in the same spirit. . . . Obviously, though, it had been too much to expect.

"I'm sorry, Emil," he said firmly, "but I think the boy's route would be better."

"You mean," said Saxo, "that you refuse to follow my advice?"

"In this case—yes. I promise you that later on you'll have plenty of chances to lead the way."

Saxo looked at the ground, scowling. Then he looked up at the Fortress, and made a move as if to untie himself from the rope. He didn't, though. Instead, he turned away with a shrug. "Yes, later perhaps we shall see," he muttered, as he followed the others across the platform.

Rudi still went first. Following the ledge that curved out over the south face, he reached its end and inched out onto the bulging cliff beyond. With Franz belaying the rope, he made the crossing without difficulty. Then he in turn belayed his uncle, and behind them came Saxo and Winter, safeguarding each other. In less than ten minutes they were all together at the foot of the great cleft.

Then up again. . . .

And, as on the ridge and the bulge, the going was far easier for Rudi, now that he knew the way and was no longer alone. Or at least it was easier until he reached the narrow shaft-like section, halfway up, and then suddenly there was a scraping noise at his back, and he stuck fast.

"It is that pole of yours," Franz called from below.

Rudi knew well enough what it was: the two ends of his staff had become wedged against the walls of the cleft. And now he was struggling desperately to free them and at the same time not lose his holds on the smooth vertical rock.

"Try to slip off your pack," Franz called. "Then you can untie the thing and leave it there."

But Rudi was not leaving the staff if there was any way to help it. He jerked and wriggled and thrust himself upward and sideways—and at last its ends grated loose.

"All right, now untie it," called his uncle. "Get rid of it. Throw it away."

Rudi pretended not to hear. Reaching a hand back over his shoulder, he tugged at the staff, trying to shift it from a horizontal to a vertical position. The best he was able to do was to get it diagonal, like a slung rifle. But at least he could now move again; and, though Franz was still shouting at him to untie and drop it, he resumed climbing on up the cleft. Now and then there was an ominous scraping of wood on stone. At the great chockstone, which called for delicate climbing, there was a bad moment when it caught in a crevice overhead. But this time a mere dipping of his shoulders released it; and beyond the chockstone there were no further difficulties. In a few minutes they were out of the cleft and on the flat top of the Fortress. The four of them . . . and his pole.

To his relief, his uncle made no further mention of it. "Not bad. Not bad at all, boy," was his only comment, and something very close to admiration showed in his eyes.

Winter grasped Rudi's hand and pressed it warmly. And even Saxo conceded, "*Ja,* it was all right. It went." Then, as an afterthought, he added: "Although straight up the wall would have been better."

They rested again, and ate and drank sparingly. The sun was now almost midway across the sky, and the mountain world around them glittered in the full brightness of noon. It was not around them that they looked, however, but only up and ahead: at the long, jagged slant of the upper ridge, the walls and crags tiering above it, the Citadel's shoulder jutting broad and white-rimmed against the blue depths of space. As Rudi had reported, there was no major obstacle. Or at least none was visible. But they knew that the mountain, before it was through with them, would exact the very last ounce of their strength and skill.

They rose. They started off again. Now their order of ascent was reversed, with Saxo and Winter going first, Franz and Rudi following. But Rudi did not mind being last. He had brought them safely this far; he had had his full share of leading; and now it was his turn to follow, while older, more experienced hands forged the way. He moved on steadily after his uncle, taking care to see that there was neither too much nor too little slack in the rope that joined them. He watched his holds and balance as carefully as when he had been out ahead. Not once, he was resolved, would he hamper or delay the others. Never would he give them cause to regret that they had allowed him to come.

Up—up they went: the first of all men to enter that secret world above the world. The first of all living things, too, it seemed, in the vast stillness of rock and air . . . until suddenly Rudi realized that the men up ahead had stopped; Saxo was pointing; and there above them, outlined on a crag, was a dark brooding shape. It was a lammergeier, the great Alpine bird of prey.

And it was staring at them, wings poised, as if in the next moment it would plunge down in savage attack. But its instinct, apparently, warned it that they were too big and too many; for when, abruptly, it took off, it was not down, but up. Its wings spread huge against the sky, as it arched out from the mountainside. It whirled and swooped and glided, no longer a hideous vulture with tearing beak and talons, but a thing of soaring beauty, wild and free. And as Rudi watched, his heart soared too—up and up with the great bird— along the crest of the ridge, above the walls and precipices, higher and higher, until it swooped over the mountain's shoulder into the blue beyond. For that was where they, too, were going. Not so swiftly as the lammergeier. Not on wings. But still—where they were going. Where no man had ever been before.

A surge of joy rose within him, filled his body and burst, without his willing it, from his lips, . . . YOOO-LEEE-OOOO-LAAAY-EEEEE. YOOO-LEEE-OOOO-LAAAY-EEEEE. . . . Wild and free as the bird, his yodel rose into the mountain stillness. The three men above looked down at him. Winter waved a hand. Then they climbed on.

Through the long afternoon they climbed. Up—up —up. Along the spine of the ridge. Out on the bordering faces, when the spine grew too jagged. Over crags and slabs, through clefts and chimneys; balancing with their axes, belaying with the rope; inching on and on up a wilderness of rock, reaching always for the next hold, the next stance, that would bring them still higher. On the more difficult pitches they moved only one at a time. Sometimes there were long waits while they searched out a route, and sometimes they chose a wrong one and had to back down and try again. But each time they at last found a way and went on to the next pitch—and the next problem.

They were really high now. Many of the lesser summits of the range were already below them, and the jutting outline of the Fortress, far down the ridge, appeared as remote as the glaciers and valleys. The air was thinning. Rudi's breathing was more rapid. But it caused him no particular difficulty, and, though they had been climbing for almost twelve hours, he was still not tired. Up ahead, the others seemed to be all right too—moving slowly but steadily onward. Now and then Winter had a brief spell of coughing, but his pace remained the same as ever. The only other sound was the clinking of their axes and boot-nails against the rock.

Hand up—foot up. Hand up—foot up. Then the climbing stopped; the rope connecting Rudi to Franz hung motionless, and there was another wait, longer than any before. After several minutes he climbed on up and found the three men standing together, with his uncle and Saxo in the midst of an agrument. Directly ahead, the crest of the ridge flared up in a smooth, holdless pitch, and it was obviously necessary to work around it, either to one side or the other. Franz was for going to the right and Saxo to the left.

"The rock is sounder over here," said one.

"But too steep," said the other.

"The holds are good."

"On the far side they are better."

The two guides faced each other, unyielding. Then they looked at Winter. The Englishman peered up on one side, then the other, and rubbed the stubble along his jaw.

"Suppose we try the left," he said.

Franz's lips tightened. "But it is obvious, my Captain, that—"

"Either side looks possible. Down at the Fortress we took our way. Here let's try Saxo's."

Franz hesitated. He seemed about to continue the argument. Then abruptly he turned away. With Saxo leading, they edged out to the left, above the south face, and within ten minutes had bypassed the obstacle and regained the ridge.

"So—you see?" said the man from Broli.

Franz said nothing. But Rudi noticed that, for a while thereafter, the rope joining him to his uncle jerked more often and more violently than it had before.

Up . . . still up . . . always up. . . .

And at last they were nearing the shoulder of the mountain. As it came closer it grew larger: a vast snow-topped battlement looming above them that blocked out half the sky. Thus far on the ascent, they had tried not to think, or look, too far ahead, concentrating on each problem as they encountered it. But now they could no longer keep their eyes from rising to that grim forbidding mass. For if the Fortress had been the first "key" to the mountain, the shoulder, they knew, would be the second; and they would either have to find a way up and over it or turn back in bitter defeat. That it was immense and formidable was plain at a glance. But if it was climbable—if it would "go"— they would not know until they reached it. From below, the perspective was too distorted for them to make out the details of its structure.

Also, the light was fading. The sun had long since slanted off behind the mass of the mountain, and the ridge lay in deepening shadow. Obviously they would

166

not be able to reach even the base of the shoulder before dark.

They had done enough for the first day. On that even Franz and Saxo were agreed. Leaving the crest of the ridge, they found, after some search, a place level and sheltered enough for a campsite; and here they dropped their packs and pitched their two small tents. They rested. Then they ate their supper of dried meat, cheese and bread and brewed tea on a small spirit stove that Winter had brought up from Broli. The warmth of the tea was welcome, for it was growing colder. The shades of evening closed, gray and solemn, about them. And when they had finished eating, it was night.

Still they sat for a while on the flat stones in front of the tents. The men smoked their pipes and talked desultorily, and Rudi, beside them, stared out across the gulf of darkness. In a vast arc around them the snowpeaks gleamed faintly, as if with an inner light of their own. Farther down were brooding rockwalls and ghostly glaciers, and, still farther, the dim outlines of forest and valleys. The valley of Kurtal was not visible—and would not be, until they came up over the shoulder—but yellow pricks of light winked up from even more distant villages, incredibly tiny and remote beyond the miles and the night. As he watched, it seemed to Rudi that he was no longer on the earth at all, but, rather, looking down upon it from an island in the sky.

There they were on their island: *the first of all men.*

He looked around him, and then slowly upward. His eyes fixed on the great shoulder rising black against the stars.

"*And tomorrow—*" he thought. "*Tomorrow—*"

CHAPTER 15

The Needle's Eye

THEY SLEPT two to a tent: Rudi with Franz, Winter with Saxo. It grew cold—bitter cold—and the stones under them were hard and thrusting. But for Rudi, at least, tiredness outweighed discomfort, and he was soon dropping off toward sleep. The last thing of which he was aware was his uncle's breathing, close beside him, and this warmed him more than either tent or blanket. After his ordeal during that solitary night beneath the Fortress, he felt as safe and snug as if he had been in his own bed at home.

Once he awakened. It seemed that someone was calling him. But then he realized that it was Winter coughing in the other tent. In a moment he was asleep again; and the next thing he knew Franz was shaking him by the shoulder.

It was still night. The men had agreed that by dawn they must actually be on their way, so as to make use of every moment of daylight. Fumbling in the darkness, Rudi laced his boots and rolled up his blanket, and when he came from the tent Franz and Saxo were already preparing breakfast. . . . Tea again. Two biscuits apiece. A bit of cheese. . . . Sitting beside Winter, Rudi noticed that he ate almost nothing and kept putting a hand to his still-bandaged head.

"It is hurting you, my Captain?" Franz asked.

Winter lowered his hand quickly. "No, it's nothing," he said. "It was only a bump."

"Perhaps with the altitude—"

But Winter did not want to talk about it. Rising, he began packing his knapsack, and the others followed suit. It had been decided that they would take everything on with them: tents and blankets as well as food and climbing gear. For, although they hoped to make the summit and back that same day, there was always the possibility of trouble, and it was far better to bear the extra loads than to risk a night without shelter on those savage heights.

"If the way is clear beyond the shoulder," said Saxo, "we can leave the things there and pick them up on the way down."

The pack-straps creaked as they slung them on. Their boots scuffed against cold stone. As they started off, the first band of gray showed in the sky above the ranges to the east.

Then they were climbing again. . . . Climbing. . . . Climbing. . . . The section of the ridge on which they now found themselves offered straightforward going, and they moved all at one time and at a steady pace. For a while there was barely enough light for them to grope their way, and they themselves were merely a dark file of shadows. But gradually the sky lightened, the mountain emerged into cold twilight, and they could see their surroundings—and one another. Rudi was again last on the rope, with Winter directly ahead. Although the Englishman kept pace with the guides, it seemed to the boy, watching him, that his movements were somehow slower and heavier than on the previous day; and when he occasionally turned to look down, his face was drawn and strained. He had had a bad night, that was sure. With his headache and coughing, probably a sleepless night. But at least he had not coughed so far that morning. And whatever his pain or tiredness, he spoke no word of complaint.

"He will make it," thought Rudi. "He *must* make it. Because, of all of us, he most deserves to make it." Watching the lean, bent figure ahead of him, he felt a glow of admiration, and of gratitude. For without Winter, where would they be now? Down in the valley, all of them. He himself at his dishpans in the Beau Site Hotel. It had been Winter, and Winter alone, who had given him his chance; who had brought them all together; who had planned and organized, pleaded and persuaded; who had led them this far up the Citadel by the sheer will and drive of his spirit. And that spirit, Rudi was sure, could not now be denied. He would make the top.

They would all make it. . . .

As they climbed, the sun rose. Its rays thawed the cold stiffness from their bodies; and, looking up at the cloudless sky, they knew they were to be blessed with another perfect day. But also, when they raised their eyes, they saw something else—and this was a different story. For the shoulder of the mountain was now close above them, and, the more clearly they saw it, the more clearly they realized that it was to be a truly formidable obstacle. Perhaps a half-hour's climb above them the ridge ended. It was not merely interrupted, as had been the case at the Fortress, but ended—for good—and beyond it the mountain soared up in what, from below, seemed an absolutely perpendicular wall. Rudi tried to estimate its height, from its base, where the ridge stopped, to where its top, the shoulder proper, loomed like a white-rimmed battlement against the sky. Two hundred feet, it might be; or three hundred; foreshortening made it hard to tell. But height alone, steepness alone, did not matter. What mattered was that there be a *way*.

Rudi bent his head. He concentrated on the next step, and the next. A half-hour passed; and in one thing, at least, his judgment had been right, for presently the men up ahead stopped and waited. Coming up beside them, he stopped too. They had reached the end of the ridge.

And now four pairs of eyes searched the mountainside above them. The first thing they saw was encouraging; for it was not quite so steep as it had appeared from farther down, and it was not smooth, but broken up into hundreds of ribs and buttresses, clefts and gullies. So far, so good. But what was good was at the same time bad, or at least utterly perplexing, for the very number of these turned the wall into a formless maze. On the ridge, except for a few short stretches, the route had been clear. There had been only one way to go. Whereas here there was a whole labyrinth of ways—or, rather, possible ways—each of which *might* bring them to the shoulder, but might also, and far more likely, be merely a false trail, leading nowhere. They peered upward. They pointed. Franz favored one route, Saxo another, and another argument would have ensued if Winter had not stopped them. It was useless to argue, he pointed out. It was useless even to theorize. No human eye, looking up from below, could thread the maze of that mountain wall; and besides, its whole upper half was hidden behind great bulges and overhangs, and it was impossible to tell which routes did, or did not, lead to climbable sections above.

There was only one way: trial and error.

First they selected a route to the left, above the south face—not because it seemed more promising than any other, but because a broad ledge curving out beneath it gave some measure of protection from the mile-high drop below. They had not climbed fifty feet, however, before they reached a blank holdless wall and had to return to their starting place. They tried again, to the right, and again the holds petered out; in between, and were stopped by an overhang. Franz pointed out a way, Saxo a second, Winter a third; and they tried them all. But with the same result. It would have saved much time, of course, if they had been able to unrope and reconnoitre separately, but the going was far too steep and dangerous for solitary climbing. Even on the rope, the man up ahead was in a precarious position, for the others could have done little to hold him up if he slipped or fell.

The three men took turns in the lead, and each time they had to back down, defeated, their faces were tense from exertion and strain. Now for the first time they were all breathing hoarsely, and their fingertips were bloody from clawing at the rock. Even Rudi, who only followed where the others led, began to feel the effect of the struggle in his his lungs and legs. For the first time his pack felt heavy and cumbersome, and its straps bit savagely into his shoulders.

They advanced—retreated. Advanced—retreated. Back at the bottom for perhaps the tenth time, Winter was overcome by a sudden coughing fit, his first of the day, and for several minutes sat with his head to his knees, while paroxysms wracked his body. The others waited, watching him with troubled eyes. And the sun, as if to mock them, shone more brightly than ever, glinting gaily on the steel of their axes and the mica in the rocks.

When Winter arose his face was pinched and gray. "I'm sorry," he murmured.

"You are all right now, my Captain?"

"Yes, all right. Let's go."

Then they tried again.

And this time, at last, they were able to keep going. Starting up a narrow chimney, they came out at its top onto a ledge which, though tiny, was yet wide enough to hold them. Beyond it were other ledges, and these in turn led to a second chimney, a belt of slabs, more ledges, a jutting crag. Not that there was anything easy about their progress. At almost every step they had to stop and plan the next one, and often they followed a wrong lead and had to backtrack. But at least they did not have to descend all the way. Each time they found another route that "went." And slowly they moved higher and higher.

They were now all on one rope; Franz first, Saxo second, Winter third, Rudi last. And whereas, on the ridge, they had often been able to climb simultaneously, it was now always a matter of one at a time. On each new pitch there was first a long wait, while Franz explored and tested, with the others perhaps offering advice from below. Then Franz began to climb, the rope gliding behind him—ten feet, twenty feet, thirty feet—before it stopped. Another wait, while he found a stance and braced himself. At last his voice calling, "Come on!" The other three following in order, with Franz belaying Saxo, Saxo Winter, Winter Rudi, until that particular stretch was behind them. And then the whole performance began again for the next one.

The steepness was unrelenting, the holds tiny and widely spaced. Often, the toe of one boot and a finger of one hand were all that held them to the mountain-side. And, although they kept trying to bear to the left, or at least straight up, the contours of the wall forced them steadily to the right. Here there was no ledge beneath them, as on the other side, but only the east face of the mountain plunging sheer to the glaciers; and Rudi, accustomed though he was to height, tried not to look down at the blue emptiness beneath his feet. For almost an hour now they had been out on the face of the rock, clinging like insects. He wished they would come to another cleft or chimney that would give at least the illusion of holding them in.

Then they did. Clambering up onto a narrow shelf, he saw, to the left, a long chimney slanting upward; and, though steep, it was cut deeply into the rock, and with protecting sides that made it almost like a funnel. The men ahead, however, had not taken it, but were still moving up the face, to the right. Thinking it had escaped their notice, Rudi called and pointed, but when Winter, who was next above him, turned, it was only to shake his head. . . . Why? the boy wondered. But he was not to wonder long. . . . A few minutes later the stillness was broken by a rumbling overhead; the rumbling rose to a roar; and, looking back, he saw a cascade of loose rocks pouring wildly down the chimney.

At least he had been right in one thing, he thought grimly. It was indeed a funnel.

On they went: over bulges, crags, buttresses. Often the rock above them actually overhung, but each time they were able to find a way up and around. The top of one of the overhangs proved to be a fairly wide shelf, and for the first time since leaving the ridge they were able to sit down and rest. When they rose to go on again, Franz and Saxo changed places on the rope. Rudi had never before seen his uncle give up the lead without reluctance.

It was not long before Saxo was put to the test, for a few minutes later, they reached a second shelf and stood peering up at a vertical wall. There was no way to work around it—that was obvious. Its surface was smooth and holdless. But up its center ran a long crack, a few inches wide, that seemed to lead to another level place, high above. If, that is—*if*—it was climbable.

"Ja," said the man from Broli, "it will go."

And while the others watched, he started up. There were no holds in the crack, any more than in the outer wall, nor was it anywhere wide enough to hold a man's body. Saxo climbed by jamming a knee into it, then an elbow, then a knee again and again an elbow, levering himself up not by any grip on the stone, but by the stone's grip on himself. It was an exhausting process. Every few moments he had to rest, and those below could hear his hoarse breathing as he held himself on by the wedge of his flesh and bone. But always he moved up again—knee and elbow, knee and elbow—until he disappeared over the top of the wall and a shout came down to them that he had reached the platform above. "Well done!" called Winter. And even Franz's face showed his admiration. For it had been a magnificent exhibition of strength and skill.

Then they, too, went up—first Franz, then Winter —and, with the rope from above to hold them, they made it without difficulty. But when it came Rudi's turn he was in trouble from the start. For his knees and elbows, smaller than the men's, did not wedge properly into the crack, and, try as he would, he could get neither friction nor leverage. He slipped— and caught himself. Slipped again—and dangled. He was not afraid of falling; he knew the rope would hold him. But even worse than fear was his frustration and shame, for this was the first time on the whole climb that he needed help from the others. He struggled, strained, twisted, clawed the rock. But it was no use. The crack would not hold him. Slipping and dangling, he was hauled up the wall—like a despised "bundle of firewood"—until at last he stood, breathless and humiliated, beside the three men on the top.

"All right, son?" asked Winter.

"Yes, all right," he answered, his eyes averted.

But once they were moving again there was little time to brood over what was past. For now they were really high on the shoulder, the climbing was more exposed than ever, and every step required the utmost concentration. More and more, though they still fought against it, they were being forced out to the extreme right of the wall. Below them were only chasms of space. And above—very near now—the farthermost tip of the shoulder projected in a sharp, almost needle-like point against the sky. Here was where they would come out: of that there was no longer any doubt. At that farthest point—at the Needle—poised like a pointing finger above the precipice of the east face. Above it, sweeping on to the left, was the broad, snow-covered flat of the shoulder. Once there, they would be both on easier ground and within striking distance of the summit. It was still only midmorning, and with luck. . . .

Yes, with luck. . . .

But would they have it? Would they be able to find a way around—or over, or under—that needle in the sky? Staring up at it, their faces were drawn and grim, for they knew that here was the second "key" to the Citadel.

Five minutes. . . . Ten minutes. . . . Another ten. . . . And there they were. There at the extreme upper corner of the monstrous wall; on a tiny platform in a sea of space, with the top of the wall curving out in a cornice above them and the Needle thrusting up diagonally to the right. Their eyes moved slowly, almost inch by inch, over the rock around them. To the left was a sheer cliff—unclimbable. Overhead the cornice —equally so. That left the Needle. As they had expected—the Needle. In spite of its thinness they knew it to be solid; otherwise it would never have weathered the winds and storms of the centuries. Its rock was sound. It would hold them. But the question was, could they hold on to *it?*

There seemed to be two possible ways of climbing: one up and around, on the outside, almost to its very tip; the other through a sort of cleft, farther in, where the base of the Needle joined the main mass of the shoulder. Neither offered much in the way of holds or stances, but the second was far less exposed than the first, and after a short discussion, Saxo, who was still in the lead, moved up to try it. For the first ten feet or so he climbed directly above them. Then the cleft deepened and bent, and he disappeared. By advance agreement, the others did not follow, but stayed where they were, so as to be in a better position to belay the rope if anything went wrong. For several minutes, however, nothing did. The rope glided up, stopped, glided again, stopped again. Finally it stopped and stayed motionless for a long time.

"What is it?" Winter called.

There was no answer.

"Doesn't it go?"

Still no answer. But after a few moments the rope began to move slowly downward. Then Saxo reappeared, maneuvering carefully down the cleft, and soon he was beside them again on the platform.

"No, it does not go," he said.

"Why? Where does it lead to?"

"Beyond the turn it cuts deeper into the mountain. There are holds; it is not difficult. But it gets darker and narrower, like a tunnel—and at last so narrow that a man cannot pass. Even when I took off my pack I could not get through. It is no good. It does not go."

"How far up does the tunnel go?" asked Winter.

"I could not tell."

"Could you see light above you?"

"No."

"Perhaps if you had gone a little farther—" Franz put in.

"If you think you can do better," Saxo told him, "—go ahead."

Franz did. Climbing up the cleft, he disappeared for a full ten minutes. But in the end, like Saxo, he returned defeated. "No," he conceded. "It is too narrow. One cannot get through."

There was a silence. No one moved. Then slowly their eyes turned to the other route—to the point of the Needle—to the tiny cracks and wrinkles that formed its only holds, slanting up to its tip above the terrible abyss.

"It's my turn now," said Winter quietly.

"No, my Captain—"

"Yes, mine."

Winter laid down his ax and unslung his pack. Changing positions with Saxo, so that he was now first on the rope, he moved out toward the edge of the platform. Behind him, the two guides wrapped the rope around their bodies and braced themselves as best they could. But it was an almost useless belay; for, once

178

out on the Needle, Winter would be both above them and off to one side, and, if he fell, he would drop so far before the rope caught him that it would either crush his ribs or—more likely—break. The guides knew it. Winter knew it. Rudi knew it. And he knew, too, that was *why* the Englishman was going first. Not because he considered himself the best climber; but because the risk was so great and he was resolved that it be his.

Winter stood poised on the rim of nothingness. He rubbed his hands slowly against his trousers. Then he swung up and out. His first hold was a tiny crevice into which he managed to insert two fingers of his right hand; the second a shallow notch which held just the toe of his right foot. For several moments he clung to these, while his eyes searched the rock ahead. Then slowly—so slowly that it scarcely seemed motion at all—his left hand moved to where his right had been and the right to another hold, farther on. At the same moment his feet shifted; they, too, were farther on, and higher. Again there was a wait. Again the groping, creeping movement. He was farther out on the Needle. Then still farther. . . .

It was a miracle of climbing. Of nerve and balance. To those watching from the platform the holds were no longer visible, and it seemed that Winter was held to the rock by the mere touch of toe and fingertip. Sometimes his body was arched out, straining, against the sky; sometimes flattened in, as if he were trying to press it into the solid stone. Once, for what seemed an eternity, he hung spread-eagled and motionless, seemingly unable to shift either a hand or a foot. But at last there was again the slow groping—the creeping—the grasping. And he moved higher. And higher.

His line of ascent was diagonally up the side of the

Needle and, if he were able to continue it, would bring
him out at a point just to the left of its tip. From here
on in to the main mass of the mountain the snow-covered upper surface of the Needle was almost level
against the sky. Indeed, as far as he could be seen
from below, it was simply an extension of the broad
shoulder, and, once it was reached, there would be no
further difficulty. . . . But the question still remained:
could Winter reach it? . . . For a time the answer
seemed to be yes. He was perhaps ten feet from
the top. Then eight feet. Then five feet. His hand
was reaching up again, and two more holds, two
more movements, would bring him to the white rim of
snow. But this time he found no holds. He reached to
the right, to the left—and there was nothing. He reached
straight upward—and there was nothing. The minutes passed, as he tried and tried again: groping, straining and struggling against the sheer rock, clinging by
finger- and boot tip above the gulf of space. . . . And
still there was nothing.

Throughout his ascent no word had been spoken.
The guides below had stood braced and tense, as they
payed out the rope. But now Franz could keep silence no longer.

"Come down!" he called. "Come down!"

Winter was trying again.

"It is no good. You are tired. Come down!"

The Englishman made one last desperate effort, but
it was as futile as the others. Then slowly he began the
descent. Coming down took him as long as going up
and was even more hazardous, because of the difficulty in seeing the holds below. Twice he slipped,
and caught himself just in time. And once it took almost ten minutes of maneuvering merely to lower
himself from one stance to the next. But gradually the

gap between him and the platform lessened, until it was a matter of only a few feet. Then once again he slipped—and this time could not catch himself. His body lurched out from the rock; he began to fall. But luckily he was now so close to the guides that they were able to brake almost immediately. For one sickening moment he swung like a pendulum over the abyss. Then they were pulling strongly at the rope, and in a few seconds he was beside them on the platform.

He had been out on the Needle for a full hour—every instant of it one of the utmost exertion and danger. Sweat beaded his forehead; and his face, always thin, now seemed as hollow as a skeleton's. One of his sleeves was ripped and his elbow bloody; both legs were trembling from the strain to which they had been subjected; and his breath came in quick sharp gasps that soon turned into a wracking cough. "I'm all right. I'm all right," he kept murmuring between paroxysms. But several minutes passed before he could speak or move normally.

Winter had had his ordeal. Now came Franz's and Saxo's.

Franz went first, following Winter's route for a way and then angling off to the left, in the hope of finding better holds. But, like the Englishman, he got to within a few feet of the top—and no farther. All his efforts, all his skill and resolution, were of no avail against that last merciless pitch of rock, and eventually he too returned to the platform: grim, panting and defeated.

Then Saxo. Big and powerful as a tiger. Unlike the others, he carried his ax with him, slung through his belt; and when he neared the top he reached up with it, above the white rim, hoping that the prong would catch and give him the means of pulling himself higher. But this, too, met only with failure. Time and again the ax went up, dug in—and slipped away. Apparently there was no ice above, but only loose snow over smooth rock; for not once did the prong catch and hold. And eventually Saxo, like the others before him had to acknowledge defeat and climb down.

Defeat. . . . It hung over them now like a gray shadow. It was in their voices, their eyes, their worn bodies. For three hours they had done battle with the pinnacle of rock that rose before them. They had struggled, risked their lives, called on every resource of flesh and blood, brain and will—and still it rose, unconquered and unconquerable. It was they who were beaten. For there was no more that they could do. Dully, bitterly, they stared up at the hateful thing that had put an end to their hopes and dreams.

"Please—"

The voice was Rudi's. And it was the first time in hours that he had spoken. Throughout the long struggle he had remained on the platform, helping when he could, trying to keep out of the way when he was not needed. As each man in turn had made the attempt, he had hoped and striven with him, suffered and despaired with him, no less than if he had been climbing himself; and now that it was over—and they were beaten—his despair was perhaps the deepest of all.

Still there was one thing he must say before they turned to go down.

"Please—"

The men looked at him.

"Please, may I try—"

"No, of course not," Franz cut him off. "If we three could not make it, how could you?"

"I don't mean that way, Uncle. I mean inside."

"Inside?"

Rudi pointed to the opening at the base of the Needle. "That way," he said. "Where you tried first."

"But it was no good. We could not get through."

"Perhaps I could. I am smaller."

The men looked at him for another moment; then at one another.

"It is a slim chance," said Franz.

"It would take a marmot to get through," added Saxo.

"And also it probably does not lead anywhere."

"Even if you can squeeze through," said Winter to Rudi, "—and even if it does come out on the shoulder—what good will it do? The rest of us can't get up."

"I will be on the rope," Rudi said. "If I get to the shoulder I will pull it up. Then I will go around and let it down over the Needle. With a rope from the top you can climb it easily."

There was a silence.

"Please," he said. "Let me look. Let me try."

For a moment the old light kindled in Winter's eyes, and as he looked down at the boy, a smile touched his worn face. He glanced at the guides, but they said nothing.

"All right, son," he said. "Go on."

Rudi dropped his pack, staff, and ax and tied himself onto one end of the rope. At the same time the others untied themselves, and Franz took the slack in his hands, ready to pay it out to its full length behind them.

"Good luck, boy," said Winter. "And don't take any chances."

Then he was on his way. Up the cleft . . . around the turning . . . up a steeper, narrower part above. For some thirty feet the climbing was easy, there were holds aplenty, and his only concern was that the rope should not foul on some projection beneath him. But then, as Saxo and his uncle had reported, the walls began to close in; soon there was one behind him, as well as in front and on both sides; and he was, in effect, crawling upward through an all-but-vertical tunnel. Rocks nudged his shoulders, chest and back, as he wormed his way past them. Then they were pressing in on all sides at once, and he knew that this must be the point at which the men had turned back, because he himself was barely able to squeeze through. As he climbed, the light had gradually faded: from bright sunshine to gray twilight, and now almost to darkness. He could no longer see his holds, but had to grope for them blindly.

Also—and worse—the rock was now wet. And the wetness made it slippery. Several times he lost his footing, and once actually began sliding downward, until he brought up with a jolt on a knob below. Soon whole streams of water were pouring down the walls, into his face and eyes and down the collar of his shirt. But if the wetness meant discomfort, and a certain danger, it also had its compensations. For one thing, it enabled him several times to squirm past narrow places which might well have stopped him, had the rock been dry and rough. For another, he realized that the reason for the wetness was that the shaft was a sort of drainage pipe for the snow on the shoulder above, and he was sure now that it went all the way to the top. If the melted snow could come down, there was at least a chance that he could get up.

The walls contracted to a bottleneck, little more than a foot in diameter. He twisted, writhed. . . . And suddenly stuck. . . . Wet or not, the rock held his shoulders as if in a vise, and the more he struggled the tighter its grip became. For a moment panic seized him. His arms and legs jerked convulsively. He tried to cry out. But the only sound that came from his lips was the quick rasp of his breath. For the first time on the long climb he was fighting for air. In that dark tunnel there was no air at all. And no light. He was caught, trapped, suffocating, in a black grave in the rock.

Coward! Fool!

He stopped his wild and senseless thrashing. His breathing was still labored, his heart pounding; but the panic was gone. He was a mountaineer again—not a frightened child—and with slow deliberation he set about finding a way to release himself. His shoulders were wedged tight. A strong push with either hands or feet would probably have released them, but they could find nothing to push against. What he was able to do, however, was to work his arms gradually upward. Inch by inch he forced them along against the walls, bending them, contorting them, trying to work them into a position above his head. Long minutes seemed to pass. Often he had to pause to rest his aching muscles. During one of the pauses he heard a distant muffled sound, and he realized that the men were calling him from below. But he hadn't the breath to answer. He concentrated on the job at hand. On the slow painful maneuvering of his arms. And at last what he had been hoping for, struggling for, happened. His right arm was above his head. Then his left. They were no longer pinioned, but reaching up, grasping. His shoulders were free, and he pulled himself on.

And still on. . . .

Up the black walls; over the wet rocks; on and on through the long twisting tunnel. The rope still dragged behind him. By now it must have been almost at its full length, and its weight pulled heavily at his waist. But at least it had not got caught. And he himself did not get caught again. The shaft had widened slightly. It bent to the left and leveled off; steepened again and bent to the right. And then, suddenly, he had stopped, he was staring upward, and this time it was neither fear nor exertion that made his heart beat faster. For the shaft was no longer dark, but filled with a grayish light, and straight above, framed by a rim of rock, was a patch of blue gleaming sky. Now at last he *could* shout. And did. And the sound of it echoed wild and free in the core of the mountain. Then he was climbing again—faster now—up, up, as fast as his strength would take him. He was lunging, grasping, pulling, shoving. He was halfway—two thirds of the way—almost there. Then he *was* there. He was crawling up onto the rim. Coming out of the shaft. He was standing in snow, in bright sunlight, on the shoulder of the Citadel. He had climbed up past the Needle . . . through the Needle's Eye.

The world seemed to spin around him, vast and dazzling. The whole other side of the mountain, that before had been hidden, was now revealed: the north face plunging away into space; the northeast and northwest ridges; beneath them, the snowfields and boulder-slopes, and, still farther down—remote and tiny, but visible at last—the valley and village of Kurtal. All this was below. And above—yes, there it was —*the summit*. Rising before him: huge and gleaming. And close now. Very close. . . .

He tore his eyes away. There were still things to be done, and even the summit must wait. Turning, he pulled the rope up out of the shaft. He coiled it around him. Then he was moving across the shoulder, toward the Needle, out onto the flat upper surface of

the Needle. He was waving and calling. He was tying
one end of the rope around a knob of rock and lowering the other down the wall below. The men tied on
the packs, and he hauled them up. Then they themselves were coming: one . . . two . . . three. . . .
They were all up, all standing together on the shoulder
of the Citadel, and his uncle had put his arms around
him and was holding him tight.

CHAPTER 16

Darkness and Dawn

"MY CAPTAIN—"

Winter did not answer.

"Are you all right, my Captain?"

The Englishman raised his head and nodded, but he did not speak. Franz took a flask from his pack and held it out to him.

"Here—drink some tea," he said.

"There isn't enough, is there?"

"Yes, there is enough."

Winter took the flask and raised it to his lips. But even with two hands he could not hold it steady. The tea sloshed down his chin and onto the front of his jacket.

They were on the broadest part of the shoulder, well in from the Needle, resting on a flat rock that broke the surface of the snow. For several minutes that was all they had done—rested—with no strength in them for talk, or even for looking ahead. But now, as Winter drank, Rudi's eyes moved up to the peak above him, and instantly his tiredness was forgotten in the bright promise of what he saw.

For, as they had hoped, there were no major obstacles between the shoulder and the summit. There would be difficulties, of course. The way was steep and exposed, and at the altitude they had now reached even straightforward climbing was no simple matter. But at least there were no further barriers like the Fortress or the Needle. The final reach of the Citadel climbed upward in a vast broken pyramid—first of snow, then of rock, then again of snow—and for the first time since they had been on the mountain the top itself was visible, gleaming white and radiant against the empty sky.

It was now—what? Two hours above them. Perhaps three. Surely not more than three. . . .

Saxo had stood up and was also staring at the peak. "We had best be going on," he said. "It is getting late."

And, as he spoke, Rudi realized with shock how long it had taken them to get past the Needle. Morning was long since gone; even noontime was gone; it was already well into midafternoon. Allowing three hours to reach the top, it would by that time be almost dusk, and they would never get down even this far before nightfall. They would have to make a second bivouac somewhere on the pyramid above, and it was lucky indeed that they had decided to carry the extra burden of the tents.

He got to his feet. Franz got to his feet. But Winter did not move. He was sitting hunched over, with his eyes closed and a hand pressed to the bandage on his head.

"It is hurting again, my Captain?" Franz asked.

Winter opened his eyes. "A little," he said. Then abruptly he stood up. "It's nothing, though. I'm ready. Let's go."

As he slung on his pack, however, he was seized

189

with a spasm of coughing. He struggled to control it, but couldn't, and for a few minutes stood bent almost double, retching and gasping for breath.

Franz watched him with troubled eyes. "Perhaps we should rest a while longer," he suggested, when Winter at last turned and faced them.

The Englishman shook his head. "No, let's get going. I'm all right now."

But as they worked their way up the snowslope above the shoulder he was obviously anything but all right. Even though the going here was easy, he slipped and stumbled at almost every step; his breathing was labored, and his eyes showed the pain that was throbbing behind them. Twice Franz, who was leading, turned back and looked at him questioningly, but each time Winter gestured to him to go on.

Then another coughing fit seized him. He leaned forward against his ax while his body shook with convulsions. Hard as he tried, it was a long while before he could stand straight again, and, when at last he did, it was only to sway and almost fall.

This time Franz came down to him, shaking his head. "No, it is no good, my Captain," he said. "We have done enough for today. Up ahead the snow ends and there is a good place for the tents. In the morning, when you are better, we will go on to the top."

"No," Winter murmured. "We must go now."

Saxo had stood by, listening and frowning. "If we camp here," he said, "we may lose our chance. Rest again, Herr Captain, and in a little while—"

"In a little while it will be too late," Franz interrupted. "Even as we are going now we could not reach the top before dark. . . . And the Captain is not strong enough. It is too risky. . . . No, we must stop here: it is the only thing. And in the morning—"

"By morning," argued Saxo, "the weather may change. It may be impossible."

Franz shrugged. "That is a chance we shall have to take."

Winter started to protest, but his words were lost in yet another spasm of coughing. And when it had passed, leaving him weak and shaken, he was forced at last to recognize the bitter truth. There was no choice for him about going on. He simply *could* not go on.

"At least you go," he told the others. "Leave me here. Go to the top. I'll wait for you."

Franz shook his head.

"Please. Go on. Go now."

He looked from Franz to Saxo. And Saxo wavered. His eyes went from one to the other and then up to the heights above them. "If the Captain insists," he began—

"It is not a question of what the Captain insists," said Franz, "but of what a guide must do. A guide of Kurtal does not leave his *Herr* on a mountain. What a guide of Broli does, I of course do not know."

Still Saxo hesitated. Then his lips went tight. He started to speak, changed his mind, and was silent.

"Come," said Franz. "There is the place." He pointed. "Up to the left. You see it?"

He went first and the others followed, and soon they were off the snow and in a sheltered hollow between two slabs of rock. "Here there is room for the two tents," Franz said. "Even if the wind blows it will not be too bad."

He set about the work of pitching them. Rudi helped, and after a few moments Saxo joined in with sullen reluctance. Winter, too, tried to do his share, but was almost immediately seized by another coughing fit and had to sit by wretchedly, watching. Whatever

191

his physical distress, he was obviously suffering even more from frustration and anger at what had happened to him.

When the first tent was up, Franz helped him crawl inside. He put a blanket beneath and another over him, placed a pack as a pillow, and made him as comfortable as possible. Then he rejoined Saxo and Rudi, and the three put up the second tent. By the time they had finished it was getting on toward late afternoon, and the sun was sloping away toward the ranges in the west.

"The Herr Captain should have something hot to drink," said Franz. "And it is best if we all eat now, before it is dark." He set up the little oil stove and sorted out the remaining food. "There is enough for tonight," he commented, "and for tomorrow morning. But by tomorrow night, whatever happens, we must be back down at the hut."

There was a patch of snow at the rim of the hollow, and, scooping up several handfuls, he put them into a pot and set the pot on the lighted stove. Then they sat and waited. At that altitude the snow began to simmer almost as soon as it had melted; but boiling water did not mean hot water, and the wait was a long one. They sat in silence. Franz watched the pot. For a while Saxo kept his eyes on the ground, then raised them and for several minutes stared fixedly at the peak that rose above them into the fading light. Suddenly he rose and paced restlessly back and forth across the hollow; then he mounted to its upper rim and climbed the rocks to a crag some thirty feet above. Here he stopped and stared upward again, remaining for several minutes before he turned and descended.

"There are no obstacles," he said. "None. It is clear going all the way to the top."

Franz said nothing. Rudi said nothing. Indeed, the boy had now not said a word since they had left the shoulder. For what was there to say? Or even think or feel? For a glorious few minutes at the Needle's Eye, he had known the intoxication of being a hero. He had been preëminent among the four of them, the essential one, the leader on whom the others had depended. But no sooner had they reached the shoulder—and Winter had become sick—than everything had changed. The fate of their venture had been wholly in his hands. Now, suddenly, it was wholly out of them. Whatever would now be done—or not done—was not for him to decide. For him there was now nothing but to wait numbly; to hope and fear; to stare up at the great summit which now loomed so tantalizingly near, and which, yet, they might never reach.

The sun sank. The water hummed in the pot. At intervals the sound of coughing came from the tent where Winter lay. Then at last the water was hot enough, and Franz, after mixing it with tea, sugar and a few drops of brandy, took it in to him. Saxo and Rudi followed, carrying bread, meat and cheese, and the three of them crouched beside the Englishman in the brown dusk of the tent.

"Here, my Captain," Franz said, "this will make you feel better."

Winter stirred and raised himself on one elbow. He slowly sipped the steaming tea and forced himself to swallow a few mouthfuls of food.

"Already it makes you stronger, does it not?" said Franz.

Winter nodded. "I'll be all right," he murmured. "In the morning—"

But his appearance belied his words. Under its stubble of beard his face was pale and sunken. His lips were bloodless, his eyes dull, and he was obviously a man who was near the end of his strength. Partly, of course, it was the result of his injury in the avalanche; partly of the lack of oxygen (which affected him more than the others) and his long struggle on the wall of the Needle. But even more—it seemed to Rudi, watching him—it was simply that he had worn himself out. Not so much physically as inwardly. Not so much in the actual climbing of the mountain as in the expenditure of will and spirit that had made the climb possible. He had given all of himself; too much of himself. And now the flame that sustained him was fading. The man who had dreamed the dream of the Citadel—who, of all men, deserved the prize of its conquest—lay haggard and spent on its desolate heights, defeated by the very intensity of his effort.

"I'll be all right," he murmured again. "I won't let you down." Then he lay back in the blankets, closing his eyes, and the others left the tent.

Outside the sun was gone. The peak rose bleak and forlorn into the darkening sky. The two guides and the boy ate their own meal in silence, and by the time they had finished it was almost night.

"We, too, had best get our rest," Franz said. "In the morning it will be hard going—whether up or down."

Saxo merely grunted. But now, at last, Rudi spoke. "What do you think, Uncle?" he asked. "Can Captain Winter go on? Can he make the top?"

No sooner had he asked the question than he regretted it—so afraid was he of the answer. But Franz simply shrugged and said, "There is no telling yet. In the morning we will know." He arose and for a few moments stood looking up into the night. A slight wind had risen with the darkness, but it was from the north —which was good—and the stars were sharp and gleaming. "At least the weather will be all right," he said, "for whatever we must do."

Saxo had risen too. Again he was to share the tent with Winter, and taking his pack, he went to its entrance.

"Call me if he gets worse," Franz told him.

"*Ja,*" said Saxo.

He disappeared, and Franz and Rudi crept into the other tent. They arranged their packs and blankets, took off their boots and lay down, side by side.

"Goodnight, boy," said Franz.

"Goodnight, Uncle."

Then there was silence. There was darkness. But, tired as he was, Rudi could not sleep. An hour passed —perhaps two—and still he did not sleep, and he could tell from his uncle's breathing that he was not sleeping either. Outside, the wind whined, cold and thin, over the rocks. At intervals he could hear the sound of Winter's coughing in the other tent.

Later—how much later he did not know—he heard footsteps. They came closer and stopped, and from beyond the tent-flap came the sound of Saxo's voice.

"Lerner—" he said.

"Yes?"

"I must speak with you."

Franz sat up, pulled on his boots and crawled outside. Rudi was about to follow; then thought better of it and remained in the tent. Through the canvas he could hear the two men talking.

"He is worse?" Franz asked.

"Perhaps not worse," said Saxo. "But no better. He will not be able to go on."

"It is not likely," Franz agreed.

"He cannot go up, but only down, and that is the end of it for him."

Franz said nothing.

"But it does not have to be the end for us," said Saxo.

"What do you mean?"

"I mean it is still possible that *we* climb the Citadel."

"We? Without him?"

"Yes. It is, at most, three hours to the top. If we start at first light we can be there by eight o'clock."

"Leaving him here alone?"

"Alone, or with the boy. It will be for only five or six hours. We will be back before noon and can then take him down."

There was a pause.

"Will you do it?" Saxo asked.

Another pause.

"No," said Franz.

"Why not? He will be all right here. And he will not object. Before we stopped, he himself said we should go on without him."

"It does not matter what he says. He is weak. He is sick. A guide cannot go on without his *Herr*."

"No harm can come of it, I tell you. We will not be gone long, and we will leave the boy with him. The weather is good—"

"The weather can change. We could be delayed. Also, if he gets worse, we will need all our strength to get him down."

"All our strength—bah! Why do we not have strength enough for both?" Franz started to speak again, but Saxo cut him off abruptly. "Do you know what is the matter with you, Lerner? You are afraid of this mountain. But *I* am not afraid. I am not looking for excuses to turn back. For years it has been my dream to climb the Citadel. Now at last I have my chance, and I will not give it up. Not for you

196

and your stupid fear. Not for a coughing Englishman. Not for anyone, or anything!"

"If you do a thing like this," said Franz—and now his voice, too, was angry, "you do not deserve to be called a guide."

"And you do not deserve to be called a climber. . . . All right, have it your own way. Stay here. Go down with your coughing *Herr*. Go down beaten, defeated, and see how you feel in Kurtal when a man of Broli stands victorious on the top of the Citadel!"

"You are a fool, Saxo! A madman! You cannot climb to the top alone."

"No? We will see about that."

There was a silence. Then the sound of receding footsteps.

"Saxo—" said Franz.

But there was no answer. He had returned to the other tent. After a little while Franz raised the flap and crept back in beside Rudi. He removed his boots and lay down in his blanket. He did not speak. Nor did the boy.

For, again, what was there to say? He could talk all night without budging his uncle an inch from his conviction and decision. This he knew. And he knew something else too—something even more shattering—and this was that his uncle was right. It was the very heart and essence of a guide's code that he must not leave his *Herr*. Least of all when that *Herr* was sick or injured. Unthinkably least of all if his going were not to the *Herr*'s advantage, but only his own. Yes, Rudi knew it. He knew it with a knowledge that was deeper than mere learning; that was part of his heritage, part of his blood and bone. A guide could *never* leave his *Herr:* that was the first and great commandment.

And yet . . .

And yet . . .

Yet this knowledge did not help him now, as he lay silent and rigid in his misery. Captain Winter could almost surely not go on. His uncle must stay with him; and he with his uncle. They had come all this way—up the snowslopes and the glaciers, up the cliffs and the ridges, past the Fortress, past the shoulder wall and the Needle—laboring, struggling, winning their way to the very threshold of conquest, only to have it turn, at the last moment, into bitter defeat. And bitterest of all for him—Rudi. For if it was Winter who had brought them to the Citadel, it was *he* who had led them up to it; who had found the way past the Fortress and threaded the Needle's Eye; who was alone responsible for having brought the summit within reach. Winter was unable to go on. His uncle was not willing. But he was both able and willing—he was burning with desire. It was more than he could bear to come so close to the fulfilment of his life's dream, only to have it mercilessly snatched away.

It was too cruel. Too unfair.

He lay in silence. He lay in torment. The wind whined, and the night crept on, and, beside him, his uncle breathed rhythmically in sleep. And then at last he, too, slept . . . and where darkness had been was the shining sky, where the tent walls had been was the white pinnacle of a mountain and, for the hundredth time—and the last time—he was dreaming *the dream*. Only now the dream was not the same as before. He was not on the pinnacle, but beneath it, struggling toward it, and the more he struggled the farther away it seemed to grow. Something invisible but monstrous had twined itself about his legs, was pressing down upon his back, seeping like a black cloud into his throat and lungs. He

198

strained forward, but remained where he was; cried
out, but made no sound. And now, through the cloud,
the peak was no longer white but dark and brooding;
it was no longer a peak at all, but something else—a
figure—the giant figure of a man. Strangling, paralyzed, he lay at the foot of a nightmare mountain
while the face of Emil Saxo looked down on him with
cold and mocking eyes.

Then all was dark again. He was awake again. At
first he thought it was the dream that had awakened
him, but in the next instant he knew it had been
something else. It had been a sound. . . . He listened,
and heard nothing. Even the wind was gone. . . . But
still he knew it had been a sound.

Carefully, so as not to rouse his uncle, he sat up and
lifted the flap of the tent. It was still night outside, but
that dawn was not far away. A few feet off, across the
hollow, he could see the dim outline of the second
the darkness was thinner than before, and he could tell
tent. No sound came from it. There was no movement.
And yet he felt—he knew—that something was different; something had *happened*. For a long moment he
sat watching, listening. Then he crept noiselessly from
the tent. In stockinged feet he crossed to the other tent
—stopped—listened again. He lifted the entrance flap
and peered in. On the left, where they had put him the
night before, Captain Winter lay motionless and asleep
under his blanket. But the blanket on the right was
empty.

Saxo was gone.

Rudi stood in the dark hollow between the tents, his
mind as numb and frozen as it had been in the dream.
He looked up at the rocks above him, but there was
only darkness; back at the tents again, crouching low in
the night. His first impulse had been to shout, to waken

Winter and his uncle, to tell them what had happened. But even as he thought of it he knew what the result would be. Winter could not go on. Without him, his uncle would not. They would remain there, miserable and impotent, while Saxo climbed on, alone in triumph, to the summit. . . . It was a thing he could not face; that he would rather have died than face. . . . For another moment he stood motionless in the darkness. Then, without willing it—almost without knowing it— he was approaching his own tent. He was raising the flap, reaching cautiously in, taking his boots and pack and ax. He was sitting on a rock, lacing the boots; rising and slinging on the pack. The pack was so light that he scarcely felt it, for now it no longer held food and equipment, but only a single piece of clothing. Only an old red flannel shirt—and, lashed to its straps, a hand-carved pole.

He did not pause. He did not hesitate. For the waking-dream in which he now moved was even more powerful than the dream of sleep. Mounting to the rim of the hollow, he began to climb the rocks above. They were steep, but the holds were sound and plentiful, and he made good progress. Around him, the night was fading. The contours of the peak emerged slowly into an ashen half-light. Every few moments, between steps, he paused and peered upward; but there was no sign of Saxo, no hint of movement in the gray frozen world that rose before him.

Once—only once—he turned and looked back. He stared down at the two tents, now far below him, and thought of Winter and his uncle lying within them, still asleep. For one shuddering moment the force that gripped him seemed to loosen its hold. The coils of the dream fell away, his mind was clear, and, for the first time since he had awakened, he was aware of just what he was doing. Cold panic filled him. What would his uncle say—and do? What would Captain Winter think of him? . . . And then came another thought, even worse than these; the thought that old Teo had left with him when he said goodbye . . . *What would his father have done in such a situation?*

Not what he was doing. That he knew.

But even knowing it, he could not stop. The moment of clearness passed; the force, the compulsion returned. The consequences did not matter. Right and wrong did not matter. Nothing in all the world mattered, except that he must go on. If it was the last thing he did in his life, he must climb on after Saxo—catch Saxo—pass Saxo; he must go on and on, up and up, bearing his shirt and pole, bearing his hopes and dreams, until he stood at last, victorious, on that white summit in the sky.

He was climbing again. It grew lighter. He moved up through gray stillness into the day that was being born.

CHAPTER 17

The Day

THE FIRST BEAMS of the rising sun struck the summit of the Citadel and kindled it into white fire. Moments later they touched the tops of the lesser peaks. and a tide of light flowed from the heights, down the cliffs and ridges, along the snowfields and glaciers, over the forests and meadows, into the valley below. Last of all it reached the village of Kurtal. Its bright rays glittered on the church spire, the shop windows and the polished brass of the telescope that stood on the terrace before the Beau Site Hotel.

Even at this hour there was a crowd around the square—for Kurtal had borne no resemblance to its usual peaceful self since Paul Tauglich had come down with word that the climb had begun. The southeast ridge of the mountain was not visible from the town. But the shoulder and all above it were in plain view; and since noon of the day before (which according to Tauglich, was when the climbers might first have appeared) a steady procession of watchers had been peering up at the heights.

So far, however, they had seen nothing. They had remained at the telescope until night closed in. Now, with the sunrise, they were back again. But they had still seen no hint of life or movement on the soaring pinnacle of the mountain.

Overnight, the mood of the town had changed. On the previous day it had had a holiday atmosphere. There had been a buzzing of excitement, a joyful pride —almost as if the peak had already been won. But now, in the first morning light, voices were muted and faces tense. True, there was not yet real cause for worry. These were mountain people, and they knew that on a mountain there can be all manner of obstacles and delays. But they knew, too—from Tauglich—that the climbers had food for only three days. If they were to succeed—if they were to appear on the shoulder and go on to the summit—it must be this morning. Or not at all.

The sun climbed the sky. It grew brighter. A hush lay upon the town.

There were hundreds of searching eyes, but only the one telescope, and this was reserved for the use of the senior guides. The single exception was Herr Hempel, the fat proprietor of the Beau Site Hotel, who, as owner of the instrument, had first priority of all, and who stayed at it twice as long as anyone else—focussing, more often than not, on an entirely wrong part of the mountain.

"Where are they? *Where?*" he demanded, his moonface clouded with worry as he reluctantly stepped aside.

The guides did not answer. Hans Andermass, then Paul Tauglich, then Johann Feiniger peered in turn through the lenses, and no one spoke until Herr Hempel took over again.

"It is that Saxo," he declared. "The man from Broli. He has delayed them."

And a moment later:

"He could not go on. The others have had to bring him down."

"If they came down yesterday," said Hans Andermass, "the men in the hut would have known it. They would have sent word here."

The crowd thickened. Every man, woman and child was in the streets.

And among them, coming along the main street toward the central square, was Frau Ilse Matt. She had been to early Mass at the church and prayed for the safety of her brother Franz. And as she now walked along she murmured another prayer: this one of thankfulness that at least her son was safe. For two days following Rudi's disappearance she had suffered agonies of uncertainty and fear, but with Paul Tauglich's appearance the worst of them, at least, had ended. For Tauglich had assured her that the boy was not on the mountain. Franz had gone, yes—he had said. Franz and Captain Winter and Saxo: those three. But Rudi had stayed safe in the hut with the support party. Though she was upset and concerned about Franz, he was at least a grown man; he could take care of himself. But Rudi—with Rudi it was different. He was a boy. Her son. Her own and only son.

And she was thankful.

Now she reached the square in front of the hotel and approached the crowd around the telescope. She did not need to ask questions. She could tell without asking that they had seen nothing yet.

"Do not worry, Frau Matt," said Johann Feiniger gently. "They are all right. They will soon appear."

"Your brother will get them there," Hans Andermass assured her.

"If only that Saxo does not spoil it all," muttered Herr Hempel.

204

There was a silence. The men took their turns at the telescope, and as each left it he slowly shook his head. Frau Matt stood by with the others for a while and then turned quietly to go on her way.

"Yes, it is better you wait at home," Herr Hempel told her. "Be calm. Be hopeful. And we shall call you as soon as—"

He never finished. His glance moved suddenly past her to Johann Feiniger, who was now at the telescope. For Feiniger's body had gone rigid. His hands gripped the shaft. In the next instant one hand was raised, commandingly, and a deathly stillness filled the square.

Then—

"They're there!" Feiniger cried. "I see them! They're there!"

The stillness exploded into a roaring shout. Through the mass sound came a volley of individual voices. "Where?" they demanded. "Where? . . . Where?"

Feiniger's hand was still raised. And now others were raised too, for silence.

"On the shoulder," he said. His eye remained glued to the telescope. "A little above the shoulder. On a slope of snow under the summit ridge."

The crowd hummed with excitement.

"How near the top?" they yelled.

"How many of them?"

"Are they moving?"

"Yes, they are moving," said Feiniger. "Up the snow. They are only specks, but I can see them clearly. Two small black specks—"

"Only two?"

"Yes, only two."

"Which two? Where are the others?"

"I cannot tell which two. I can see nothing but—"

The rest of what Feiniger said was lost in the hub-

205

bub. Herr Hempel was trying to push him from the telescope, but he would not budge. Voices sounded from all sides—questioning, clamoring.

"Where can the others be?"

"They have turned back."

"Or fallen."

"You told us they went four on one rope," said Hans Andermass to Paul Tauglich.

"Yes—when they started. But they could have changed higher up."

"If they changed, how would they split up?"

"Captain Winter with Saxo, probably."

"And Franz with Rudi."

"Yes."

"Perhaps the boy could not make it," said Andermass. "Then Franz would have had to stay with him and—"

He stopped. His words hung in the air. He realized that Frau Matt had not left, but was standing there watching him.

"I—I mean—" he stammered—and again stopped.

There was a silence. For a moment the telescope was forgotten, and all eyes turned to the small, faded woman who stood there alone among the guides of Kurtal.

"You mean," said Frau Matt very quietly, *"that my son is on the Citadel."*

Andermass did not answer. No one answered. And her gaze moved slowly to Paul Tauglich, who stood awkwardly among the others.

"You lied to me," she said.

Her lips trembled. Her face was chalk white. In the next instant, it seemed the storm within her would break out in a flood of anguish and anger. . . . But the instant did not come. Instead, a strange thing happened

—a remarkable thing happened—that the people of Kurtal were to remember for years to come. . . . The trembling of her lips ceased. Her face grew calm. And her voice, when she spoke again, was even quieter than before.

"You lied to me," she repeated. "You all have lied to me. . . . But that is all right. I am not angry. . . . It was kind of you to try to spare me worry for my son."

She paused.

"No, I did not want him to go. I have not wanted him to be a guide. And all of you know the reason. . . . But it was not a good reason. I know that now. I think I have known it in my heart all along. No, it was not you who were wrong in lying, but I in causing you to lie. In being afraid to face the truth. In trying to live my Rudi's life for him, instead of letting him live his own."

Again she paused. Her slight body grew more erect. Her eyes looked out at them, clear and proud. "Very well," she said, "now he is living his own. He is on the Citadel. He is doing what he must do—what he was born to do—and if it is God's will, so be it. . . . I am a woman of Kurtal; the widow of a guide; the sister of a guide. Now I am to be the mother of a guide. May he be the best and bravest."

For a moment she looked up at the shining mountain, then back at the men around her.

"I shall go again to the church," she murmured.

Five thousand feet up, the four men at the high hut were also watching the mountain. Unlike those below, they could not see the summit pyramid, but only the southeast ridge as far as the shoulder; and, having no telescope, they could not, in any case, have been able to locate the climbers. Yet still they stared up from outside the doorway—as if the rising sun would reveal some sign or portent on the heights above.

"The weather still holds."

"Ja."

"The upper snow should be firm."

"Ja."

"If they camped last night above the shoulder, they should already be—"

They talked, not because they had anything to say, but rather to break the stillness. For the stillness had deepened until it was monstrous and unendurable. It was almost impossible to believe that human beings lived and moved in that dead, frozen wilderness that soared above them into the sky.

The previous day, according to plan, Andreas Krickel, Peter Tauglich and Klaus Wesselhoft had gone up to the base of the ridge. They had reached it about noon and remained for five hours, their eyes straining upward for some sign of the descending climbers. But there had been no sign. And in the late afternoon they had had to start down, in order to reach the hut before dark. Meanwhile Old Teo had waited. And waited. He had stared up at the peak until his neck ached and he was almost blinded by the fierce sunlight, and then he had gone into the hut and with loving care prepared a welcoming supper. But when at last, toward nightfall, he had heard footsteps and rushed outside, it was to find only the three who had set out that morning. And they had scarcely eaten at all. Teo himself had scarcely eaten.

"We will celebrate tomorrow night," they had said.

"Yes, tomorrow."

And then they had lain down in their blankets, to toss and turn through the endless night.

Now it *was* tomorrow. The third day. . . . The last

day. . . . Once again they laced their boots, slung their ropes, picked up their axes. But this time, as they came out from the hut, there were not three of them, but four.

The other three looked at Teo Zurbriggen. "No," said Andreas Krickel. "It is too far for you. Too steep."

Teo shook his head. "I can make it."

"But—"

"I will not hold you back—I promise. I have done it before. And I can do it again."

The others argued, but it was no use. "If not with you, then I will go alone," said Teo. "I cannot sit here another day, waiting, like an old woman." He looked at them steadily, and a light kindled in his sunken eyes. "I was a guide of Kurtal when you could not climb to your mothers' laps. And I say to you that I am coming."

"All the way to the ridge?"

"Yes, to the ridge. And if necessary, farther. *Up* the ridge—to the Fortress—straight on until we find them."

The three younger men were silent. Teo jerked his rope tight over his hunched shoulder. "Come on," he said. "What are we waiting for?"

At dawn of that day Franz Lerner had awakened in his tent, above the shoulder. For long hours after the argument with Saxo he had been awake and brooding in the darkness; but at last the tiredness of his body had outbalanced the turmoil of his thoughts, and he had slept. Then, the next thing he knew, he was awake again, and the tent was filled with gray twilight. He raised himself on one elbow, turned—and saw that Rudi was not there.

At first this did not startle him. The boy could have

gone out to prepare breakfast, or to relieve himself, or simply because he was awake and restless. But then Franz saw something else. Rudi's pack was not there either. . . . Sitting up with a jerk, he pulled on his boots and, without pausing to lace them, crept quickly from the tent. The hollow outside lay empty in the dawnlight. The rocks above it rose empty to the sky. Crossing to the second tent, Franz lifted the flap and peered in. Captain Winter lay where he had last seen him, wrapped in his blanket. But Saxo, like Rudi, was gone.

As Franz stood there, Winter stirred and mumbled. Then he opened his eyes.

"What is it?" he asked.

Without answering, Franz dropped the flap and turned away. For a moment he stood as if rooted to the rocks. Then, mounting to the rim of the hollow, he followed it around, searching. He looked on all sides. Clambering onto a nearby crag, he stared up at the walls of rock above. His lips were compressed into a thin bloodless line, and his hands opened and closed at his sides.

There was a movement below, as Winter crawled from his tent. "What is it?" he asked. "What's happened?"

Franz came down to him. "You must not move about, my Captain," he said. "Go back inside and rest."

"What's happened?" Winter persisted. He looked about him. "Where are they?"

"They have only—" Franz hesitated; stopped. There was no use lying, he thought. There was no lie to tell. "They have gone," he said.

"Gone?"

Franz nodded.

"You mean up?"

"Yes."

"How do you know? Have you seen them?"

"No. But where else would they go?" Franz recounted briefly what Saxo had threatened the night before. "And now he has done it," he said. "And the crazy boy has gone with him."

"Rudi—with Saxo? Like this? I can't believe it."

"Where is he then?" asked Franz grimly.

There was a silence. The dawn was brightening. Above them the rocks rose bleakly into gray stillness.

With a sudden movement Franz leapt back onto the crag on which he had stood before. "Rudi!" he shouted. "Rudi!"

His voice reverberated and echoed, but there was no answer. He cupped his hands and yodeled. But there was no answer. For perhaps five minutes he remained on the crag, calling and peering upward. Then he descended slowly to the hollow.

Winter had disappeared into his tent. Franz approached it, stopped and stood motionless, in terrible indecision. The Englishman was his *Herr*—and too weak to go on. It was his first duty as a guide to stay with him. But if he was a guide, he was also a man. And the boy was his sister's son—his own blood kin—climbing now, wildly, crazily—perhaps to his death.

Or perhaps—he thought suddenly of Saxo—perhaps not to death at all, but to the summit with the Boaster of Broli. For a moment he thought not of the boy, but only of Saxo—Saxo, in his pride and his arrogance, standing triumphant on the crest of the Citadel—and his fists clenched to whiteness and the veins throbbed in his temples.

No, he could not stand by, helpless and beaten. It was more than flesh and blood could bear. . . .

He reached for the tent flap. But at the same instant it was opened from within and Winter emerged, carrying his ax and pack.

"All right," he said quietly. "I'm ready."

Franz stared at him. "Ready?"

"To go after them."

Still Franz stared. He shook his head slowly. "No," he said. "No, my Captain. You are too tired. Too weak."

"The weakness is over. I'm better now."

"Yes, better—and that is good. But still you must rest. You must save your strength for the descent." Franz paused. "This is what we will do, my Captain. The weather is good. You are no longer so weak. Though I do not like to leave you, you will be all right here for a few hours, and I shall go up alone—"

"No, Franz," said Winter. "We shall go up together."

"But—"

"But nothing. I am better. I can make it."

The two men stood facing each other in silence, and for the first time that morning Franz really looked at Winter. Outwardly he was much the same as on the previous night. There were the tattered clothes, the bandaged head, the hollow cheeks under the stubble of beard. And yet, Franz recognized, watching him—yet there was unmistakably a change. It was not an outer but an inner change; a thing that could not so much be seen as simply felt. It was in his bones, in his blood, in his heart. And in his eyes. . . . Yes, Franz thought—most of all it was in his eyes: no longer dull and clouded as on the night before, but burning again with their old bright fire.

"Come on," said Winter in his quiet voice. "We're going to the top."

For one last long moment Franz wavered. Then he turned abruptly and went to his own tent. He laced his boots and got his ax and pack and rope. Returning to where Winter waited, he tied them both on to the rope and tested the knots.

"We will go slowly, my Captain," he said. "Slowly and carefully. And when you are tired we will rest."

Winter nodded. Franz studied the rocks above, chose his route and began to climb.

There was bare stone, then patches of snow, then stone again. The gradient was not too steep, the going not difficult, but at the height which they had now reached the air was so thin that they gasped and panted at every step. Every few minutes they paused and leaned motionless on their axes, breathing deeply. And at intervals, as on the previous day, Winter broke out in fits of coughing. But after each brief rest he was again ready to go on, and when Franz turned and looked at him questioningly he nodded and murmured, "All right."

It was not, as Franz had feared, a matter of hauling up "a bundle of firewood." For the Englishman, through the sheer force of his will, had made a remarkable recovery; and the guide was now having his troubles too. Mountain man though he was, he had never before been so high. Already, with perhaps a thousand feet to go, the summits of the surrounding peaks were well below them, and it seemed they were no longer in the earth's atmosphere at all, but in the blue ether of outer space.

They climbed on. The tents vanished below them. Soon, through the distortion of distance, the broad snow-covered shoulder appeared as far beneath them as the glaciers and valleys. There was no wind. Only stillness and space. And minute by minute, space grew brighter, bluer—until at last there was a great golden glow and the sun was cushioned on the ranges to the east.

There was a chimney, slabs, a crag, more slabs. Then they came to a long strip of snow, and here they stopped again, staring down at the footprints in its surface. There were two sets of prints—one large, one small—and both bore straight up the snow and vanished among the rocks above. They craned upward, but saw nothing. They tried to shout, but only a hoarse croaking came from their throats. Then they were coughing: this time not only Winter, but Franz as well. They leaned forward, heads bent against their axes, until their breathing eased. Then they moved on again.

Above the snow there was a stretch of more difficult climbing, and they moved one at a time while the other belayed the rope. Beyond this was more snow, more footprints. And still farther on, a steep pitch of ice-coated rock. Franz climbed it first—very slowly, very cautiously—then turned at the top and held the rope for Winter.

"Easy now. Watch it," he said.

"I can do it," said the Englishman.

And then the only sounds were the deep rasp of his breathing and the scraping of his boot-nails against the ice and rock.

The top of the pitch marked the end of the particular section of the peak on which they had been climbing. Standing side by side, they looked at the awesome prospect ahead. Directly before them, the mountain narrowed. Its cliffs and buttresses seemed to fall away, to vanish, and all that was left was a thin ridge twisting on into space. The slant of the ridge was not steep—

considerably less steep, indeed, than the stretch over which they had just come—but on either side the walls dropped off almost vertically into the immense chasms of the north and east faces. For perhaps a hundred feet that was all there was: a saw-edge of rock, a cat-walk in the sky. Then the mountain broadened again. Mighty ribs of granite flared up from the abyss and joined together to form the base of a solid pyramid. It was a snow-covered pyramid: huge, symmetrical, gleaming. It rose in a gentle slope to a white point in the sky, and ended—in the summit of the Citadel.

The two men stopped. They sat on a slab and rested. Above them the sun, now well on its morning journey, burned like a great eye in blue-black space. And around and beneath them the world of the Alps spread in a vast panorama of peaks, glaciers and valleys. There was no cloud, nor even a shred of mist. Every major summit of the range stood up clear and glittering in the crystal light. To the west, in distant France, the dome of Mont Blanc seemed to fill half the horizon. To the north and east rose the tall hosts of the Swiss Pennines and the Oberland—Monte Rosa, the Dom, the Weisshorn, the Jungfrau and scores of others—incredibly white and vivid against the blue immensity of sky. Beyond them the land rolled away endlessly toward Germany, toward Austria; to the south, for uncounted miles across the plains of Italy.

But it was not at the world beneath them that the two men looked. It was at the narrow, slanting ridge that lay ahead—and at the shining pyramid beyond the ridge. The side of the pyramid was a smooth slope of unbroken snow, and, from the distance at which they saw it, any moving shape should have been visible. But they saw no shape; no movement. In the white stillness there was no sign of the two climbers who had gone before them.

They did not speak. Whatever their private thoughts may have been, they kept them to themselves. Perhaps Saxo and Rudi had circled to the far side of the peak. Perhaps they were resting, and hidden by a drift. One thing certain was that they were up there somewhere.

Or else . . .

They sat in silence. They got up. They went on. Franz leading, Winter following, they inched out onto the spine of the narrow ridge. It was climbable—of that there was no question—but it was also a tightrope no more than a foot in width. One slip, one misstep to either side, and they would have been twisting in space for a fall of a vertical mile. Franz moved, and Winter belayed. Winter moved and Franz belayed. They got a third of the way across—halfway—two-thirds of the way. Only ten yards or so separated them from the base of the pyramid. . . . When, suddenly, Franz stopped. . . . For a long moment he stood motionless, looking at something at his feet. Then he gestured, and Winter came up behind him. The two stared at the knapsack that lay before them on the ridge.

A roughly cut staff was lashed to its straps.

Crouching, Franz opened the pack. It contained only one item—an old red flannel shirt. The men's eyes met, held, broke away. Instinctively they looked down into the emptiness on either side of the ridge. To the left, above the east face, was a smooth vertical wall; to the right, another wall, not quite vertical, slanting down to a narrow ledge some twenty feet below. But the ledge was empty, and beneath it the north face dropped away so steeply that it could not be seen.

Franz stood as if stunned—frozen. But Winter's face

was clouded with the thoughts that struggled in his mind. "No, Franz," he said at last. "He didn't fall. He couldn't have."

The guide looked at him numbly.

"If he'd fallen, the pack would still be on his back. How could he have taken it off first?"

"But—"

"Think of it. It's impossible. That he took off the pack and *then* fell. . . ." Winter's voice was hoarse and strained. "No. He didn't fall. He took it off and went on. He decided he could climb better without it and left it here, to be picked up on the way down."

Franz thought it over, and hope kindled in his eyes. For what the Englishman had said was well reasoned.

"Yes," he murmured. "That is possible. He could have—"

Then he paused. He was again looking at the pack. And slowly he shook his head.

"No," he said. "No." He pointed at the staff; at the red shirt. "These he carried the whole way up the mountain; the whole way from Kurtal. And we knew why he carried them. He would not leave them here."

There was a silence. Winter started to speak—and stopped. Then at last he muttered: "Still—he couldn't have fallen. It doesn't make sense."

"Nor does the other," said Franz.

They stared dumbly at the pack. At the ridge. At the gulfs of space beside the ridge. At the white crest of the Citadel that rose beyond it.

They raised their heads and shouted. But there was only the croaking of their own voices. And then silence.

They shouted again. And again. And still there was silence.

"They must be ahead," said Winter. "They must be!"

Franz said nothing, but after a moment moved slowly forward. The Englishman started to follow, then paused and looked once more at Rudi's pack.

"Wait," he said.

Stooping, he took out the red shirt and tied it around his waist. He unfastened the staff from its bindings and secured it to his own pack.

"All right," he said.

And they moved on.

CHAPTER 18

The Heights

THERE WAS the stillness. There was the mountain and the sky.

The sky was bright now. The sun was up. But when it had risen—and how far he had come—Rudi did not know. He had climbed beyond time, as he had climbed beyond the world, and all that existed were rock and sky; the next step . . . and the next . . . and the next. Sometimes he looked down, but what he saw had no meaning. Beyond an ocean of space, the earth spread vague and formless, like a landscape in a dream. And sometimes he looked up, but the peak of the mountain gleamed so brightly in the sun that he quickly had to turn his eyes away.

Yet each time he was nearer to it: at least he could see that.

Nearer and still nearer. . . .

His legs were all right. His lungs were all right. He did not cough or gasp. But he knew that the altitude was affecting him, for there was a pace beyond which he could not force himself—and the pace was slow. The rocks glided by. Patches of snow glided by. In the snow, at intervals, were the footprints he was looking for, and then again he would look up. But all he could see was a white glare filling the sky.

"He is already there," he thought despairingly. "Saxo is there, standing alone on the summit, and I shall meet him coming down in mocking victory.

"And the others are now awake," he thought. "They know I am gone. And what I am doing."

A wave of guilt rose through him and passed, and where it had been were pride and defiance. Why should he not be doing it? he asked himself, almost fiercely; he who, alone among the four of them, had found the way up the mountain. He was doing what he had to do—what he had been born to do—and nothing could stop him . . . nothing. The staff was lashed to his back. The red shirt was in his pack. Soon now he would be carrying them up that final white crest in the sky, as he had so often before in his dreams.

Only this time it would be no dream.

There were steep slabs, crags, a chimney, more slabs. There were rock, snow, footprints, rock again. There was the next step . . . and the next . . . and the next. Once he thought he heard a sound—above? below?—and his body tensed as he listened; but as soon as the sound of his own footsteps stopped there was only immense unbroken stillness. He had never known such stillness before. It was a thing that did not exist in the familiar world of men and animals, life and growth, but only in this high secret world above and beyond it.

"But I am not afraid," he thought. "No, I am not afraid."

He climbed on. Through the stillness. Through the terrible aloneness. Up and up, toward the blue shining sky. He came to a pitch of steep ice-glazed rock; scaled it; reached its top; stood on the top, looking ahead at the thin saw-edged ridge that led on to the final pyramid of the mountain. . . . And now, suddenly, he was no longer alone. . . . For halfway up the ridge was Emil Saxo.

The guide's back was turned to him. He was moving slowly up the rocks between the precipices of the north and east faces. Rudi stared at him. His mouth opened, but his voice seemed frozen in his throat. For hours he had been hoping and struggling to catch up with the man from Broli, but now that he had at last done so he did not know what to say or do.

At last two words came:

"Herr Saxo—"

In the stillness his voice did not seem his own at all.

The guide stopped, turned and looked back at him, motionless. Standing above the boy on the ridge, he seemed not a man but a giant. Against the white glare of the summit beyond him his face appeared almost black.

He stared down at Rudi, but did not speak.

"Herr Saxo—wait—"

Still the other did not speak. Rudi hesitated a moment and then began climbing toward him. As he moved he had to keep his eyes fixed on the thin edge of rock, but when he stopped and looked up again he was within a few feet of Saxo. The guide was still watching him, and now he could see not only his outline but his features. The broad leathery face; the small cold-blue eyes; the lips drawn tight across his face like two white strips of ice.

"What are you doing here?" Saxo asked.

"I have come—to join you—"

"Join me?"

"To go to the top."

221

The man's glance moved past him, down the mountainside. "Where are the others?" he said.

"They are back at the tents."

"You came alone?"

"Yes."

Saxo was still scanning the rocks below, as if he suspected a trick. Then he looked back at Rudi. "That is too bad, boy," he said. For now you will have to go back alone."

"Go back?"

"Yes—go back. To the sick Englishman. To your old woman of an uncle. You are better than either of them, boy: that I will say. You are a good climber, and one day you may be a great one. But that day is not yet. The Citadel is not for you—yet. I am going to climb it alone, do you understand? Not with a kitchen-boy from Kurtal. Not with any Kurtaler. Or any foreigner. I am going to climb it myself, only I—for the honor of Broli—and the name of Broli will be known in the world as long as the Citadel stands."

There was a silence.

"No," Rudi murmured. "No—"

"Go back, boy," said Saxo. His eyes were like blue stones.

"No—"

"Go back!"

Saxo turned. He began to move again along the knife-edge of the ridge. For a moment Rudi stood where he was, and then quickly moved after him. "Herr Saxo—" he pleaded.

The guide paid no attention.

"I cannot go back. Let me come with you. Please—"

He was close behind Saxo now. He reached out and touched his arm. And Saxo wheeled on him in anger. . . . Or rather he started to wheel. . . . For at his first motion his foot caught between two stones, and he was jerked violently to one side. His ax clawed the air; his free hand groped for support. But he found none. The full weight of his body sprawled on the ridge, struck a loose rock and dislodged it; and in the next instant the rock, and Saxo with it, were sliding down the precipice of the north face. There was a hoarse, choked-off cry, the crash of stone on stone, then silence. And Rudi was alone on the ridge.

For a moment he could not move. He could not even breathe. Mountain and sky spun around him, and he thought that he, too, was going to fall; but with a convulsive effort he managed to throw himself flat, to grasp a boulder, to cling to it until the spinning stopped. Then, numbly, he raised his head. He crept to the edge of the ridge. He looked down the north face. . . . *And saw Saxo.* . . . The rock that had slid off with him was gone; apparently it had fallen—or was still falling—all the way to the base of the mountain. But the guide had landed on a ledge not more than twenty feet down the face, and though the ledge was narrow it had been enough to hold him. He was there—and he was alive. As Rudi peered down, he pulled himself up slowly from the sprawling position in which he had fallen and crept in as far as he could from the rim of the ledge.

"Are you all right?" Rudi called.

There was no answer.

"Are you hurt?"

Still no answer. Leaning out from the ridge, he saw that Saxo was crouched close in against the mountain wall; and with one hand he was pressing his arm tightly against his body. Yes, Rudi thought, he was hurt all right. Not dead, by a miracle. But hurt. Perhaps badly.

His eyes moved over the twenty feet of rock that separated them. They were almost vertical—but not quite. Almost smooth—but not quite. There was sufficient angle, and enough cracks and holds, for a good climber to make it, either up or down. If he had had a rope there would have been nothing to it. He could have belayed it around a rock and lowered an end to Saxo, and the guide would have been up in a minute. But, climbing alone, he had brought no rope. Saxo had no rope. And whether the latter, with an injured arm, could climb the delicate stretch on his own was, to say the least, doubtful.

The boy looked at the guide, at the wall, back at the guide again. The climb, the summit, even the fierce resentment of Saxo that only a few moments before had burned inside him: all were now forgotten, or at least pushed off into a remote corner of his mind. Whatever the cause, whoever the blame, the helping of another climber in trouble must always—*always* —take precedence over everything else.

Saxo was getting slowly to his feet. He was looking up at the wall. "To the left," Rudi told him. "Here on the left the holds are best."

The guide swayed a little. His left arm, which he had been holding, dangled limp at his side, and there seemed also to be something wrong with one of his legs. Moving along the wall, he selected a place, paused a moment and began to climb. He got one foot onto a narrow projection and his good hand into a crevice above. He pulled himself up, found two more holds, moved up again. Then he stopped. Directly above him, now, the rock was perfectly smooth. To the right it was smooth. Only to the left, at almost arm's length, was there a series of cracks to which a man's fingers might cling. But it was Saxo's left arm that was the injured one.

For several moments he stood motionless; then slowly tried to raise his arm. But it was no more than a foot from his side when he dropped it again with a hoarse gasp of pain. He did not raise it again. Instead, he tried to maneuver himself, so that he could reach over with the right hand. But it was no good. His footholds, alone, were not enough to hold him, and the instant he let go his present handhold he began to slip. Peering down, Rudi could see that his face was covered with sweat. He began to curse in a harsh rasping whisper.

He let himself down. He tried again at another point. And then at a third. But each time he soon came to a place where it was necessary to use the left hand. And each time he ended up motionless, pinioned to the wall. Back on the ledge, he tried another tack. Instead of challenging the wall head on, he moved off toward one end, then the other, searching for a route that might lead off to either side. On the right, there was only smooth rock and space; but to the left of the ledge (Rudi could not see this section, because it was blocked off by an overhang) there was apparently some hope of escape, for Saxo spent a long while there before reappearing directly below.

"It does not go?" asked Rudi.

"No," said Saxo.

It was the first reply he had made since he had fallen. And he said no more. For a while he stood motionless, holding his injured arm. Then again he moved slowly back and forth along the ledge. He was not like a mountaineer any more. He was a prisoner. A caged animal.

"I will come down," Rudi said.

Just how he could help he was not sure. But at least he must make the attempt. It had now been perhaps a half hour since Saxo fell. He had tried every way to get up, but could not, and there was no choice as to what Rudi must do.

He studied the wall beneath him. It was far too sheer to descend facing outward, so he swiveled himself around until he was lying prone on the ridge with his feet dangling. He searched for a foothold, found it, and let himself slowly down. But the hold was shallow, the wall steep, and as he leaned out to look for the next step below, the pack and staff on his back, light though they were, seemed to be pulling him relentlessly off into space. Creeping back onto the ledge, he unslung them and laid them on a rock. He would retrieve them when he came up again.

Then again he was prone, dangling, groping with his toes. He found the first hold, then a second, then a third. When he looked down the ledge seemed no more than the merest ribbon against the gulf of space. But he contrived not to think of space. Only of the ledge. Of the next hold—and the next. And at last he was half-climbing, half-sliding down onto the band of rock beside Saxo.

He was there. Now what? The trick, of course, was to make it possible for Saxo to climb the wall. He could not carry him. He could not support even a fraction of his great bulk. All he could hope to do was to substitute in some way for Saxo's left arm; to act as a lever and a balance; to hold him against the rock when he could not hold on for himself. He studied the wall from below. Then he looked at the guide. Sweat still covered his broad face. His eyes were clouded and his lips twisted with pain. His left arm was not only limp, but hung at a peculiar angle that made Rudi sure it was broken.

"I have a big handkerchief," he said. "I will make a sling for you."

But Saxo shook his head. "I am all right. I do not need your help."

Rudi tried to reason with him, but it was no use. "Then if you will go first up the wall," he said, "I will try to help you from below."

The guide hesitated. He did not want this help either. But he had no choice. Approaching the wall, he climbed up to where he had been before, and Rudi, coming up after him, tried to support his feet while he swung his sound hand over to the holds on the left. It was no good, however. The instant Saxo's weight came down on his shoulder he began to slip and slide, and no effort of will, no straining or clawing of rock, could stop it. When they returned to the ledge they were both panting heavily, and there was an ugly bruise on Rudi's shoulder where Saxo's boot-nails had ripped through to the flesh.

They tried again—this time with Rudi going first. Climbing halfway up the wall and holding on precariously by one hand and one foot, he leaned far down and sought to support Saxo by grasping him under the bad arm. But this, too, was no good. For one thing, the pain to Saxo was so great that he groaned aloud. And, also, they could not get the proper leverage to swing him over to the crucial holds. The guide ground his teeth; his face contorted; with all the mighty strength of his good arm he struggled to thrust himself up and over. But it was not a question of strength. It was one of balance. And balance they could not attain. They made a final effort. Rudi leaned down until one hand reached Saxo's belt. The guide strained upward.

227

They slipped. They swayed. For one ghastly instant they lurched out from the wall, and it seemed that the two of them, clinging together, would topple off into space. Then Rudi let go. They clung to the rocks and gasped for air. And again they returned to the ledge.

Through all of it they had not spoken. They did not speak now. They sat on the ledge, and Saxo held his injured arm, and Rudi looked up at the wall above them. It was no prison wall for him. The holds were there, plain to view, and he could go up it more easily than he had come down. In less than a minute he could be back on the ridge, slinging on his pack and staff, moving on along the ridge—to the summit pyramid—up the pyramid. . . .

His eyes fixed on the shining crest of snow. Then he tore them away. He saw that Saxo was watching him.

"Go on," said the guide.

Rudi said nothing.

"Go on. You have won; I have lost. Climb to the top. Claim your victory."

Still Rudi said nothing. He sat motionless, and his face was without expression. But within him there raged a struggle fiercer than any he had had with the mountain. Thought and emotion met, conflicted, tangled, and seemed almost to tear his mind to shreds. . . . He had left the others; why not Saxo? But that had been wrong, and two wrongs did not make a right. . . . This was different, though: Saxo was not a *Herr*. Not even a friend. He was a ruthless enemy. But (again *but)* he was crippled. He was alone. . . . The top was so close. So close! He could climb quickly, return quickly, rejoin Saxo. But (always *but)* then what? Then he would have to go on down, get his uncle, bring him up. But

228

by that time it would be late in the day. And would his uncle leave Captain Winter?

His brain spun. He closed his eyes. When he opened them he looked at Saxo, and the guide was sitting hunched over with his bad arm dangling to the ground and the other hand covering his face.

Rudi stood up. He moved to the right end of the ledge and looked down into space. He peered from the outer rim, and there was only space. Then he edged to the left, onto the section of the ledge that, from above, had been hidden by the overhang. He reached the end, looked down again—and froze, motionless. *For on this side there was a way out.* From the very corner of the ledge a deep fault in the east face slanted down through the solid rock toward the distant shoulder where the tents were pitched. It went all the way to the shoulder: Rudi could see that for certain. And it appeared everywhere climbable; in fact, easier and less steep than the ridge up which they had come.

Obviously this was what Saxo had seen before, when he had disappeared under the overhang. He had said, "No, it does not go," and for himself alone he had probably been right. But for the two of them it was a different matter. It would go. In the whole stretch of the great crevice there was nothing as steep or difficult as the twenty feet of wall above them. Even with a broken arm a climber could make it—if there were a second climber to lead and steady him.

Still, it was not with joy, or even relief, that Rudi stood there staring, but rather with the bitterest disappointment. For though the cleft was a way out, it was not a way up—but only down. Its slanting course descended unbroken across the mountainside, with no access to the main ridge until it joined it at the shoulder, about a thousand feet below. With Saxo's injury

229

it would take them hours to reach the tents. There would be no time to start again that day. Nor would he have the strength; nor would his uncle let him. With two men incapacitated—and their food gone—there would be no next day. They would go down, defeated.

Here, at this place and this moment, was his last chance for the top. His only chance. It was now or never.

He came back to the center of the ledge. Saxo was again holding his injured arm, and his face was twisted with pain.

"Go on," he said, "Go on up, you fool!"

Rudi stood silently.

"You've won, boy—don't you understand?" The guide's voice grated like iron on stone. "Go on. Get your damned shirt and pole. Carry them up. Put them on the top."

Rudi scarcely heard him. He scarcely saw him. A cold numbness had closed around him, and within the numbness he stood alone. Once more his eyes went up to the wall above the ledge, to the jagged line of the ridge, to the junction of the ridge and the summit pyramid. They moved up the pyramid, up the white slopes, up the gleaming pinnacle to a point in the sky—and stopped. And that was all there was in the world: the point and the sky, the goal and the dream, the white dream rising into the blue stillness of space.

Then, through the dream, through the stillness—a voice. But whether it was Saxo's voice, or his own, he did not know.

"Go on," it said. "To the goal. To victory. All Kurtal will hail you; all Switzerland will hail you. You will be a hero. The conqueror of the Citadel. Your father's son."

His father's son.

230

Rudi lowered his eyes. The mountaintop was gone; the dream was gone; the numbness of dream was slowly dissolving, and in its place was clearness. Clearness as deep and cold and pure as the mountain sky.

He turned, looked at Saxo and pulled his handkerchief from his pocket.

"I will make a sling now," he said quietly. "Then we will go down together."

The ledge receded above them. They crept and slid and stumbled down the long slanting cleft in the mountainside.

As Rudi had judged, it was climbable. It "went." But their progress was terribly slow. With Saxo's useless arm, even the simplest of maneuvers became a formidable problem, and, besides, the guide's leg, which he had also hurt in his fall, now began to trouble him seriously. He limped, lurched, seemed to have lost all sense of balance. Rudi had to help him almost constantly: now going ahead and leading him by his good hand, now following behind and gripping him by his belt. Soon his own arms were aching from the strain. His shoulder, already bruised by Saxo's bootnails, seemed shot through with darts of fire.

Suddenly he remembered something. His pack. He had left his pack on the ridge before climbing down to Saxo, and there it still was. . . . All right, he thought, there it was. What matter? . . . It contained only one thing. Only an old red shirt—and, slung through the straps, a rough-cut pole. He had no need of them now. There they would stay, lost and forgotten, as high as he had been able to bear them. High on the great mountain where his father had died. And his dreams.

He bent to the next rock, the next step. He was going first now, descending a few feet at a time and then turning to help Saxo down after him. The process was repeated ten times, twenty, thirty times, each almost exactly the same. And then, suddenly, not the same—for Saxo slipped. His good hand reached out for Rudi's, but missed it; reached for a hold, but missed it; and the next instant his weight bore down on the boy and the two slid together down the rocks. Luckily they did not slide far. There was a level place a short way below, and they landed with a jolt. But the jolt alone was enough to make Saxo cry out in agony. And when Rudi regained his feet his own body was trembling with shock and tiredness.

They rested. Saxo sat motionless, pressing his broken arm, and his usually red face was as gray as the mountain rocks. After a few moments he bent his head and closed his eyes. He seemed almost to be sleeping. Rudi, too, sat still, except for the spasmodic twitching of his muscles and the quick panting of his lungs. He struggled for air, for control of his body. He struggled with all his strength, but now at last, he realized, his strength had begun to ebb.

"I can do it," he thought fiercely. "I can do it. . . . Because I *have* to do it."

He looked down, along the great cleft in the mountainside, and there below was the shoulder, jutting white and immense against the distant valley. Then he looked up, to see how far they had already come: along the slant of the cleft—to the ledge—to the thin line of the ridge above the ledge. And suddenly his body was no longer trembling, but rigid. His heart seemed to have stopped. For on the ridge were two human figures. Outlined against the sky, they were moving slowly along its crest toward the base of the summit pyramid.

He could not, of course, see their faces. But he did

not need to. They could not possibly be any other than his uncle and Captain Winter. He sprang to his feet. His mouth opened to cry out. In that stillness of rock and ice they would surely hear him. If he waved they would see him. In half an hour—perhaps less—they could work their way down to the ledge, down the cleft, to where he now stood. Then there would be three of them to help Saxo. There would be a rope, a whole team of climbers. To reach the shoulder and the tents would be no problem at all.

His mouth was open—to shout. But no shout came. Instead, his eyes moved on past the two figures: to the end of the ridge, to the snowslope beyond, up the white flanks of the slope to the shining point that was its summit. That, too, they could reach in half an hour, or less. . . . If he did not call.

Only if he did not call.

Still he gazed upward, motionless. The figures had reached the upper end of the ridge, the base of the pyramid, and now they were no longer outlined against the sky, but against the whiteness of snow. They crept slowly higher. . . . And, abruptly, Rudi turned away. Saxo was still sitting with head bent and eyes closed. The boy approached and touched his shoulder.

"Come," he said. "We will go on."

The guide looked up at him, and his eyes were clouded. "I cannot," he murmured.

"You must."

Saxo shook his head. "No, I am done in—finished. Leave me here, boy. Save yourself."

"Come! Come!" Rudi pulled at his good arm. "Give me your hand. I will help you. I will get you down."

"You cannot do it."

"Yes, I can do it."

Somehow he got Saxo to his feet. They were moving

on again. They were climbing, slipping, stumbling, crawling, inching down the endless rock of the mountainside. Now he was holding Saxo by the hand; now by the belt; now supporting what seemed the whole of his weight by a shoulder propped under his armpit. For a while the guide muttered and groaned. Then he was still. His eyes, though open, were glazed and unseeing, and he had lost all control over his movements. Rudi maneuvered him along the deep slant of the cleft: allowing gravity to pull him downward, using his own strength to brake and prevent a fall.

Or at least a bad—a fatal—fall. For they were falling constantly. They were lurching, slipping, falling a foot, two feet; scraping against rough rock walls, clawing for holds, landing among sharp stones; creeping on again, slipping again, falling again. There was blood on their hands, on their faces. Their clothes were in tatters. And still they crept, stumbled, fell: on and on, down and down. How long it went on Rudi did not know—and would never know. Time had ceased to exist. Even pain and tiredness no longer existed. Now there was only numbness. Only the gray rock slipping past. Only the next step, and the next, and the next, and the blind instinct to go on.

It was steep: terribly steep. Then not so steep. Then steep again. The rock bulged; they swung out over space; Rudi knew he could not hold on. . . . And held on. . . . They fell and lay sprawled upon a crag; he knew he could not stand up again. . . . And stood up. . . . Then the angle eased off once more. It was almost level. It stayed level. He was half-dragging, half-carrying Saxo across a broad shelf of rock. He was looking down again—down the mountainside—searching for the shoulder. But he could see no shoulder. *They were on the shoulder.* Ahead was snow;

beyond it the sharp, flaring point of the Needle. To the right, and a little above them, was the rim of the hollow in which the tents were pitched.

Rudi turned toward it. He took a step—and a second step—dragging Saxo after him. But Saxo staggered and fell. Rudi bent to help him up. And fell too. He tried to rise, but couldn't. He lay still, while mountain and sky spun around him. He closed his eyes and there was darkness.

Then at last, beyond the darkness: sounds—voices. His eyes were still closed, but he knew that two figures were bending over him. They were picking him up, carrying him, laying him down again, but this time not on the cold rock of the mountain.

The world came back. He was in a tent. He looked up at his uncle and Captain Winter, and he tried to speak.

"Don't talk now. Rest," said Winter.

But there was something before rest.

"You went after me?" he murmured.

"Yes," said the Englishman.

"You went—all the way?"

"Yes, all the way, Rudi."

"That is good, my Captain." His eyes moved slowly to Franz, and he tried to smile. "Yes, that is good, Uncle," said the son of Josef Matt. "We are guides of Kurtal, and we got our *Herr* to the top."

CHAPTER 19

The Conqueror

Down . . . down . . . down. . . .

They had fed him tea and chocolate. They had made him rest for an hour. But an hour was all; for their food was now gone, and they had to be off the mountain by nightfall.

"You can do it, boy," his uncle had said.

"Yes, I can do it."

And they had started off.

They left the tents where they were, so as to travel as light as possible. They roped up, all four together. Rudi went first, Winter second, Saxo third, Franz last. Franz's position was the hardest, for Saxo was all but a dead weight on the rope, and often, after letting Rudi down, Winter would turn and, from below, help maneuver the guide over the steeper pitches. They moved slowly, but steadily. And they moved in silence.

The Needle, where before they had struggled for so long, took only a few minutes to descend; for now there was no need to bother with the "eye." Rudi crept out to the edge of the projecting rock, let himself over, dangled—and was gently lowered to the platform below. Then came Winter. Then Saxo, hanging limply. Finally Franz, by means of a second rope doubled over a crag. On the platform Saxo swayed and fell. Winter and Franz picked him up.

"I—I cannot—" murmured the man from Broli.

"Come on. Move," said Franz.

And they moved on.

Down . . . down . . . down. . . .

There was the wall below the shoulder. The endless wall. There was the rock gliding past—cliffs and ledges, knobs and crevices, crags and clefts—as if in the gray blur of a dream. Again and again Rudi slipped and stumbled; a dozen times he was on the verge of falling; but he scarcely knew it until he felt the bite of the rope around his ribs. In the numbness of dream through which he moved, only the rope was real. The rope that held him, grasped him, sustained him. The rope that was life itself.

"To the right now—"

"To the left—"

"Straight ahead—"

At intervals a voice came down to him, and he obeyed blindly, mechanically. From the Needle on, he scarcely saw his uncle, for Franz remained always above, directing and supporting them. But at the end of each pitch another familiar figure appeared beside him—a lean, haggard figure with a bandaged head and a wracking cough. "Good boy," came Winter's voice. Over and over: "Good boy." Then he braced himself and belayed the rope, while Rudi descended.

"He is done in too," the boy thought. "As done in as I. I must not make it hard for him. I must not slip or stumble."

Then he was slipping again, stumbling again. He was not climbing down the mountain, but simply being lowered down—"like a bundle of firewood." At last they came to the base of the wall and the beginning of the ridge. The shoulder was high above them; they were passing their first campsite; then the place where Franz and Saxo had stopped and argued. . . . Saxo. He had not thought of him for hours. What had happened to him? Was he still with them? . . . He looked up. Yes, he was still with them. There he was, about fifty feet behind, swaying drunkenly on the rope while Franz held him from above. Another "bundle of firewood."

Left. Right. Straight ahead.

Down. Down. Down.

Or *was* it down? It no longer seemed to him that he was moving at all, but rather that the mountain was flowing up past him. It flowed in a gray stream—a stream of rock—endlessly repeated, endlessly the same. And then, at last, no longer the same, for they had again reached a place which he recognized. He was on the flat slabs on top of the Fortress. He was descending the cleft through the Fortress. He was on the ledge below the cleft, edging around the bulge above the precipice of the south face. The rope steadied him from behind, but it was not enough. He was losing his grip, slipping, falling. He was reaching out blindly, despairingly . . . groping, grasping, clinging . . . clinging at last, safe and secure . . . not to the rock, *but to a hand*. The hand pulled him on. He was on the platform below the Fortress. *"Lausbube—"* a voice was saying. "Dishwasher. Kitchen rat—"

Teo Zurbriggen held him in his arms, and tears streamed from his old sunken eyes.

Ridge. Snowslope. Glacier.
Sunlight. Dusk. Dark.

Then the hut. Lights and voices. And sleep—sleep—sleep.

When he awoke it was light again. The hut was full of men. There were his uncle, Winter, Saxo. There were Old Teo, Andreas Krickel, Peter Tauglich, Klaus Wesselhoft. They made him eat and drink, and slowly he felt the strength returning to his body. They thronged about him, talking, and slowly their words took form and meaning through the fading numbness of his brain. Krickel was shaking his hand. Then Tauglich. Then—awkwardly, almost shyly—Klaus Wesselhoft. "Hello, Angel-face," said his old tormentor. But this time he said it differently.

Then Krickel and Klaus were leading Saxo toward the door. Two slats of wood held his bad arm motionless. His left leg was swollen and rigid. But he was able to walk slowly, with only a little help from the two beside him.

"We will have him down in Broli by noon," said Krickel. "Then we will come around by the valley and be in Kurtal in time for tonight's celebration."

They reached the door, and the others watched them in silence. Then Saxo turned. For a long moment he looked at Winter, for another at Franz. And the silence deepened. "Come," said Krickel. But still he stayed where he was. His gaze moved to Rudi. Limping slowly back across the room, he stopped before him and put out his good hand.

"Will you take it, boy?" he asked.

Rudi hesitated. He looked up into the grim face; into the eyes that were no longer cold as stone, but clouded and filled with pain. The hand waited. And he took it.

"You saved my life," said Saxo. "You could have climbed to the top, but instead you saved my life. I

239

thank you. I salute you." He turned to Franz and Winter, and for an instant the old defiance glowered in his glance. "And you thank him too," he said, "you conquerors of the Citadel!"

He limped back to the door, and the two men waiting there led him out.

There were crowds as high as the base of the Blue Glacier. There were crowds on the boulder-slopes, on the forest trail, on the green meadows below. It was no mere file of weary climbers that made the descent to Kurtal—but a triumphal procession.

And the town itself was as it had never been before in all the years of its history. The church bells pealed. A band played. Every shop was closed, every human being on the streets: men, women and children, guides and hotel workers, tradesmen and housewives, natives and tourists. The air was split with shouts, cheers and singing, as Kurtal went mad in its pride and its joy.

In the main square stood the mayor and the town council. But Rudi scarcely saw them. All he saw— suddenly—was the small figure darting toward him through the crowd; the figure of his mother, the face of his mother; his mother flinging herself upon him, embracing him, holding him tight. And now he was holding her too. Her shoulders trembled under his hands. He was trying to comfort her, speak to her. But the din was too great. Then she raised her face. He saw her eyes, and her tears. But in the same instant, too, he saw beyond the tears—to what lay behind them— deeper and stronger and more shining than tears. And he knew that there was no need to speak.

The crowd surged around them, bore them on. Ahead, a group of guides had hoisted Captain Winter and Franz onto their shoulders and were carrying them across the square toward the terrace of the Beau Site Hotel. The mayor had already reached the terrace. He was waving his arms and calling for order. Herr Hempel was calling for order. But their voices were lost in the shouts of the crowd, the blare of the band, the clanging of bells. A stagecoach rumbled into the square—then a second, then a third—and their occupants poured out and swelled the throng already there. "There are more coming!" voices cried. "Dozens more! Hundreds more!" From down the valley they came. From neighboring valleys. From the plains and cities to the north. Already the news of the great event was spreading across the length and breadth of Switzerland.

A roar like the ocean. A cheer like a wave. . . . Then suddenly, magically, silence. . . . On the hotel terrace, before the crowd, stood the conquerors.

"Herr Captain Winter, Guide Franz Lerner," said the mayor, "—we hail you with pride. Soon all this country—and your country, my Captain—and all the world—will hail you. Your feat will be remembered and honored as long as mountains stand and there are men to climb them." He paused and pointed upward: beyond the crowd, beyond the rooftops, beyond the valley, to the great peak that soared above them. "There it is," he said. "The Citadel. Unclimbed, unconquered through all the ages, until you, by your skill and courage, have won it. There it stands above our valley of Kurtal; there it will stand forever; and all men will know it by your names. As your triumph and your prize. As your mountain."

Captain Winter was slowly shaking his head.

"No, you are wrong," he said. "Not our mountain."

241

The mayor stared at him. The crowd stared. Not a whisper broke the stillness that filled the square.

"It is Rudi's mountain," said Captain Winter.

A murmur ran through the packed throng.

"Rudi's?"

"Rudi Matt?"

"How? Why?"

"Did the boy reach the top?"

Winter walked to where Rudi stood beside his mother. He put a hand on his shoulder and led him out to the center of the terrace.

"Here is the conqueror of the Citadel," he said.

Rudi could scarcely breathe. His bones were like water. The crowd and the square spun around him. "I?" he whispered. "No, my Captain—not I. I only—"

His voice faded. He no longer had a voice. Winter was leading him again. Then they had stopped again, and before him was the long brass telescope of the Beau Site Hotel.

"Look," said the Englishman. "You will see. . . . Then all the world will look, and it will see."

Rudi bent to the eyepiece. There was a circle—a circle of blue—and, rising into the circle, a wedge of dazzling whiteness. . . . "It is the dream," he thought wildly. "I am asleep, and it is the dream again." . . . But he was not asleep. It was not a dream. The brass of the telescope was hard and real to his touch; Wintere's hand was tight and warm on his shoulder; the image in the lens did not fade, but grew steadily brighter. Across the miles of space he saw the mountaintop, clear and gleaming. From its highest point there rose a pole. And from the pole, tied by its two sleeves, a red shirt streamed out like a banner against the shining sky.

He straightened slowly. He stared at Winter and at

his Uncle Franz, standing beside him. "You carried it up," he murmured. "You put it there."

"No, Rudi," said Winter, "you put it there. You and your father."

The crowd was stirring again. The mayor was talking. Herr Hempel was talking. Around them everything was turmoil and confusion. But in the midst of it Rudi stood dazed and motionless, and once more his eyes went up to the distant summit. Without the telescope there was no pole, no shirt; only the whiteness of snow and the blueness of sky. And then even these were gone. His eyes were blurred and sightless. He turned quickly away.

An arm was around him. Winter held him close. "You'll climb it many times, son," he said.

"Yes, all through your life," said Franz. "Wait and see."

His eyes cleared and he looked at them. He looked past them at his mother. He looked at the guides of Kurtal, standing in the front rank of the crowd. Off to one side was the small gnarled figure of Teo Zurbriggen, and somehow, amid all the excitement, he had contrived to slip into the hotel and put on his cook's cap and apron.

The mayor was waving his arms again. Cheers shook the square. "They are taking us to the town hall," said Franz. "The governor of the canton is coming. And later—"

"Yes—later," said Rudi suddenly. "I will come later, Uncle. But first, please—you will excuse me—I must go now—"

"Go? Go where, boy?"

"With Old Teo. He is waiting—see?" He turned and darted off through the crowd, and the others looked after him in bewilderment. "There is work to do," he called back. "I must help him. I promised. After so long a time there must be a thousand dirty dishes."

That is the story they tell of the old days in the valley of Kurtal; of the conquest of the great mountain called the Citadel; and of how Rudi Matt, who was later to become the most famous of all Alpine guides, grew from a boy into a man.

About the Author

James Ramsey Ullman's vivid stories of mountaineering do not come only from his imagination, for he is himself an experienced climber—with two sons who share his love for high places. Jim, Jr. has climbed the Matterhorn and Longs Peak in Colorado with his father, and Bill has gone with him to the top of Wyoming's Grand Teton.

Other titles you will enjoy

56036 JUST A DOG, by Helen Griffiths. Illustrated by Victor Ambrus. An abandoned mongrel pup roams the streets of a large city, facing hunger and fear. After many adventures, she finally finds the home and security she seeks. ($1.75)

56004 GAME OF TRUTH, by Edith Maxwell. Trapped in a boarded-up summer hotel during a blizzard, three teenagers and two strangers pass time by playing the Truth Game, which turns ugly and dangerous as long-hidden secrets are revealed. ($1.75)

29987 BIG MUTT, by John Reese. Illustrated by Rod Ruth. When a blizzard hits the North Dakota Badlands, an abandoned dog kills sheep to live, and the ranchers set out to hunt him down—but Dwight is determined to save the outlaw dog. ($1.75)

56103 JUST DIAL A NUMBER, by Edith Maxwell. When a prank phone call leads to death, four teen-agers are plunged into the nightmare of keeping their guilt secret. (1.75)

(If your bookseller does not have the titles you want, you may order them by sending the retail price, plus 50¢ for postage and handling, to: Mail Service Department, POCKET BOOKS, a Simon & Schuster Division of Gulf & Western Corporation, 1230 Avenue of the Americas, New York, N. Y. 10020. Please enclose check or money order—do not send cash.)

56081